DUST COVERED LIES

DUST COVERED LIES

A NOVEL

CATHERINE M. O'CONNOR

TCU Press

FORT WORTH, TEXAS

Library of Congress Cataloging-in-Publication Data

Names: O'Connor, Catherine M., 1961– author.
Title: Dust-covered lies : a novel / Catherine M. O'Connor.
Description: Fort Worth, Texas : TCU Press, 2024. | Summary: "Set in Texas
   during the 1870s and in the 1930s at the height of the Dust Bowl, Dust
   Covered Lies tells the story of Frances Abbott, or Frannie, an orphaned
   immigrant who faces a terrible choice that will haunt her the rest of
   her life. Frannie is a teenage champion markswoman when she and her
   autistic and artistically gifted brother, Juan Esteban, set off on a
   scientific hunting expedition on the Colorado River led by a dangerous
   con man who claims to be a French zoologist. When a murder is committed
   and Juan Esteban's life is in danger, Frannie lies to protect him.
   Determined to take her secret to the grave, Frannie and her brother flee
   to the dust-covered Texas panhandle to escape the one person who could
   reveal the truth about their past"— Provided by publisher.
Identifiers: LCCN 2024032867 (print) | LCCN 2024032868 (ebook) |
   ISBN 9780875658834 (paperback) | ISBN 9780875658940 (ebook)
Subjects: LCGFT: Novels.
Classification: LCC PS3615.C5847 D87 2024 (print) | LCC PS3615.C5847 (ebook) |
   DDC 813/.6—dc23/eng/20240719
LC record available at https://lccn.loc.gov/2024032867
LC ebook record available at https://lccn.loc.gov/2024032868

TCU Box 298300
Fort Worth, Texas 76129
www.tcupress.com

Design by Julie Rushing

For my parents

ACKNOWLEDGMENTS

Thank you to my beautiful and burgeoning family for your devoted support of my writing efforts. You have cheered me on, and I'll be forever grateful. Having a family that believes in you is everything. I would especially like to recognize the Wootens. Your example of unshakable dedication and unconditional love has inspired this novel in so many ways.

To my many wonderful friends who took the time to read my work: you are the best, and I can't say enough about my writing group—Betsy and Alison. Your comments were always valuable and unfailingly made the writing better. We did this together—this is *our* accomplishment—thank you.

TCU Press has been a fantastic partner on this debut novel. Their staff offered guidance and support that has proved to be immeasurable. I am especially grateful for Dan Williams, Abigail Jennings, and for Kathy Walton—my wise editor.

Lastly, to my husband Jim and my children—Claire and Patrick—you have always lifted me up, and I love you beyond words.

CHAPTER 1
LEILO, TEXAS

1934

"All rise!" Those words give me a shiver. I've had a recurring nightmare since age fifteen of a moment that changed my life. And when I wake in a cold sweat, I don't shake it off, because it wasn't just a dream. It was real— and at age seventy-two, I'm still watching my back.

That's why I'm living on these dusty panhandle plains in a bump-in-the-road town called Leilo. Leilo's one of those places that has nothing going for it—on this open prairie, it's flat and hot in the summer and freezing cold and windy in the winter. Few trees manage to survive, just the weed species that ranchers and farmers hate, like mesquite and hackberry, and even those look like they've been beaten with a stick.

Despite its negatives, Leilo suits me just fine. When my brother and I moved here in 1876, we weren't looking for beauty or comfort. We were looking for a place to hide.

I was nineteen and he was eighteen when we slogged from Cedar Bend, Texas, over five hundred miles north to Leilo with a horse and cart. I'll never forget the day we arrived. Though the atmosphere above felt ethereal, what lay before us was a vision of decay and wreckage. But it was ours, and I felt a sense of freedom that I hadn't felt in years.

Our new home, a two-room wood slat house that leaned with the prevailing wind, sat about thirty feet from the road. Behind it was a wooden privy with a rickety door that hung only from its bottom hinge. Inside the house, floorboards were missing, and the roof had holes open to the sky, but we patched it up as best we could and moved in our meager possessions:

a table, two chairs, an oil lamp, a few pots and pans, a set of tin cups and plates, and my rifle.

I organized our furniture around a potbelly stove near the east wall and hung my Jaeger rifle above it. It was the only place with any character within an overall setting of deterioration—peeling paint, creaky floors, and patches of curling, yellowed wallpaper.

A productive well was our biggest asset, and over a few months, we built a shed from lumber that was strewn about—most likely, remnants from a barn that had been slapped down by a tornado.

For over fifty years, wheat farming kept us going—until the dust put an end to it. These days we survive on the small patch of land we still own because the rest went to the bank. We tend to our garden and hen house, and of course, Juan Esteban does what he always does—he draws.

Seems to me, he's documented almost every living creature on these dusty plains. Where he spotted a prairie chicken, I'll never know, 'cause they're almost extinct around here. From memory alone, he drew that bird in full plumage with its body erect, head and tail feathers skyward, beak slightly open, like he was king of the plains.

As for me, I do the best I can to keep our past hidden. Private, stubborn, and peculiar—that's what I'd call myself.

My stubbornness keeps us alive on the bare minimum. Most folks out here hang their hats on hope—hope for rain, hope for one good crop to help pay off the bank loan. But I've found hope to be an unreliable companion. It'll pass through your fingers like sand, and you're left with nothing. At least stubbornness provides a sturdy foundation. And a good dose of peculiarity keeps unwanted attention in check.

As for others, some have different words to describe me: crazy old bag, lunatic, murderer, the list of unpleasantries goes on, but I don't let it get to me anymore because I chose my path with clear eyes.

I stood before that judge and lied through my teeth to protect my brother and me from the one scoundrel who could reveal our past.

~

My recurring nightmare is a reliving of my day of reckoning—August 19, 1873.

The place was Clearwood, Texas, a settlement in the Piney Woods of central Texas, population 150 or so.

The courtroom was nothing more than a lean-to shed made from cedar posts with a picket roof. Normally a goat shelter, it offered little shade for the twenty or so townspeople who gathered under a blistering sun to witness my trial called to order.

I sat at the front, on a stool, facing a table that tilted to one side. I had watched as two men carried it from the schoolhouse down the street and situated it a few feet from the corn crib. All four legs had been gnawed on by some sharp-toothed creature—tiny incisions made a crisscross pattern in the pine.

Though I faced away from the crowd, I felt a collection of eyes scrutinizing my every detail —the unwieldy wisps of brown hair that refused to stay in my bun, my tattered dress with strings at the hem and holes in the elbow, my undersized shoes with toes poking out. And I was sure I wasn't the only subject of interest.

Behind me in a stained shirt and wool pants was my younger brother Juan Esteban. His hair was roughly cut for the occasion. Celia, my adoptive mother, had taken a razor to it in an attempt to civilize what was formerly his long black mane. Next to him, Celia wore a dress made of the same cloth as my own—once a cheerful pattern of orange flowers now appeared faded and tan-colored, like dead bouquets. Pop, a reverend, held her hand. He was in his usual black attire, his expression the same as the one he wore when presiding at funerals.

My older brother John Joseph—stern-faced, blond, and lean—was near Pop. He gripped my sisters' small hands as if they were about to wade into a swift current. Usually chatty and wiggly, Cora and Marie Isabel looked hollow-eyed and dazed.

My family's and my own anxiety had no impact on the crowd—their mood was anything but somber. Men in dirty overalls conversed about yesterday's downpour and the rising river that had washed out the bridge at Frederick's crossing. Children played tag among their mothers' skirts, wrapping their small bodies in cottony hiding places. Boys threw rocks at a tin can and cheered when someone hit it with a *clank*. There was laughing coming from the shade of a low-branching live oak, then a scuffle over a bottle of whiskey.

I knew no one in the crowd except the red-headed *vermin* at the center of the scuffle.

"All rise," the bailiff bellowed as the judge appeared from behind a makeshift backdrop—a moth-eaten blanket wired to the rafters.

When I rose from my stool, my knees wobbled, but I dug my toes into the dirt to stiffen my stance and gritted my teeth to prevent any unwanted chattering.

Deep creases in the judge's neck, his stooped frame and frayed robe revealed the extent of his weariness—hundreds of miles on horseback to cover his rugged circuit. Clearwood was just one of his twenty stops to sentence the guilty and release the innocent in a frontier where the difference between right and wrong—black and white—felt mostly gray.

Mine wasn't the only case on the docket. Before me, there had been a horse thief, a money swindler, and a woman accused of public indecency. All were proven guilty.

By the time my case came up, the judge leaned into the table like he needed its support. His drawn mouth, combined with the way he grimaced and rubbed his temples, foreshadowed the fact that my fate would be decided in less than fifteen minutes.

"Miss Frances Abbott, how do you plead?"

I stiffened my back. "Guilty, as charged," I said.

The judge raised his heavy head and wagged it back and forth, "You understand, Miss Abbott, you are making this plea in spite of your lawyer's advice."

"Yes," I said. I stared straight at the judge with a determination that made my hair stand on end, both in fear of what lay ahead but also in astonishment at my own resolve.

Mr. Grimes, the attorney Celia and Pop had hired for a hog and two chickens, sat on a stool next to me and adjusted his wire-rim glasses. He was young, maybe half a dozen years older than me, and had a nervous twitch—constantly blinking like something was about to hit him in the face. The day I met him, I knew I was in trouble. His mannerisms and his unseasoned appearance made me wonder if he was capable of presenting a persuasive argument.

"Please your honor, one more chance," my attorney said. The judge obliged.

Mr. Grimes leaned over and whispered. "Frannie, for your parents' sake, plead not guilty. We'll take this to trial. The jury may have empathy, and there's a big chance you'll get less time."

"I won't," I said, "I can't."

The judge sighed and wasted no more time. "Are you standing with your previous plea, Miss Abbott?"

"Yes."

Murmurs filled the air like a hive of buzzing bees.

"Given the nature of your youth—fifteen years of age—and the circumstances of your crime, I sentence you to two years for the murder of Dr. Pierre Duvalier."

The hive grew louder. A woman screeched, "Hang her, you coward! She's a cold-blooded killer."

"Shut up," a man yelled back. "She's just a girl."

A garbled shout came from the shade. "She's a *liiiiiarrrr!*" followed by a bone chilling laugh—like it was straight from the devil's tongue.

"Order!" the judge shouted with surprising strength. "We will have none of that!"

He looked at a sheet of paper and then at the bailiff. "Done?" he said.

The bailiff nodded.

"This court is adjourned," the judge said. He slammed his gavel, shed his robe, and hobbled toward his horse.

A woman patted Celia's shoulder to comfort her and then sighed and said, "Sorry, Reverend," as if she were envisioning my descent into hell.

John Joseph dropped my sisters' hands and hugged me so tight that my shoulder blades almost touched. Cora whimpered and pulled on John Joseph's shirttail as if the undercurrent was tugging at her feet. Juan Esteban took a step closer and stood by my side, staring blankly toward a tall pine tree where a squirrel chattered and flicked its tail. He didn't hug or say anything. He didn't like touching—he was repelled by it. He didn't talk either, but he understood. We both knew that he loved me, and I loved him—that was all we needed.

The sheriff from San Saba shook the hand of the sheriff from Clearwood. It had been agreed, out of mercy, that I would serve my sentence closer to home—not ninety miles away in San Saba, where the crime had been. Clearwood was the closest town with a jail.

"Now's the time," the Clearwood sheriff said.

When I reached out to hug Celia, she grabbed me, pulling me tight against her chest. I could feel the dampness of her collar against my neck.

"I'll visit as much as I can," she said.

She stroked my cheek with her fingers, and I could smell the dirt under her nails—earthy, like the soil in her garden after a shower.

"It's a ways," I said. "You don't have to . . ."

John Joseph interrupted. "We *will*, Frannie."

The twenty-mile trip back to Cedar Bend—our home—was along a rocky road that made twenty feel more like one hundred. You could make it in a morning if you had a healthy horse. We didn't—we had a slow donkey named Doris, so it would take my family much of the day to get back.

I turned to face Juan Esteban. "Before you know it, I'll be back," I said. He looked at his feet with no emotion.

"Help Celia with the cooking and tend to the chicken coop. And don't stop drawing. I'll want to see what you've done when I come back."

I could tell he was thinking by the way he shifted his eyes, then he looked up as if he was asking me a question. I understood.

"Draw a painted bunting like the one we saw on the river," I said.

The crowd had mostly dispersed when the sheriff reached for my arm.

With his sunburned forehead, pocked skin, and stubbled beard, he had a rough appearance that contrasted with the softness of his blue eyes.

"Come on. I ain't gonna handcuff you. Just stay in front of me, so I can keep watch on you."

Together we walked down the dirt road toward a wood frame building with a limestone wall surrounding it. We entered through a wooden gate into a courtyard with no trees, nothing but swept earth and a clump of trampled yuccas. I looked up at the sky, wondering if the buzzard circling above was a premonition of worse things to come.

"Back there's the latrine," he said. "Since they're only men here, just holler and I'll make sure you got your privacy. Food will come six am, noon, and five pm. There's a bucket in your cell for washing and whatnot." He cleared his throat as if the "what not" was embarrassing.

I nodded.

"If you want to write letters, I'll arrange for pen and paper and make sure they get sent out. And my wife makes dresses. I'll see to it that you have another."

"Thank you," I said.

He turned to walk away, then looked over his shoulder and adjusted his wide brimmed hat. "I don't like having a girl in here—something ain't right about it."

~

I took that sheriff up on his offer to provide paper and pencil and wrote a journal of events that led to my jailing—the real truth, not what I told the judge. I did it to keep my sanity while in prison and to remind myself of who I really was, despite what others thought.

These days, I keep the journal under lock and key in a steel box under the floorboards of my house here in Leilo—no one knows about it except me, and I plan to keep it that way.

Lately, I've been preparing for the possibility that I might die before Juan Esteban. At age seventy-one, he's only one year younger, but he's tall, sturdy, and healthy looking. I'm just the opposite—shriveled, bent over, and my lungs are failing. Mostly because of the dust, but my pipe doesn't help—Pop's pipe. It gives me comfort, reminding me of him, and since comfort is elusive, I'm not giving that up.

I plan to meet with a lawyer and set up a will, so there's money to care for Juan Esteban if I go first. He's my *only* concern.

As for the journal that holds my story and my secret, I'll probably burn it for Juan Esteban's sake.

CHAPTER 2
THE VOYAGE

1868

The beginning of my path to this jail cell started at sea. It was October 12, 1868, and I was ten when my parents and I boarded a ship in Liverpool bound for America. The *Isaac Web*, a three-masted sailing vessel, was captained by a gruff, dark-haired fellow with a scar that swooped downward from his right earlobe to the corner of his mouth.

Our family, along with thirty-five other families—mostly English like us, some French, and a few German—were packed tight in steerage on a forty-day voyage. Our only privacy was a tarp thrown over a wire, and our stacked bunks were nothing more than prickly hay mattresses atop creaky warped boards.

We learned that our fellow passengers were much like the citizens of the English hometown we had left behind—farmers, laborers, carpenters, tailors, masons. Among the children, I was the only girl my age, but even though I wore a crinoline-lined dress with puffy sleeves, I found my place among a group of boys who roamed the decks like a pack of wild dogs.

The only person who appeared out of place was a fellow named Dr. Pierre Duvalier. The day we boarded, he strode down the bridge wearing a stove pipe hat, lavender waistcoat, and green bow tie. It was the lavender that set him apart—like an exotic bird—as the rest of us were dressed in shades of gray as dull as the leaden sky.

"*Dépêchez-vous.* Hurry up!" he shouted and used his cane to swat the baggage boys who lugged his overstuffed canvas duffels that spilled with equipment and odorous contents.

Once on deck, Duvalier spoke to the captain with an air of authority. "I am a professor, from le Muséum National d'Histoire Naturelle en Paris, and I hope that you will allow me certain accommodations while on board."

The captain frowned and growled, "No special treatment," but he changed his tune when the professor slipped him three silver coins.

As word spread of the professor's claimed royal connections to the House of Orleans and his self-professed academic accomplishments as an expert in taxonomy and zoology, some of the ship's passengers began to show interest.

One morning, after playing chase from stem to stern with my pack, I stopped to catch my breath and listened as the professor spoke about his pursuits to a cluster of men. "Zoology is my primary specialty. I am on an expedition to bring back specimens—animal skins for stuffing, sketches, and anatomical analyses—for the gallery of natural history."

He curled the waxy tip of his mustache. "Europeans have an insatiable appetite for scientific knowledge of the new world. Alexander Wilson's *American Ornithology* was a start, then of course John James Audubon followed with his *Birds of America*—like myself, Audubon was an esteemed Frenchman. Very fine works indeed, but Monsieur Audubon chose the English to engrave."

He clicked his tongue. "The French—we will elevate the science to *une haute connaissance*—how do you say, a higher knowledge? You see, drawing is one thing, but bringing an animal to life with inspired taxidermical expertise is another; that is an experience, not just art. Consider the panther . . . the glint in its eye, the snarl, the sharp teeth . . . as if you are about to be attacked, taken down, by tooth and claw. *N'est-ce pas?*"

"What other species do you hope to acquire?" a short German man said.

"My intent is to collect the top of the food chain." He spread his arms to demonstrate their size. "Bobcats, cougars, bears, wolves . . . these will be of greatest appeal."

As the professor spoke, I began to consider the wildness of America with a tinge of apprehension, but mostly with a sense of excitement.

On the fifteenth day of our trip, the wind died, and the only movement was our constant bobbing among green-colored ocean swells. It was sweltering below, so most were on deck when the professor got to work. He convinced the captain to release a rowboat for fishing—"to catch *des specimens*," he said.

Myself, a boy named Otto, and another named Steffen hung on the ship's rail as they lowered the professor and a young mate to the water. The mate, who was hairy-armed, shirtless, and wore his cap backwards, appeared slapdash compared to the professor's attire in neatly rolled-up shirt sleeves and bow tie. While the professor uncoiled a strip of heavyweight fishing cord and then tied on a string of hooks, the mate did the dirty work and baited the hooks with kitchen slop.

For a while, the professor caught nothing, then suddenly there was a great tug and thrashing at the surface. The professor shouted, "Mackerel!"

A crowd gathered as he and the mate gripped the line and pulled in three silvery fish. While the professor took measurements and jotted notes, the mate slit the fishes' bellies and dumped the guts overboard.

Then the professor pulled out a small box filled with metal tools and selected a sharp knife that glistened in the sun. Carefully, he peeled away the skin and scales from head to tail then brushed turpentine on the skin's underside and laid the flesh out to dry.

By then, guts and kitchen slop were pooling beside the boat, and I held my nose as the smell wafted over the deck, but kept my eyes on the water. The mate launched another line as the water rippled with schooling fish, then like a flash the mackerel dispersed, and all was eerily quiet until a long shadowy form darkened the water near the boat.

The professor stared. "*Un requin!*"

"*Es ist ein hai,*" Otto yelled.

"What is it?" I said gripping the ship's rail with excitement. Steffen translated, "Shark!"

The line went taut, and suddenly the mate's eyes were wide with panic.

"Pull!" the professor shouted at the mate. The cord whined against the boat's edge as the shark swam away. The mate let out a shriek as the rope ripped through his hands. He released his grip, and the professor reached to grab it, but within seconds the line was limp.

The professor's face flushed red like hot iron. He threw his hands in the air and shook his fist at the mate.

"*Mon spécimen!*" he yelled. His eyes flashed with fury. "You let it get away!"

While the mate stared wide-eyed at the rope burns that made pink streaks across both palms, a blunt force slammed into the boat and sent the professor crashing to the floor. As the professor clamored to regain footing, the shark surfaced again, this time with mouth wide open.

A woman behind me screamed. I watched in disbelief as the shark's double row of teeth clamped down on three mackerel at once—just two feet from the boat.

The mate scrambled for a weapon while the professor lunged for the line.

When the professor looked over his shoulder, the mate was holding a harpoon high above his head.

The professor yelled, "Not the harpoon! Use the club. Beat the head—save the skin!"

Bug-eyed with fear, the mate plunged the harpoon into the shark's mid-section and blood spurted and spilled down its slick underside. The shark rolled, then whipped his tail at the water's surface.

The professor held tight, then yelled again. "The club! Dammit!"

Instead, the mate reached for his knife and stabbed the shark's upper body. More red streamed from the shark's back, then it dove again. The professor struggled to hold on as the rope uncoiled, then the shark emerged on the opposite side. The mate leaned over and continued to stab like he was possessed by the devil—the tail, the head, the gill.

With every blow the professor shouted, "Drop the knife!'

Picking up an oar, the professor swung it at the mate's head. The boy fell backwards. The professor lunged to grab the knife just as the shark yanked on the rope. The boat lurched, sending bodies and oars flying.

The professor was now on top of the boy, struggling for the knife. Then, like he'd been struck by lightning, the boy's mouth popped open, but no sound came out. The knife had pinned the mate's arm to the boat's hull.

The professor stood over him and shouted, "*Stupide!*"

When the professor pulled the knife from the mate's arm, blood gushed from the wound, and I turned away from the gore to catch my breath. When I looked back, the mate was writhing in pain, and then there was a flash of light and a splash. With a look of disgust, the professor had pitched the knife overboard.

"For God sakes, help the poor chap," a woman screamed.

The captain shouted, "Tie the lines, so we can get the boy!"

"Wait!' the professor yelled. He stared at the water until the shark slowly appeared, then lolled at the surface.

"Secure the lines, you bastard!" the captain roared. "Forget the shark!"

"I will not!" the professor said and picked up a rag and threw it at the mate. "Wrap it."

The professor took his time while tying nooses around the six-foot-long shark's body, then cinched them tight and shouted, "Pull her up!"

The boat was next. Once it was even with the rail, the crew unloaded the mate and lay him on deck as the professor swaggered toward the captain and sneered, "Your mate is useless!"

Enraged, the captain lunged at the professor, grabbed his shirt collar, shoved him against the mast, and clamped both hands around his throat. My father and several men wrangled in, grabbed the captain's arms, and pulled him off the professor.

The captain pointed his finger in the professor's direction. "This man is a criminal. He attacked my crewman!"

The professor calmly adjusted his collar and smoothed his hair, then stepped toward the captain and muttered, "You, *monsieur*, are no better than your mate."

That afternoon, the professor cut off the shark's head, propped open the jaw, and left it to dry on deck—a gory reminder of the day's events.

And what happened to the mate was even more grim. After an attempt at amputation, gangrene set in, and a week later he died.

Some aboard said the professor was right to berate the mate for his insolence, and that the knifing was an accident, but others saw the professor's actions as intentional and cruel. Even Father and Mother disagreed. Mother sided with cruelty, Father the opposite. The morning after the mate died, my gang resumed their raucous games, but I spent the morning alone at the ships rear, staring at the heavy gray clouds and bubbling wake, feeling sad for the mate.

As for the captain and crew, there was no more hat tipping or "Good day, Sir" as they passed the professor on deck. But the professor was unfazed. He had other plans to revive his reputation.

～

Reluctantly, my mother was the first to sit for a portrait, but my father insisted.

"I can capture her gentle grace with a drawing," the professor said. "But she must wear her finest." Then he cupped his hand near his face and whispered to Father, "For a small fee of course."

Father seemed pleased that Mother would be the first—as if the professor had plucked her from the crowd for her unique attributes.

The day was fair when Mother changed into her favorite dress and wore her ivory brooch. The dress, made from lilac-colored fabric, had white lace cuffs and gold-colored needlework at the waist and necklines. Mother's aura changed when she wore it—as if it were the only time she felt beautiful.

She sat in a chair near the main mast, and the professor sat opposite her with paper and charcoal in hand. While the professor worked, Father strolled the deck, but I climbed the ratlines and observed from above—out of the professor's view.

The professor tilted his head and looked at Mother pensively. "Madame, if you please, sit straight and lift your chest some."

Mother adjusted her position.

"Lovely," he said. "But alas, the dress is a bit off at the bust. Too high perhaps—may I?" but before Mother could respond, he reached out and gave the dress a tug near her bosom and smoothed it with his long fingers.

When Mother blushed, he said, "Don't be concerned my dear lady. I am an artist—looking only for the right composition."

Mother nodded but did not smile.

The professor resumed his drawing and chatted as he worked. "I must say, your brooch is charming. Where did you get such a beautiful piece?"

"It was a wedding gift—from my father. Irises were his favorite flower. "

"*Fleur de lis*—is it valuable?"

Mother shifted in her chair as if she were uncomfortable. "My grandfather was a botanical engraver, so such pieces have meaning to us."

"Ah yes, botanicals," the professor said. "Once a fine craft, but a bit passé, wouldn't you say?"

Mother stiffened. I recalled the flower prints in our dining room and their delicate curling petals in bright blues, pinks, and yellows—corn cockle, forget-me-not, primrose, and ragged robin. To me, they were the most beautiful thing in our home, and I remembered the argument my parents had before we left.

"We must take them—to remember my family," Mother said. "And they will be Frances's one day."

"You and she will have the brooch," Father said, and then his voice turned gruff. "We don't have room."

I remember trying to convince him, not only for Mother's sake, but for my own. "I will carry them, Father," I said, but Father wouldn't budge.

My mind returned to the present when the professor cleared his throat and lowered his voice. I cupped my hand over my ear to hear.

"As for your brooch, Madame, you must be very careful. When among strangers, you never know if thieves are aboard."

My eyes widened as I added thieves to my list of the wild and treacherous things that might lie ahead in America.

"I keep it safe . . . hidden of course," Mother said.

The professor chuckled. "In your undergarments I presume?"

Mother blushed again and glanced down.

"Ah, of course, your hem," he said.

Mother furrowed her brow.

The professor smiled. "Not to worry, your secret is safe with a gentleman."

Father reappeared and looked over the professor's shoulder. "I must have a look."

The professor held up the sketch for both Father and Mother to see. "Time and money well spent?"

"Indeed," Father said. "You've captured her countenance quite well."

Mother's expression made clear that she didn't like it, perhaps because he accentuated the downturn of her mouth and the beak-like nature of her nose, but I knew it was mostly because she had not forgotten the professor's cruelty.

I didn't like it either. Something about her appeared solemn and distant—as if she sensed something bad was going to happen.

$\sim$

"Land ho!" a ship's mate shouted from the crow's nest.

On the horizon, a hazy slice of land turned into sand-covered barrier beaches, then marshland as far as the eye could see. Long-legged birds— egrets and herons—waded at the edges as sea gulls swooped and fought over fish scraps.

"We'll dock in an hour!" the captain shouted.

The crew scurried about pulling on ropes, climbing the main and mizzen masts, and binding sails for landing. Passengers marched like ants as they hauled out their sour-smelling bags and mildewed trunks, then laid them in the sun near the ship's bridge.

Father set ours down, then stood and gazed across Galveston Bay with Mother by his side. I perched on a crate to get a better view of the harbor and the bustling wharf.

The professor put two bags next to ours, then came back with a third and clumsily dumped it at his feet. There was a strong smell of turpentine and dead fish, and the shark's head poked out with its sunken eyes and sharp teeth.

Mother waved her hand near her nose, then whispered to Father, "Must he put it so close to ours?" She spun on her heel and left.

The professor slapped my father on the back. "At last, my friend, we are here. What are your plans?"

"We're headed to Bastrop County, where we have a title on a piece of land," Father said, "And you?"

"I'll stay in Galveston to secure supplies and find an assistant to help with the skinning and hauling, then I'll move south along the shore. An alligator would be a good start—and an ocelot too. After that, I'll head west to the hills and high prairies."

"Are you not afraid of the Indians?"

"I am indeed," the professor said. "I will need a skilled guide—I intend to skin, not be skinned myself."

The professor pulled out a leather folder filled with cigars and offered one to my father and the two chaps to his right.

"A parting gift," he said. "To my shipmates! May I do the honor of lighting each of yours?"

After a few minutes of chatting, the cigar smokers strolled away, leaving the professor alone. Father left to find Mother, but I stayed and counted the docked ships and the dozens of other ships waiting in the wings. Soon the professor left too, and when I looked down at the bag with the shark's head, a trail of smoke curled upwards from its open mouth. Then an orange flicker emerged from an eye socket.

"Fire!" I screamed.

Within seconds our own bags were smoking.

The captain shouted. "Get water!"

Mates lowered and pulled up pails, then tossed them into the flames, but it wasn't enough to keep the fire from spreading.

"The bags," the captain roared, "Throw them overboard!"

"No," my mother shrieked. "My dress, my brooch!"

Father ran toward the fire and grabbed Mother's bag and kicked at the flames. His sleeve cuffs caught, and he frantically tamped them out. When his jacket started smoking, he tore it off and threw it over the rail. He reached in his own bag and pulled out his Jaeger rifle, then handed it to me.

"Hold this!" he said, before whipping around and throwing his bag over the edge.

I clutched the rifle by the wooden stock because the metal was too hot to hold and stared helplessly as Mother's bag was consumed in fire. A mate scooped it up and hurled it as Mother and I stood open-mouthed watching the flying flames. Seconds later, the bag was nothing but a snuffed-out sinking lump.

At that moment, I knew that the rifle and whatever money Father carried in his pockets was all that we had. Mother sat with her head in her hands while Father surveyed the wreckage and waved his arms explaining to confused passengers what had happened. Knowing that I had been given charge of our most valuable possession, I gripped the rifle so tight that my knuckles turned white.

When we docked, the flames were out, but deck boards were still smoking. My pack had dispersed, and I didn't have time to say goodbye as shaken passengers hurried to disembark. During the commotion, I spotted the professor, in his lavender jacket, on the dock, and watched as he swiftly maneuvered through a sea of horse-drawn carts and fish mongers. At the time, I thought little of his urgent departure, but later I would understand his haste.

CHAPTER 3

GALVESTON

1868

When we set foot on dry land on that warm and breezy November day, the port was roiling with activity, making our ship life feel restful. Loud chatter and shouting in a cacophony of languages mixed with the squawking of hundreds of sea birds created a frenzied chorus. Mother held a vice-like grip on my hand as we pushed our way through the well-dressed and coiffed, swerved around clusters of the slovenly and rank smelling, and gave wide berth to the slumped and blathering forms clutching empty liquor bottles.

Adding to our path of chaos were dogs, cats, chickens, goats, pigs, and cattle, and in their wake the smell of manure and feces was mixed with the overriding scent of dead fish, salt, and seaweed. Mother moved in a hunched-over gait while clutching her handkerchief over her nose and mouth, but Father wouldn't give in to the unpleasantness and walked with long strides and head held high as if he were landed gentry. I, on the other hand, was so glad to be on land that none of it, bad smelling or sweet, made a difference to me.

We headed north to an area where the crowds began to thin, and Father purchased a newspaper from a barefoot, red-faced boy while I gawked at the market stalls, developing an immediate craving for food—fresh apples, pears, meat—no more salted fish and potatoes or mush for breakfast.

After begging Father to buy something edible, we sat on a bench near the water's edge and shared a bruised pear, a half loaf of bread, and a hunk of cheese.

For a few minutes, Father shuffled through the paper looking for a place to buy provisions and spoke in a confident voice, trying to dislodge Mother's gloom.

"We can buy new clothes. All is not lost," he said. And as if our future were crystal clear in his mind he added, "We'll stay here for five days, select an affordable inn, buy the goods we need, a horse, a wagon, and then head west."

Perusing the local headlines, my father read the news in a dramatic yet jaunty voice. There was a lost cow that had washed up dead in the bayou, a barefooted burglar who stole jewelry from a house on Centre Street, and the arrest of a man who commandeered armfuls of fabric from a seamstress shop.

"What kind of place is this?" Mother muttered, but after our meal her voice sounded more weary than distressed.

Father was unperturbed. He yawned, leaned back, spread his arms across the back of the bench, then closed his eyes and let the unseasonably warm sunshine wick out the moistness that had weighed down our clothes for over ninety days.

A few moments later, Mother placed her head on his shoulder—the long days at sea, the tension between the professor and captain, the fire, the loss of their belongings—especially the brooch—had taken their toll. She let out a long sigh and dropped her shoulders as if she had taken her last breath.

While they dozed with their faces to the sun, I slipped out of my shoes and jumped from the boardwalk to the wet sand below and searched splits and cracks in the wooden timbers for crabs and mussels and collected shells in colors and shapes that I had never seen before. Some were perfectly formed and looked like angels' wings with a wash of purple, but most were just pieces of shells with streaks of red and ochre and undersides the color of moon glow.

I was beneath the boardwalk between the water's edge and bulkhead when I heard a *tap tap tapping* of a cane overhead and voices coming my way. Two men were in conversation, one with a rough gravelly voice, and another that was without a doubt *his voice*—the professor's. Not far from where I was below, they stopped, and I could see the soles of the professor's boots through the gaps in the deck boards.

"A scout. Do you know of one?" the professor said.

"That depends," the man said. "Information will cost you."

"Everyone's an entrepreneur here," the professor said. "You can't even get a simple piece of advice for free."

There was quiet for a minute except for the rush of a gentle wave that lapped over my toes then I heard the distinct sound of clinking coins.

"That should be plenty," the professor said.

The other man cleared his throat. "One more will do—if you please."

I heard the professor slap another coin in the man's hand, then he rammed the tip of his cane against the board above my head and roared, "Tell me, damn you!"

I jumped sideways and let out a slight squeak, not unlike a sandpiper's call, and hoped that the men above didn't hear.

The gravelly voiced man coughed, then spat. "There's a fellow that drifts around these parts by the name of O'Brien. He knows his way around with the Injuns and all . . . speaks Comanche I think, or Apache . . . they all sound the same to me, but . . ."

The professor interrupted tersely. "What's his first name?"

"Jasper," the man said.

"Where can I find him?"

"Probably around Austin or other towns near the edge of Indian territory."

"You mean I have to search far and wide to find this Jasper O'Brien? My money buys me nothing more specific than that?"

The man paused, then spoke. "Settle down, mister. I ain't finished. I know another fellow too, but he's out in Del Rio."

"That's almost Mexico," the professor said incredulously.

The gravelly voiced man puffed out a breath. "This here's big country. It ain't like your little rinky-dink France. Go to Austin, and I guarantee you'll find O'Brien. Try the brothels and the saloons. He'll either be there or somebody will know where he is. But just so you don't get uppity and come looking for me later with that Frenchie lip of yours, I'm going to tell you the facts. He knows this territory, but he's also a scoundrel. Card cheater among other things."

The professor laughed mockingly. "Aren't all you Americans scoundrels? The bigger the scoundrel, the bigger the dimwit!"

The man didn't laugh, but I heard his feet shuffling like he was agitated.

"I can handle him," the professor said. "Dimwits are easy to outsmart."

The gravelly-voiced man said, "Hmmm," as if he were visualizing an unpleasant circumstance, then he coughed and added, "Well, you can't say I didn't warn you."

As they walked away, I heard the professor ask, "What does this so-called scoundrel look like?" and I heard the man say something about red hair, but the rest of his description was inaudible due to a wave that slapped against the sand, then retreated with a shimmering sound.

I waited for their footfalls to become more distant before peeking my head out from under the boardwalk, and I saw the professor and the man— one of the slovenly types—turn on a nearby street and disappear around a corner. To my right, Mother and Father were still napping. Father had his hat tipped over his eyes, and Mother's body was slumped against his torso, and her head dropped downward against her chest.

I continued my search for shells and wondered if on our trip westward we'd run into the professor again—I knew Mother would be unnerved by his re-emergence, but there was something about his line of work—the newness and wildness of it—that made my heart quicken. I continued my own search for foreign creatures and had two pockets full of treasures when Mother and Father roused from their drowsiness. It was as if for an hour they were overcome by a spell that smoothed any hard edges, as the ocean had done to the tumbled shells in my pockets.

Neither my parents nor I had any way to know that the peace they felt that morning would be short lived.

~

Our troubles began at a boarding house west of town where the rooms were cheaper, but the air was still and water from late-afternoon downpours pooled in low spots beside a crushed-shell road.

When we arrived at dusk, we were still weary from the trip but relieved to have a room of our own. The sky behind the board-and-batten house was ablaze with streaks of pink and orange, and tidal pools shimmered in the glowing light as striped-winged nighthawks scoured the marsh grasses and sandy patches for insects.

Our first impression of our accommodations as a place of beauty and calm was transformed within minutes. As we walked down the matted sea grass path toward the porch, our surroundings turned into a swarm of all things biting—gnats, flies, mosquitoes—from which there was no escape. When the boarding house attendant showed us our room, which consisted of nothing more than a low-ceilinged space with three cots side-by-side, a small wooden table, a candle, and a wash pan, the room was already filled with mosquitoes that had penetrated the cracks in the wood siding.

And after we blew out the candle and crawled into bed that night, we soon found that the thin woven net that hung from the ceiling and draped over our beds offered little protection. Mosquitoes buzzed incessantly in our faces all night, and the next morning, despite our efforts to bury our heads under our blankets, we were covered in swollen red spots.

Mother couldn't hide her irritation when she asked the housekeeper with exasperation, "Do you have other nets *without* holes?"

The woman, who wore a dirty dress and had a drawn face with dark circles under her eyes, shrugged unsympathetically, "You get what you pay for."

Shortly after this exchange, Mother and Father had an argument that seemed to rattle the room's wooden siding.

"This is intolerable!" Mother said. "We must move to another inn!"

"We cannot," Father said in a loud, firm voice. "We can't afford it. We need to save our money for supplies."

For the remainder of the morning, neither Father nor Mother was interested in each other's company, and since Father was the less irritable of the two, I chose to accompany him to investigate the purchase of a wagon and horse instead of going with Mother to the market for bread, butter, and beans.

Together we endured six consecutive days of unpleasant conditions, but it was on the seventh day that everything changed.

That evening, when Father and I came back with news of a rancher at edge of town with a fine mare for a reasonable price, Mother was in the bed under three layers of blankets, shivering, with beads of sweat sprinkled across her blazing red forehead. She had a faraway look in her eyes and didn't seem to recognize either of us.

With a panicked expression, Father paid the house attendant to go for a doctor, but the doctor didn't come until the next day, and the attendant moved elsewhere for fear of catching whatever Mother had, leaving us with nothing but a half loaf of bread, a jar of honey, and a bucket of fresh water.

When the doctor arrived, Father was applying a wet towel to Mother's forehead, and I was standing in the doorway fidgeting with worry. He knew immediately what her illness was and covered his nose and mouth with his handkerchief. He only examined her for a few minutes, then stepped into the hallway, opened his leather bag, and handed Father a glass tube with three doses of quinine.

With a long face he said, "Not sure if it will help. She's pretty far along." Then he shook his head and said, "I'm sorry."

Father stayed by Mother's bedside the next day when swelling and pain entered her fingers, arms, and legs, and when she started vomiting blood, he got a fever of his own and barely had enough energy to make it to the latrine. I was no longer allowed in the room for fear of my becoming ill, so I assembled a pallet in the hall outside their door and talked through the keyhole. Sometimes I went outside and cupped my hands over my eyes and peered through the window to see their faces. What I saw was horrifying—Mother's cheeks were hollow, and her bones pushed out against her skin. Sometimes Father would come to the window, and we'd touch fingers through the glass.

He could barely lift his head off his pillow the day Mother died. Out in the hall, I had just awakened.

"Good morning," I whispered through the tiny hole. There was a long silence, then I heard his voice—weak and thin.

"Your mother's gone to heaven," he said, then there was more silence as my eyes swelled with tears.

I heard his cot creak as he turned on the mattress. "I need you to do something," Father said. "Remember the preacher we met at the grocer on Market Street?"

"Yes," I said, trying to sound strong, but my voice quavered.

"He's staying at an inn on Centre Street called Stiles House. Go find him and deliver this."

Father groaned, and then I heard two footsteps and another groan as he slipped an envelope under the door, then he fell back onto the bed.

I tucked the letter in my waist pocket and put on my shoes but didn't waste time tying the laces.

"I'll be right back," I said.

I heard him take a deep breath, "You're a good girl."

My mind was spinning as I ran through the streets of Galveston, swerving around horse-drawn wagons and all kinds of carts with goods for sale. When I reached Main Street, I asked a boy for directions. His hair was blond, and he wore a bloodstained apron as he pushed a cart filled with pink-skinned fish.

"Stiles House. Do you know where is?"

He raised a freckled arm and pointed his finger to the right. "Two blocks down, then take a left. You'll see a blue sign hanging from a post."

I took off running and heard him yelling behind me, "Redfish, redfish here. Nickel a pound."

When I found Stiles House, there was a man dressed in black wearing a wide-brimmed straw hat. He sat on the porch in a rocking chair. Next to him was a dark-haired woman who was fanning her neck. A blond-headed boy who looked a few years older than me sat on the steps, wearing rolled-up pants and an undershirt. He was whittling a stick into a sharp point.

I stopped at the wooden gate before entering. "Reverend Cranston?" I said.

"Indeed, I am," the man said.

"And you?"

"Frances Abbott . . . you may not remember, but my father, mother, and I met you at the market."

"Ah yes," he said and smiled. He stood up and walked toward me. "I remember now. Just off the boat from England. I'm surprised you're still here with so many sick."

"We had to get supplies. Then my mother . . ." I began to tear up.

"What's wrong, child?" he said.

I dropped my head and let my hair fall over my face, trying to hide the drops coming from my eyes. "My mother died, and my father is . . ." I couldn't finish my sentence, so instead I handed him the letter. He adjusted his glasses, opened the envelope, read the note, then folded it again and turned toward the woman.

"Celia, please get some tea for this young lady. And John Joseph, introduce yourself. I will be back after a while."

Celia walked to where I was standing. I didn't look up, but I could hear her skirt luffing like a sail in the breeze as she approached, and then she put her arm around my shoulder and accompanied me to a porch that was surrounded by a mixture of pink and red roses.

"Sit, child," she said. "Along with the tea, perhaps I can find a muffin leftover from breakfast." She went inside.

As I sat, the musky scent of roses mixed with the smoky air from neighborhood chimneys. I wiped a tear away and gave my best effort to prevent another from leaking out.

The boy stood up and held out his hand. "I'm John Joseph," he said. "I'm twelve, how about you?"

"Ten." I reached out and gave him a handshake. His hand felt clammy, so I withdrew quickly.

"I'm sorry for your troubles," he said.

I nodded but couldn't get a word out. He started whittling again. "I'm making a spear—in case we need it. We're headed west tomorrow. Who knows what we'll run into? Maybe I'll spear a rattlesnake, or coral snake, or a giant scorpion. I hear there all kinds of things that'll bite, sting, and raise the hair on your head."

I held my head in my hands wishing he would stop talking about such things. Despite my interest in wild creatures, at the moment, I didn't need anything else to be fearful of.

"They're Indians too, you know? Pop says the soldiers have chased most of 'em up north, but he's keeping his gun handy just in case, and he's taught me how to use it. I've got good aim. Killed a rabbit just yesterday."

Celia returned with a corn cake and a mug of tea in hand.

"For God's sake, John Joseph. What are you rattling on about?" she said.

"Just Indians, snakes, guns, and stuff." He was jogging his knee up and down like he was ready to take off in a sprint.

"Well, shush about that. Frances doesn't want to hear about such things."

She sat down in the rocking chair beside me and put the cornbread and tea on a small wooden table. I pushed my hair behind my ears and took a nibble of the muffin but was too upset to eat, so I cupped the warm mug in both hands and took two sips of tea that tasted like it had been thinned down and reheated.

"Frances is a pretty name," Celia said.

"It was my grandmother's," I said.

John Joseph jumped in. "Anybody ever call you Frannie?"

I looked at him from the corner of my eye and hesitated for a moment before saying, "My father does."

"I like the sound of it," John Joseph said. "Mind if I call you that too?"

"Okay," I said, but down deep I wasn't sure I was ready to be so friendly.

He held up his stick for me to examine. "Wanna whittle?" he said. "I've got an extra knife you can use. I'll show you how."

Whipping his head to the side, he flicked his straight blond hair back from his eyes, dug into his pocket, and pulled out a penknife. "This one's kind of small compared to mine, but it'll do the trick—good for beginners."

He held the knife flat in his palm. His hand was dirty and calloused.

I shook my head. "That's okay, I don't want to," but he seemed not to hear.

"Now when you open it, you have to be extra careful. Hold it like this and open the blade away from you." He put his dirt-caked thumbnail in the knife's etched slot and pulled open the blade. "And when you close it, you gotta watch your fingers. I made that mistake once and almost lost my pinkie." He looked up at Celia. "Right, Ma?"

Celia gave him a stern look. "I'd prefer not to remember such things, John Joseph."

She stood and took a deep breath. "I need to continue packing. Frances, you let me know if you need anything, and John Joseph, be considerate of Frances's feelings. She's probably not in the mood for your jabber."

"I will, Ma." After he watched Celia close the screen door, he held up his finger and showed me his scar and whispered behind his cupped hand. "It bled like a son-of-a-gun, but Ma bandaged it up good."

He walked out into the yard and snapped a twig off low-hanging branch. "This will do for starters," he said, then sat back down on the porch steps, curled his toes around the board's edge, and slapped his hand on the wood. "Come sit next to me. If you want to learn, you gotta get closer."

I could see he wasn't going to leave me alone, so I moved to the steps, gathered my dress, and sat down.

He held the open knife between his thumb and index finger. "Put the blade near the tip of the wood, make a shallow notch and slide the knife forward. Always push away from your body. Don't want to stab yourself."

He held out the knife. "Here, you try."

I took it, followed his instructions, and pushed shavings off the stick's tip.

"That's right," he said. "Soon you'll have your own spear to protect yourself."

Though I knew he was just being friendly, my patience was wearing thin with the constant spear talk.

"What if I don't want a spear?" I said.

He looked at me with disbelief. "What? Everybody needs a spear. Heck, on our way from Mississippi to here, I speared a frog . . . you can eat a frog you know—and I speared a catfish—they're better eatin' than frogs—and a lizard, too, but I didn't eat that. I'd only eat that if I was starving to death. Why don't you want one?"

I straightened my back. "I don't need it."

"What do you mean?"

I decided to stretch the truth. "Because I have a gun," I said.

He turned his head sideways and laughed. "You don't have your own gun. No ten-year-old girl has her own gun. It's your papa's."

"I do," I said. I could feel my courage growing stronger. "Papa gave it to me."

He looked me straight in the eye and pursed his lips before saying, "Can you shoot it?"

I met his gaze straight on. "Yes. He taught me how."

"Hmmm . . ." John Joseph said. He cocked his head and carved off a few more wood chips. "Well, if you say so," and I could tell that he still didn't believe me.

As we waited for Reverend Cranston, I sat and listened to the squawk of seagulls as John Joseph whittled.

After a few minutes, I picked up the pen knife and started working on a point. I decided that a little whittling wouldn't do any harm, mostly because I felt guilty about my white lie.

~

It was over an hour before the reverend returned. When he finally arrived at the front gate, he held the Jaeger rifle in one hand and my bag in the other. I got up and ran to meet him because I was anxious to hear about Father.

He laid my bag and the rifle down and held my shoulders with his thick hands. He took a deep breath as if he wasn't sure what he was going to say, then glanced at Celia and then back at me.

"It's going to be okay. Your father and mother are with God, and you are with us. We'll take care of you."

I couldn't see Celia's face, but I heard her clear her throat. John Joseph sat quietly as the reverend spoke, but I could see that he was eying my belongings and the Jaeger rifle that leaned against the fence post.

At the time I didn't care what he thought about the gun. And my excitement about what lay ahead had vanished.

All I could think of was wanting to be back in my English hometown. I wanted to walk beside my mother on our slick cobbled streets and feel the cold and drizzle against my face. I wanted to be home where everything was the same—not different. And I couldn't fathom how my parents, once so sturdy and strong, could be felled so quickly, like trees in a windstorm, and why someone small like me could be spared and left alone—an orphan in a new world.

CHAPTER 4
WESTWARD

1868

Before dawn the next day, Reverend Cranston, Celia, John Joseph, and I left town in a mule-drawn wagon. As we traveled along roads made of compacted sand, I cried quietly and listened to the whoosh of waves as they pushed, curled, and bubbled at the bay's reedy edges.

John Joseph lay sprawled in the corner of the wagon making slight purring noises as he slept. I could tell by Celia's expression that she wanted to comfort me, but I wasn't ready to receive tenderness from a woman I barely knew. Instead, I pulled my knees tight to my chest to protect myself from the unknown.

I heard the reverend whisper, "It will take time, Celia."

"She's so distraught. We must do something," Celia said, but the last of her words were carried off with the rush of a wave in retreat.

There was a land breeze as we slogged through the salt marsh. The squishy sound of mule hooves, mixed with the *chick chick purr* of seabirds, was the backdrop to my quiet despair. Three times, the wagon wheels came to a stop, and John Joseph and the reverend got out to push.

Sitting on the bench, Celia snapped the reins and clucked. "Hye, mule!"

The mule snorted, hunched its shoulders, groaned, and pulled. All the while mosquitoes clouded around our faces in a swirl of high-pitched buzzing, reminding me again of the sad days before and of my loss.

John Joseph handed me a blanket. "Put this over you," he said. "It may help a little."

Celia untied her apron and wrapped it around her head, and John Joseph and the reverend covered their faces with spare shirts, leaving a button open to see. With the blanket over my head and body, I sat in the bed of the wagon. After a time, the smell of salt air cleared my head, and I began to feel better. Through a moth-eaten hole, I watched gulls and terns as they dipped and skimmed the water's surface with urgency in their flight. The sun hovered on the eastern horizon, and the shallow water was awash in pink. By mid-morning, the wind picked up, most of the mosquitoes vanished, and with their absence our spirits rose. The reverend sang, and John Joseph and Celia joined in:

> *Or, if on joyful wing cleaving the sky*
> *Sun, moon, and stars forgot, upward I'll fly,*
> *Still all my song shall be,*
> *Nearer, my God, to Thee.*

I shed my blanket and turned to face the breeze. To the west, the horizon was crowned in billowy gray clouds. As we passed from marshland into a prairie spotted with low scraggly trees, a strong puff of wind blew my loose hair across my face.

John Joseph stood up in the wagon bed and braced himself with his hands on the reverend's shoulders. His white shirt flagged in the wind as Celia retied the ribbons on her bonnet and tugged them tight against her chin.

"Weather's coming, Pop," John Joseph said.

Celia's singing quieted, and I had a prescient awareness that in this new land even a stirring wind could be foreboding, but the reverend continued with a strong, steady voice that somewhat calmed my fears.

In less than a minute, a chill hit us as if someone had opened an invisible door to the arctic.

"A blue norther!" the reverend shouted. "I've heard of these. Unpack the coats, Celia. It's winter in Texas!"

"What'll we do next?" John Joseph shouted. His words were now barely audible against the stiff wind.

"Find shelter," the reverend boomed. "Look out for a house or a shed."

John Joseph scanned the horizon, and I stood up and looped one finger through his suspender strap to brace myself.

He gave me a nod like, "I gotcha."

For what seemed like forever we saw nothing. Then to the north, I spotted some upright timbers near a clump of trees.

"Over there, sir," I said. "I think I see something."

The reverend adjusted his glasses and squinted. "Where child, I don't see."

"There, Henry," Celia pointed. "I can see it—just barely."

John Joseph held his hand over his eyes. "I can't see anything."

"Just beyond the trees," Celia said, then she turned to me and smiled. "Your eyes are like an eagle's. Lucky for us," she said. "We would surely have missed it. We Cranstons are a bit nearsighted."

The reverend turned his head my way. "Eagle-eye, that'll be your nickname."

John Joseph poked his father. "What will you call me, Pop?"

Celia laughed. "How about chatterbox?"

John Joseph grumbled. "I need a better name than that . . . like maybe . . . lion heart!"

"We will see," the reverend said. "There will be plenty of time for everyone to exhibit their talents."

Though I was shivering, I felt a flicker of warmth inside, as if a small fire had newly kindled.

~

That night we sheltered in a one-room abandoned log cabin about fourteen feet wide and long—there were no windows, just one door that sagged on its hinges and couldn't be closed, leaving the cold air to flow freely inside. John Joseph and I gathered wood and stacked it on the dirt floor next to fallen chimney cobbles while Celia coerced a few flames from a pile of dried grass. Before long, we had a roaring fire and huddled close to each other wearing all the clothes we had, overlaid with blankets. The reverend smoked his pipe and sipped coffee while the rest of us quietly nibbled on biscuits.

John Joseph broke the silence with a question that had dominated my own thoughts.

"Pop, what do you think happened to the folks that lived here?"

The reverend leaned back against a log and crossed his legs. "Hard to say, Son."

John Joseph wasn't satisfied. "Do you think it was Indians? Killed 'em and scalped 'em?"

I shivered and pulled my blanket close as I looked around the room for the gunny sack that held my Jaeger rifle. The reverend gave John Joseph a stare that said, "Enough," then took a long puff on his pipe and blew out a string of smoke.

"All I know is we don't know. Be at peace now and thankful that we have a nice warm fire and a place to rest."

Before long, all was quiet except for the popping of the fire and the hoot of a screech owl.

I lay awake for what felt like hours due to the seed John Joseph had planted. I made sure the Jaeger rifle was close by, even though I didn't know how to use it. When sleep finally came, it was fitful and light. My dreams were tumultuous and fragmented, agitated by the repetitive squeak of the cabin door that sounded like an out-of-tune violin playing a broken melody.

~

The next morning was blustery, cold, and clear. Wind tumbled across the prairie, bending the sparse trees and sending dry brown leaves into flight. The sky had an endless quality that made our wagon feel small and vulnerable, but we saw nothing and no one for hours except a herd of white-tail deer grazing in the distance. Later the wind calmed, and I noticed a varmint rooting at the edge of the road.

"Look!" I nudged John Joseph with my elbow.

"What?" he said.

I pointed again toward a creature I had never seen before—tiny upright ears, gray scaly outer armor with a foot-long extension that looked more like a medieval club than a tail.

"Armadillo!" John Joseph shouted.

He grabbed his spear, jumped from the wagon to the ground, and took off leaping and high stepping through the bronze-colored grasses. It was clear from the thrashing at least fifteen feet ahead that John Joseph was losing ground.

"He's a fast critter!" he shouted over his shoulder. The reverend laughed, but Celia shook her head, "For God's sake, Henry, don't encourage him."

Strangely, I found myself rooting for John Joseph.

"Get him," I yelled, but as soon as the words left my mouth, John Joseph stutter-stepped and leapt to the side, then let out an *eek* and a *whoaaaa*! His eyes were wide.

"What?" Celia called.

Within a split second he was racing back toward the wagon with a speed that was twice as fast as his former pursuit. *Snaaaaaaake!*

The reverend glanced at Celia with a grin, "Perhaps Chicken-Heart?"

For the first time I caught a glimmer of a smile cross Celia's lips.

∿

It was another full day before we encountered the floodplains of the Colorado and then a boat landing. There, a brown-skinned boy with no shirt or shoes dipped a pole into shallow waters and ferried us across the river's blue-green surface.

The reverend shouted to the boy. "Cedar Bend—is it far from here?"

He pointed to a thicket of trees across the river. *Allá*, he said.

∿

Cedar Bend—a post office, two churches, and an assortment of loosely scattered log houses—was our new home. The Methodist clergy house—our house—was on the far west side of town on ten acres of land.

To say it wasn't much was giving it more credit than it was due. Celia's mouth turned into a hard line when she witnessed light pouring through cracks in the chinking and a spot in the roof where shingles had given way against the weight of a broken branch. Gloms of dry dirt covered the beams where red wasps had nested, and as we stared upward at what remained of our roof they coasted in and out of their holes, oblivious to our presence.

But the reverend didn't seem disappointed, and within a few months, our one-room log house expanded to two—"the saddle bag," as Reverend Pop called it, with the new room on the other side of the chimney.

The day the new room was finished and the patching was complete, Reverend Pop, as I started to call him, hung my Jaeger rifle above the door threshold. "That's your gun, Frannie. We're putting it up there in a place of honor—to remember your parents. I know it was special to your father, and if you'd like, I'll teach you how to use it."

"I thought you already knew how," John Joseph said.

I looked at Reverend Pop with an expression that was a mix of begging forgiveness and pleading for support.

"She does," Reverend Pop said. "I meant I just need to show her how to set up a target range so it's safe. Don't want to fell one of our citizens when we're practicing. Gun like that fires a long way. Right Frannie?"

I nodded, trying to appear confident.

It was on my eleventh birthday that Reverend Pop took it down and said, "Let's polish her up. Gotta take care of a fine gun like this."

He showed me how to rub a rag in a circular motion until the walnut stock with its intricately carved scrollwork gleamed. John Joseph was right by my side watching as Reverend Pop handed me a small brush to grease the gun's firing mechanism with a thin layer of lard.

"Sperm whale oil's better for cleaning a gun," John Joseph said.

"Money's too tight for that," Reverend Pop said. "Lard will do for now." Then he attached a leather sling that he had fashioned to fit over my shoulder.

"There you go," he said. "You're a real frontier girl."

John Joseph looked me up and down like he approved of what he saw, then rubbed his hands together. "Now let's shoot that thing!"

"Hold on a minute," the reverend said. "You two go outside and pick a good spot a ways from the house, then mound up some dirt to shoot against."

John Joseph flew out the door like his pants were on fire and shouted over his shoulder, "Come on, Frannie!"

I followed more slowly, trying to appear nonchalant, as if the whole gun shooting thing was old hat. When he rounded the corner at the back of the house, he stopped in his tracks and looked from side to side, then pointed.

"How about over there, Frannie? Outside the fence."

I nodded.

Our "shootin' range," as John Joseph called it, was just beyond our barbed wire fence in a field of low grasses that our goats had cropped clean to the nub. We erected an old fence post and nailed a piece of tin to it.

When we were done, John Joseph shouted for Reverend Pop and Celia to come out.

"I'll sit on the porch and watch from here," Celia said.

As Reverend Pop, John Joseph, and I headed toward the range, John Joseph walked backwards in front of me, giving me advice. "Now remember, get your stance right, stand with your feet apart, bend your knees, and lean forward over your left knee to steady yourself."

"She knows all that, John Joseph," Reverend Pop said. "After all, it's her gun." Then he winked at me when John Joseph wasn't looking.

He didn't tell John Joseph about our secret. Reverend Pop had already given me a dry run shooting lesson when John Joseph was in town running an errand for Celia. He showed me how to pour grains of black powder into the barrel, push in the patch and lead plug, use the ramrod, pull back the flintlock, sprinkle a little powder in the touch hole, then secure the gunstock tight against my shoulder.

"This gun's known to shoot accurately for a long way, but it'll kick like an ole mule, so you have to stand firm," he said.

Even though I did everything Reverend Pop said, I was nervous as I held the gun and aimed at the target about thirty yards out. Reverend Pop moved in close behind me when I raised the barrel, took aim, and squeezed the trigger.

Bam!

John Joseph was too busy staring at the target to notice that Reverend Pop had grabbed my elbows to keep me from falling. When he turned back around, I was standing straight again.

"Close, but you're in the dirt . . ." John Joseph said, "by about two feet. That wasn't bad, though."

He flicked his hair. "Can I shoot it, Pop?"

Reverend Pop looked at me, "All right with you, Frannie?"

I passed him the gun.

"Now John Joseph, this gun's a little different than ours," Reverend Pop said, but John Joseph interrupted and held up his hand.

"I got it. I got it," he said, then proceeded to load. When he was finished, he looked at me and smiled. "Watch this."

He got into position, and I could see his muscle flex as he pressed the gun against his shoulder. I plugged my ears and closed my eyes when he squeezed the trigger.

BAM!

When I opened them, John Joseph was on his back, and the gun was in his lap. "Holy smokes!" he said.

Reverend Pop let out a laugh, and when I saw Celia smiling in the shadow of the porch overhang, she put her hands around her mouth and shouted.

"When you get more meat on you, you'll hold your own just like Frannie did."

John Joseph got up, dusted himself off, and when he handed the gun back to me, his face was flushed. "Dang, that was a wallop! How'd you keep standing?"

Reverend Pop was still laughing when he gave me a nod of approval.

"I've just had a little more practice—that's all," I said.

When Reverend Pop and Celia grinned at each other, I knew then that they had been in cahoots on my behalf.

On that day, I dropped the Reverend and kept the Pop. Celia had already insisted that I call her Celia instead of Mrs. Cranston, but I had been reluctant. But when she cut a big slice of rhubarb pie and slid it on my plate during my birthday dinner, I made it a point to change my ways.

"Thank you, Celia," I said.

John Joseph ate his pie like a water bird swallowing a fish—he was too busy talking to chew. "We'll go hunting tomorrow, and I'll teach you how to bag a rabbit. It may take a few attempts, but you'll catch on."

That night, I pulled the blankets up close to my chin on a cot next to John Joseph's and listened to his talk with a renewed sense of excitement.

"We'll head down to the gulley, and I guarantee there's a coon back in there. Who knows what we'll see?"

Oddly, his words made me think of the professor, and I wondered if he had taken down that alligator he wanted. As I lay there, I imagined a pitch-black night—warm and dense with fog—a man poling a skiff through swampy waters while the professor held a lantern against the darkness searching for movement: a tail, eyes shining behind a long snout. I thought about the alligator's speed, its powerful thrust, and its giant snapping jaws—the images I had seen in drawings in books at school and read about with wide eyes. Would he use a pistol, or would he take it with a club—as he tried with the shark?

I turned my head toward John Joseph next to me. "Have you ever seen an alligator?" I asked, but he didn't answer. All I heard was the soft purr of his snoring.

CHAPTER 5

CORA, MARIE ISABEL, AND JUAN ESTEBAN

1868–1871

Over the next three years, John Joseph and I came to know our land—the prairie and woodlands—like the backs of our hands. We knew to hunt for deer at dusk in the draws and eroded gulches near the creek. We knew the best chance to get a rabbit was in the morning or evening at the edges of our fields where the hedgerow offered safety and a source of food for cottontails. We named the two racoons that gathered regularly at our corncrib after dark—Wild Bill and Jesse James—and made sport of chasing those bandits, knowing full well that they'd be back after bedtime. We developed a fondness for the armadillos that nosed in the grasses near our fence line—they didn't seem to care how close we got, and unless we made a sudden move, they wouldn't run off. We steered clear of places where we had seen rattlesnakes and watched out for the slithering movement of a water moccasin when we swam in the creek.

But those years brought more excitement than that—our family took on a wildness of its own. It would no longer be just John Joseph and me running around. By 1871, there were six of us. Word got out that Pop and Celia took in orphans, so I now had two sisters in addition to John Joseph. Cora and Marie Isabel—ages six and four—showed up with nothing but their given names and a sad tale.

On the day the girls arrived, John Joseph overheard Celia and Pop speaking in hushed tones about an Indian raid and how Cora and Marie

Isabel were hiding in the root cellar when their parents were killed, but when I asked more about what happened, he tightened his lips and refused to tell me.

"You don't want to know," was all he said, and by the tone of his voice I decided that maybe he wished he hadn't heard either.

When Cora and Marie Isabel were out of earshot, Celia sat us both down and told us in a quiet voice, "Cora and Marie Isabel are family now, so make them feel at home."

In keeping with Celia's wishes, John Joseph and I made a pallet for the girls between our cots so they could sleep together, and we could watch over them. After their bed was made, they sat cross-legged with knees touching, then pulled the quilt over their heads and huddled in a tight knot, whispering as if they were in a world of their own.

With an offering of biscuits and honey, I was able to coax them from their hiding place. As Cora licked at the honey, I noticed her wide face, thick lips, and deep-set brown eyes that blended with the gray of her dirty cheeks and clothing. Unlike Cora, Marie Isabel's complexion had a weary brightness. With chapped red cheeks, blue eyes, and delicate lips she appeared like a spring flower emerging from rocky soil.

Later, I took them to the barnyard to introduce them to our animals in hopes that their moods might brighten upon meeting our donkey Doris, Sheila the pig, Giuseppe the goat, and our herd of chickens that Celia warned me not to name, but I did anyway.

"The red rooster's Jacob, and that black one's Esau 'cause they peck and chase each other a lot, and that red hen there is Ethel . . . mainly because she looks like an Ethel. She's our best egg layer, and the rest I just call chickens."

Marie Isabel spoke to me directly for the first time. "Why don't you name them too?"

I scrambled to think of something besides their true destiny and did my best to put a homey shine on my chicken tale.

"Sometimes they like to go visit their chicken friends down the road and 'cause their chicken coop is nicer they stay and then become a new family just like us."

41

When they both smiled, I felt as if I had discovered a glimmer of light within a dark cave, and before long they were immersed in the hay, petting Giuseppe with long gentle strokes from head to tail.

The next summer, a new brother came along when a man from Lockhart dropped off a boy named Juan Esteban.

The man, introducing himself as Mr. Slocum, spent only a few minutes speaking with Pop and Celia under our live oak tree. He kept swaying back and forth as if he were in a rush to get away. Mostly bald, with just a fringe of stringy hair draped over his yellowed collar, he spoke in a hoarse voice and nervously coughed into his shirt sleeve several times.

I was scrubbing shirts on a washboard when I overheard snippets of their conversation. Juan Esteban wasn't near them. In a dirty white shirt and pants that were above his ankles, he sat on his haunches beside the tree trunk where a lightning strike had seared a deep black scar.

"This is unexpected —no one told us." Celia said.

Mr. Slocum wrung his hands and uttered broken sentences. "Yes, Ma'am, you see, he was my wife's child . . . before we married. . . . Well, Alma, my wife, that is . . . she passed, and . . ."

He lowered his head and gripped his forehead between his fingers. "It's been difficult you see. He can't do nothing to help me in the fields . . . believe me I've tried to teach him . . ."

At first, I thought Mr. Slocum was grief stricken, but when he raised up, his brow was furrowed, and his lips were drawn up tight like he was angry. "The boy just looks for bugs all day long and draws with his finger in the dirt . . . useless sh—" He caught himself before finishing his thought and glanced at Celia before dropping his eyes and saying, "Excuse me, ma'am."

Pop broke in. "We understand, Mr. Slocum. Life is hard, but we're all God's children."

Celia turned and walked toward Juan Esteban and knelt in front of him. She reached out to touch his arm, but he turned away and wedged his shoulder into the oak's scar.

Mr. Slocum's face turned red, and he shouted, "Juan Esteban! Where

42

are your manners, boy?" Then he turned to Celia. "I'm sorry, Mrs. Cranston, you see how he is."

Celia stood up. "No need for apologies, Mr. Slocum. I was too abrupt. Things take time."

Mr. Slocum looked at Celia with a desperate expression. "If you please, Mrs. Cranston . . . I know it's a burden."

I saw Pop raise his eyebrows as if a log dam was about to break.

Celia raised her chin and straightened her back. "Mr. Slocum, no child is a burden."

"Well, I mean . . . "

"Consider the subject closed," she said. "Of course we will."

She stood up and brushed her apron and spoke to Juan Esteban in a soft voice. "It's okay, child," she said. "In due time —whenever you're ready."

When Mr. Slocum left, Pop was the only one to shake his hand and say goodbye. Celia had already gone inside and was banging pots in the kitchen. I heard her mutter.

"A burden. For God's sake."

I moved my wash bucket a little closer to the window when Pop went to investigate the racket.

Celia was irate. "Did you see the poor child's hands and arms, John? There were switch marks all over them. Mr. Slocum must have . . . " Then her voice was quiet but fierce. "I should have given *that man* a piece of my mind."

I peered through the window as Pop took her into his arms. "He's in good hands now, Celia."

Outside, John Joseph was already introducing the rest of us to Juan Esteban.

When we gathered around to say hello, Juan Esteban stood with shoulders slumped, hands dangling at his side, then turned his head the other way. I couldn't help but notice how black his hair was, and in profile, his nose appeared thick and flat. Even though he was just a year younger, he was easily a foot taller and sturdy looking compared to the rest of us.

"How come you're not talking?" Marie Isabel said.

I shushed her. "Maybe he's just shy."

Cora walked up to him. "It's ok to be shy. I was too when I first got here."

John Joseph jumped in when Juan Esteban stood expressionless. "If you'd like, you can come hunting with Frannie and me sometime, seeing that you're almost Frannie's age and all. She's a good shot, and I'm pretty good too." He pointed out across our pasture. "We have a shootin' range over there. You can watch, or if you want, give it a try sometime."

While John Joseph was talking, I watched Juan Esteban. Instead of looking at John Joseph, he turned his head the opposite direction and stared intently into the nearby cedar breaks.

"Come," I said. "Follow me. Cora, Marie, and I will introduce you to our animals." Marie and Cora jumped up and down with delight and took off ahead of us chattering, "Doris, Jacob, Esau, Ethel, you get to meet our new brother."

I waved for Juan Esteban to join us, but he didn't move. Then I heard a flutter of wings about twenty paces away and noticed him observing a house wren scoot and peck its way up the shredded bark of a cedar tree. He stood still and watched as if in a trance, but when he heard Doris's bray in the distance, he followed in my footsteps.

～

Celia and Pop found out quick that school didn't suit Juan Esteban. The kids teased him and our teacher—Mr. Benson—sent home a note saying he was too dumb to learn. That didn't sit well with Celia.

She threw off her apron, and without taking the time to fix her hair in her usual going-to-town bun, she marched to the school, looked Mr. Benson in the eye and with a stiff lip said, "It appears that you don't have the perseverance to foster his unique mind."

So instead of going to school, Celia made it my job to try to teach Juan Esteban the alphabet.

"Maybe he just needs more time than most," she said.

She set up a table for us under our live oak tree, and every morning before school, and every afternoon when I got home, I opened my reader and tried to teach Juan Esteban how to write. I felt proud that Celia had chosen me for the task, and my optimism was high, even though progress was painfully slow.

Every letter that Juan Esteban crafted was like a miniature piece of art. The pitched lines of an "A" were perfectly straight and met at the peak with a crisp dot. His cross stroke was exactly halfway, as if he had used a ruler to measure the midpoint. Then he added a curl at the base which gave his A an extra flair.

By comparison, my own "A" looked more like a broken saddle horse.

He worked in silence with his head low and his thick arms wrapped around his paper, as if his work was a secret. It wasn't until he raised his head to the sound of a hawk screech or a woodpecker tap that I could see what he was doing. Usually beside the letter he had been tasked to draw was another more complicated piece of art. Next to Q was a bumble bee with the intricate webbing on its wing delicately illustrated. Near W was a pattern of arc-shaped pencil strokes that eventually turned into the scalloped edges of a swallowtail's wings.

One day when Juan Esteban got up and disappeared into a scrub patch for a few minutes, I stared at his drawings in amazement, and when he returned, he had a single red berry in his palm. He placed the berry on the paper between the butterfly's wings and pressed it ever so slightly, creating a brilliant orange dot.

The dot—its color, its vibrancy—and the drawing's delicacy reminded me of the botanicals in my English home.

From that day on, I didn't press Juan Esteban to draw letters—I worked on my homework while he drew. I concluded that letters were a waste of time compared to his drawings, which appeared to be inspired by some deep understanding. Something not taught—rather a gift.

As for my reputation as a teacher, I was somewhat concerned. In case anyone came over, I tucked a piece of paper under Juan Esteban's elbow that displayed a few sentences in my own chicken scratch as evidence that I was trying.

Celia was the only one to show devoted interest. When she took a break from her washing or cooking, she inspected the stack of papers that began to accumulate. In addition to my own letters would be an even larger collection of creatures: centipedes, grasshoppers, ants, pill bugs.

The day the tarantula was finished—to me, Juan Esteban's finest yet—Celia came over.

Her eyes were big when she held up the paper and examined the spider's thick body and hairy legs. "Where in the world did he see that?"

I shrugged my shoulders and shook my head. "I don't know."

Then her eyes got even bigger. "Good heavens, was it in the house?"

She tapped Juan Esteban on the shoulder. "Where was it, Juan Esteban? Show us." He turned his head to the side like he was thinking but didn't get up from the table.

For the first time I saw a look of frustration cross Celia's face. "It appears that he's spending more time on insects than on his letters. Are you not helping him?"

"I am, but I kind of think the drawings are another way of writing, so I decided to let him do that."

Celia blew air from her lips. "Please Frannie, he can't speak with just pictures. He needs to learn to write too—so we can understand him."

"I'm trying," I said, "but he's stubborn. He only wants to draw."

The harsh clip in her voice had vanished, and she held out her hand for Juan Esteban. "Come with me," she said. "Let's learn something new."

Though he wouldn't hold her hand, he got up and followed behind her.

~

Before long, Juan Esteban was put in charge of dinner. Celia had nurtured his obsessive focus and applied it to kitchen work. When he was chopping vegetables, he was manic. Every carrot slice had to be the same thickness and every potato cube no bigger than a quarter inch. If someone tried to steal a bite, he'd nearly slice your finger off like it was just another carrot. And he didn't take special orders—whatever was on his mind was it.

He made the same potato and mustard green hash for the third straight day, and we kids grumbled when he dropped the iron skillet on the table with a thud.

In unison, we said, "Not again . . ." but Pop cut us short and gave us each his convincing stare.

"Looks delicious, Juan Esteban, thank you."

From that day on, we knew to eat what came our way with no complaints.

And since Juan Esteban was contributing to the family workload with his cooking, Celia seemed less concerned about developing his writing skills, so he spent the rest of his free time drawing.

As for me, I kept working at my shooting skills along with John Joseph. We extended the firing range to a hundred feet and upgraded our target to a rusty tin panel with a bullseye drawn in chalk. Juan Esteban was always near but didn't show an interest in the shooting. He'd find a spot about twenty paces behind us under an old mesquite and either draw or scratch around with a stick looking for creatures. Occasionally, he'd let out a rough "*huuuuh*" like he was clearing his throat, but mostly he was silent.

When I hit the bullseye dead center one spring afternoon when the sun was so bright that I had to squint while aiming, John Joseph put his arm over my shoulders. "You're a dang sharpshooter!"

When I hit it two times more consecutively, a big smile crossed his face, his eyes sparkled, and he rubbed his hands together. "I have an idea, Frannie—and big plans for you."

He spent the next few minutes filling me in and finished with, "Wanna do it?"

I bit my lip. "Yes!" I said.

CHAPTER 6
SCHÜTZENFEST

1871

As a girl—just thirteen years old—competing against ten men in the *Schützenfest*, I turned some heads when I stood in line to sign up for the shooting contest wearing my best dress and carrying my Jaeger rifle. John Joseph and Pop were by my side to make sure the judges didn't turn me away.

It was a breezy but warm October day with puffy cumulous clouds billowing against a bright blue sky, and the trees that shaded our line held their leaves and showed no color change. The smoky smell of pork sausage and roasted pig's knuckles filled the morning air, and there was an overriding mood of jocularity among those present. Children dashed to and fro, and men huddled in circles around smoking pits as women fussed over long tables laid out with pickled vegetables, rounds of rye bread, heaping bowls of fresh corn, and an assortment of pies and strudels.

When Pop held out a few coins to pay my entrance fee, a gray-bearded man in a bowler and green jacket said, "I don't know, Reverend Cranston. Rules don't allow women or girls."

Pop adjusted the thin black tie he always wore as if the words he was about to speak descended from a higher order. "We live in a new world now, Wilbur. Maybe there should be new traditions."

Wilbur looked me up and down like I was a heifer in a livestock show while he chewed on the soggy nub of his cigar. "I guess it won't hurt. Good for a few laughs."

When I turned toward John Joseph, I could see the muscles tensing up in arms like he wanted to give that man a shove, but Pop contained him with a look.

Pop smiled. "Well, that's mighty generous of you, Wilbur."

As we walked away, John Joseph whispered. "The winner gets the money from the entry fees. You can do this Frannie, show 'em what you got."

The festival—an all-day event—was our county's cobbled-together version of a festival that's been held for centuries in Germany, and since there were plenty of Germans settlements nearby, people were inclined to take a day off from their toil for a brief spell of cheer and camaraderie. The day's activities started with a morning parade where the shooting competitors followed a serious-faced oompah band that hit all the wrong notes at the right time, then marched past the previous year's winner—the *Schützenkonig*—the king.

Last year's king, thumb-like in stature, barely waved as the parade passed but forced a flat smile to appease his enthusiastic courtiers. Compared to the jubilant crowd, he looked like a thistle among tulips.

Not to draw attention, I held back at the parade's tail and tried to make myself invisible in the shadows of pot-bellied fifty-year-olds. Among non-competitors, there was no waiting for lunch to tap into the ole man Wagner's latest brew. And by the time the marksman tournament started at 11:00 a.m. sharp, the crowd was sour breathed from kraut, brats, and bitter ale, and ripe for the shooting performance.

The shooting range was 150 feet long across a grassy meadow facing west toward an escarpment at the edge of a grove of live oak trees. A handcarved wooden eagle, wired to the top of a dead tree trunk, added status to the event. Below the eagle was a target—a two-foot diameter white circle painted on wood and nailed to the tree. Six red rings encircled a two-inch black bullseye.

During the competition, each contestant took turns with five shots for three rounds—the most bullseyes won.

Among the competitors, the mood was tense. Those waiting their turn stood in a semicircle around the designated shooter, cradling their rifles.

I looked down the line and most held repeaters—Sharps and Spencers. My Jaeger rifle was the only single-load cap lock in the bunch. I picked a spot at the end of the arc next to a tall thin man with a red mustache that wrapped upwards toward his ears and merged with his sideburns. His mustache was an unusually *orangey* red—the color of a carrot after it's rinsed and peeled.

He wore a brown jacket, dusty leather riding chaps, a wide-brimmed straw hat, and boots caked in mud as if he had ended up here after a wrong turn during a cattle drive. When I took the spot next to him, he looked at me and my gun with an unnerving smile as if my presence in the lineup was a joke.

Three shots in the air from Wilbur's pistol launched the event, and the crowd, with arms raised, let out a cheer that wafted across the meadow like a battalion's call to *charge*. The cheering continued until the first contestant took his position within a circle of fieldstone and fired five shots—all five hit the dirt behind the target and sent up a puff of dust.

A man shouted, "Whatcha aiming at George? Those yonder hills?"

Laughter filled the air until a handsome young man in lederhosen with a turkey feather in his cap entered the circle, loaded, and raised his gun. He fired slowly and steadily with several seconds between each shot—each one hit the target with a thud.

The crowd came to a hush as Wilbur waddled his way up a set of stairs that led to a platform draped in ribbons. He raised and focused a pair of binoculars, then thrust two fingers into the air. "Two bullseyes, ladies and gentlemen!"

The crowd erupted into a swell of hurrays. A man's voice boomed, "Atta boy, Max!"

Max raised his rifle and pumped his fist. Then he turned toward a cluster of pink-cheeked young women and gave a bow. The cluster turned into giggles and a series of curtsies.

Not to be outdone by a youngster, one of the pot-bellied shooters, in a woolen vest that strained at the buttons, took his turn.

Bam! Thud. *Bam!* Bullseye! *Bam!* Thud. *Bam! Bam!* Bullseye. Bullseye.

Wilbur raised his binoculars. "We have three, folks! Let's hear it for our two-time champion, Leo Lowenbaum!"

Serious-faced and dripping with sweat, Leo returned to his spot in line. Behind him, a woman of similar stature and plumpness patted him on the shoulder. He didn't turn around.

One by one the contestants shot, but no one outdid Leo. Finally, it was the red-mustached man's turn. He walked toward the circle with narrowed eyes.

Someone behind me whispered, "Is that a Henry rifle?"

He leaned his gun against his hip, then stretched his arms in the air and rotated his shoulders and gazed up into the trees as a gust of wind rustled the leaves above. Gripping the barrel with his gloved left hand, he slowly and carefully pushed each cartridge into the chamber with his right thumb, then looked at me as if he were giving me a lesson on how to load and shoot.

A shout came from near the beer keg. "While we're young, cowboy!"

He waited a few more seconds, then raised his firearm, and without hesitation pulled the trigger: *BAM, cock, BAM, cock, BAM, cock BAM, cock, BAM.*

People stood with mouths open. Even without binoculars, everyone could see that the black dot had taken a beating. Wilbur shouted. "Four of five, ladies and gentlemen!"

He rested his gun lengthwise across his shoulders, then casually hung his elbows over the stock and barrel and yawned as if this event was barely worth his time. When he nodded at me and paused as if seeking a compliment, I nodded back but tightened my lips.

By the time it was my turn, the crowd was still buzzing over the red-headed man's marksmanship, and hardly anyone paid attention as I opened my powder horn, poured black powder into the barrel, pushed the ball in with my short starter, then rammed the ball into the powder load. But when I pulled back the trigger, at least one person was watching.

A wobbly drunkard yelled. "Take cover! *Wir haben ein Mädchen.*"

A fidgeting cluster of teenage boys had moved nearby to get a better look at me, and I heard the red-headed man ask one of them, "What's that garbled crap mean?"

"Take cover. We have a girl," the boy answered, and the whole group turned into a snickering mass.

In response, the mustached man let out a growly laugh, then tipped his hat back on his head and observed me with an amused expression, as if he couldn't wait to enjoy the hapless spectacle he was about to witness.

I looked at John Joseph standing at the front of the crowd to my left. He squinted and gave me a nod.

As I held my gun tight against my shoulder, nerves set in—when I squeezed the trigger, I pulled the barrel just a hair. The first shot kicked up a puff of dust to the left of the target. As I reloaded, John Joseph watched me with calm steady eyes.

I aimed. *BAM!*

Wilbur raised his binoculars as I reloaded and shouted. "She nicked the bullseye . . . it's a good one."

I took aim again two more times. *BAM!* Load. *BAM!*

Two more good ones. Wilbur boomed, "The young lady has four. Damn good for a girl!"

The boys behind me were still fidgeting, but instead of laughing they were whispering, elbowing each other, and pointing toward the target with a collective response of wide eyes and raised eyebrows.

I felt myself tensing up again as I reloaded, and I heard the red-headed man kick the dirt with his feet, creating a dusty swirl behind my back. I felt certain he was trying to intimidate, so I briefly closed my eyes to settle my thoughts.

"Hang in Frannie!" Pop shouted. "Lean into it—stay steady."

To my right, a full-bellied fellow unleashed a long burp—*arrrrrrrrup*—that sent those who heard into convulsions. I paused a second to let the riotous laughter settle, then stared at the target, gripped the barrel, squeezed, and fired.

BAM!

I'm not blaming the burp, but my second round was weak—two out of five. I saw John Joseph frown when my last one hit six inches wide of the bullseye and left me with a total of six. The man with the mustache and Leo did better, and by the end of the round, they were neck and neck with seven good ones each heading into the final.

In short order, the red-head finished off Leo—nine to eight—and the boys behind us started hooting and howling like a pack of hyenas. The mustached man tipped his hat to his fan club, which made them howl even louder, and a few of the other contestants were already shaking the red-headed man's hand and slapping him on the back as I was preparing for my turn.

As if the whole thing were already over, even Wilbur blurted out, "Looks like that cowboy's got it in the bag! Maybe next year, Leo!"

While I loaded the powder, the red-headed man squatted about five feet away from me and flicked twigs and leaves my direction as he bit the tips of his mustache with his lower teeth.

When I rammed the rod one last time, he dropped his head and hid his face behind his straw hat, then whispered. "That's my bag of money, girlie. Go back home and play with your dollies."

My first instinct was to pick up a fist full of dirt and throw it in his face, but that wouldn't prove anything. "Concentrate," I thought. "You got this, Frannie."

My hands were shaking when I took my position, so I leaned my rifle against my hip and cracked my knuckles to settle. I saw John Joseph lick his lips, and Pop gave me a nervous smile. Celia fiddled with her necklace, and my sisters Marie and Cora jumped and clapped while Juan Esteban covered his ears.

First shot: a flat-out miss.

I reloaded, took a deep breath, closed my eyes again, then opened and fired.

"Bullseye!" John Joseph shouted.

The crowd became more interested, and there was a flurry of whispers like the sound of wind blowing through a cottonwood tree.

Marie Isabel squealed, and then I heard Cora shush her like a school-marm. John Joseph followed up and in a cool and steady sounding voice and said, "She's all yours, Frannie."

All eyes were on me, so no one paid attention when Juan Esteban left our huddled family and walked across the field past the ring of contestants, past Wilbur, and past the cluster of boys, toward me with his elbows tucked close to his chest and his hands over his ears. I could see him coming out of the corner of my eye, and even at age twelve he appeared more man-like than boyish with his strong-looking frame, pitch-black hair, and bushy eyebrows. He was wearing his usual black pants, dark blue shirt, and as he drifted toward me his presence felt like the cooling shadow of an approaching cloud. He positioned himself about eight feet behind me and stood—sturdy footed—as if he had grown out of the earth itself.

I felt an ease overcome me as I remembered the innumerable hours of practice with John Joseph urging me on and Juan Esteban there with his quiet presence.

I took a deep breath. I had three shots left. I raised my rifle, then aimed with a confidence that I had never felt before. It was as if my next three shots were a single fluid motion. *Squeeze, BAM . . . load, squeeze BAM . . . load, squeeze BAM.*

And then there was silence—a deafening silence—as if every living creature had taken pause.

During that moment, I couldn't see anything because of the cloud of smoke that engulfed me. I waved my hand to clear it away, and when it drifted left toward the red-mustached man, I shaded my eyes with my other hand and squinted at the target.

I realized that the protracted silence was a communal state of shock. The black circle was nothing but a gaping hole.

Then like a thunderclap, I was surrounded with uproarious cheers. The crowd surged toward the target to get a closer look. The cluster of boys sprinted at the head of the pack, racing to be the first ones there.

Wilbur held up his binoculars, took a long slow look, then lowered them and jostled his head as if he were shaking out the cobwebs. He raised the binoculars again and stared, then suddenly whipped his cane high in the air.

"Damned if we ain't got a winner—ten bullseyes!" he shouted. He hit the palm of his hand against his forehead. "Our new King, Frannie Abbott!"

Wilbur glanced around the crowd looking for Pop, and when their gazes met, Wilbur raised his eyebrows as if asking permission, and with a smile that showed every tooth in his head, Pop nodded.

"Hand that girl a beer!" Wilbur said.

The same drunkard that had shouted before wobbled toward me with a newly tapped brew and shoved a mug into my hand. He drenched the front of my dress with a slosh, then looked back at the mostly dispersed semicircle of manhood and shouted, "Maybe you boys should try dresses next year!"

In the excitement of the moment, I took a larger than expected gulp that caught in my throat, and I coughed and spewed the beer right back on him. He looked down at his splattered wet shirt and burst out into a roaring laugh.

"You got guts kid—a sharpshooter and a beer guzzler to boot. Never seen anybody hit ten." He raised his mug. "Cheers to you, Missy," then he chugged it down, wiped his mouth with his sleeve, turned and staggered back towards the keg.

After the beer mishap, several of my fellow contestants came over and expressed words of congratulations like *good shootin', well done, or gotta hand it to you*, then shook my hand. Some asked to look at my gun and nodded with approval at the quality of the walnut stock and carved scrollwork.

Feeling uneasy about the closeness of the bodies that surrounded us, Juan Esteban moved to the shade of a elm tree, examined the dirt patch near its trunk, then poked an ant hill with a stick and watched as their tiny red forms dispersed in all directions.

After the last contestant left, I found myself alone with the red-headed man nearby. For a moment, he didn't say anything but wore a smirk that appeared to be chiseled into his stony expression.

He pursed his lips and spat to his right. "I hate losing when money's on the line—especially to a girl," he said.

I'm not sure how I mustered the courage to set him straight, but I met his gaze and said, "The best shot won."

His nostrils flared and he snorted. "Sassy little thing, aren't you?"

His breath was a foul mix of tobacco laced with whiskey. He took a step toward me.

"Gimme a look at that antique of yours?"

I hesitated but handed the gun over.

He took off his glove and ran his dirt covered fingers over the stock and barrel, raised the gun to his shoulder, then rested his thumb on the hammer as if he were about to pull it back. Maybe he was trying to make me nervous, but I didn't like that he was holding onto the gun longer than seemed necessary, so I reached out to take it back, but he wouldn't let go. As we both gripped the gun, he stood over me smiling with a yellowy grin.

Everything about him gave me a shiver, so I yanked the gun away and turned to leave, but after one step, he whispered, "Maybe we'll meet again."

The way he said it made my stomach turn, but before I had time to give it further thought, my family surrounded me with their swirl of chatty exuberance.

Marie Isabel and Cora jumped up and down and chanted, "Frannie's a king!"

Pop gave me a kiss on the cheek and Celia smiled and patted my hand. By my expression, John Joseph sensed that something was wrong, put his hand on my shoulder, and stared at the red-headed man with a steely eye.

"This fella bothering you, Frannie?" he said.

The man put his hands up and took a step back. "Whoa there, fella . . . just having a friendly conversation. Complimenting her on her shooting, that's all."

John Joseph gave me a look. "Is that right, Frannie?"

I didn't want to stir the already boiling pot, so I nodded, but I could tell John Joseph knew I was holding back. He took a step toward the man with his chest pushed out and thrust his fists into his pants pockets so forcefully that I thought the seams would split.

At that point Pop spoke.

"Settle down, John Joseph." he said, but he didn't take his eyes off the red-headed man.

"Maybe you better move on, Mister," Pop said.

Noticing Pop's black jacket, tie, and pants, the man took two wide strides backward.

"Sure enough, Preacher. I certainly don't want no trouble with a man of the Lord," he said.

Pop nodded and waited for the man to turn and move away while Celia grabbed Cora and Marie Isabel's hands and waved for Juan Esteban to follow.

John Joseph took my arm to shepherd me away, but when I looked over my shoulder to see where the red-headed man had gone, he was standing by his horse and rooting in his saddle bag. When he noticed me watching, he pulled out a whiskey bottle, unplugged the cork with his teeth, then shouted, "Here's to you, girlie! *Arriva durchee!*" He took a long, slow slug, finishing off the bottle, then bashed it into pieces against the trunk of a live oak.

John Joseph turned and glared, but as we got further away, he gave me a playful punch and said, "I knew you could do it," then threw his arm over my shoulders and started chatting about how I "really showed 'em," and then started in on "just think about all the things we can buy with that money."

I had to hand it to John Joseph. He had a temper, but he also had an infectious enthusiasm—even if it was *his* plan to spend *my* money.

Together we walked toward a cheering crowd, and it wasn't long before several strong-looking men gathered around, hoisted me onto their shoulders, and paraded me toward a stage with a "so-called" throne made of splintery looking wood that was painted purple, gold, and green. And in a raucous celebration, I was officially given my royal title. Made for a man-sized head, the crown dropped below my eyes—a rather laughable coronation to most, but for my family and me, it was pure glory. I held my Jaeger rifle high and ascended my throne feeling confident and admired.

I thought of my real parents in that moment and wondered if they would have been as proud. Father most definitely, mother maybe somewhat, given her understated way, and I smiled to myself. I also thought about Juan Esteban.

He didn't care to share in my royal celebration in the same way as the rest of my family. I knew the noise was hard on his ears, and the celebrants hovered too close for his comfort. Instead, he stayed at the fringes, and I was certain he was looking for new subjects to draw—that was expected. But I learned something new about myself and Juan Esteban that day. I needed him as much as he needed me.

CHAPTER 7

THE SALESMAN

1934

I'm not as good a shot as I used to be. When I won the Schützenfest, I was in my prime, but seven decades of living takes a toll on the eyes, particularly out here on these open panhandle plains with the sun glaring in your face all day long. So it's a fact that my eyes aren't as keen anymore—that's what good shooting's all about—that and a steady hand. Just a few years back, I could still hit a peanut off a fence post from a hundred yards out, but these days, I'd probably have to settle for a walnut. All in all, still pretty decent for an old lady.

And I don't use my Jaeger rifle anymore. It hangs on the wall for the memories, but for safety, I keep a pistol around. We're about two miles from town, and every now and then, suspicious-looking types pass our way. It's not the folks in cars I'm wary of—it's the people on foot. There's something about a person's gait that gives me a hint of their intent. The slow and bent over just want food, which I am happy to oblige, but the ones with a clip in their step and an unusually positive air want something more. I watch those types with my eagle eye.

I haven't fired my pistol since '29— I had to make an exception when a man selling medicinals entered our yard with a fake grin, fat attitude, and a suitcase full of stuff that was supposed to fix your ailments.

I was in my rocking chair, and Juan Esteban was sitting at his table on the porch drawing some kind of caterpillar to add to the half-dozen other caterpillars in his collection.

"Nice day ain't it, Ma'am and Sir," he said.

"Not really," I said.

Minimizing conversation was my usual tactic, so I didn't elaborate on what I was thinking—that 103 degrees with no breeze is damn unpleasant. Others might have taken a cue from my cool tone, but this fellow had a brassiness that beat all.

"Got some tinctures here that'll take care of warts, bunions, and cold sores. Might come in handy for a person your age. I'll show 'em to you."

I didn't take to his pushiness or his comments about my age. "You saying I look like a toad?" I said.

Then he opened the gate and waddled down our sidewalk dressed in a black suit with off-color patches and carrying a beat-up leather suitcase.

"Leave our property," I said. "We don't want what you're selling."

He kept walking. "Lookie here . . . it'll change your life."

"My life's just fine."

Then he said, "Trust me, if you know what's good for you, you'll hear me out 'cause I got a special today."

My head jerked to the side when I heard those words: *trust me*. Trust is a word I abandoned long ago from anyone outside of family.

"Leave our property," I said.

When he took another two steps our way, I opened the side table drawer where I kept my Smith and Wesson. But when he laid his suitcase on the sidewalk and bent over to open it, that was the last straw. I decided it was time to send a message.

I whispered to Juan Esteban, "Cover your ears. This won't take long."

Juan Esteban wrapped his big arms around his head and bent over his lap. I picked up the gun and—*schoom poof*—fired one near his left foot. A chip of concrete kicked up just shy of his big toe.

"What the hell, lady?"

Schoom poof! Another at his right foot.

Then when I shot between his legs, he let out a squeal. "You crazy old bag!"

I glared at him. "You aren't very smart, are you? Insulting a woman with a gun."

He reached down, grabbed his suitcase, and started running for the gate.

I couldn't resist. I had three bullets left, so I let them fly. Took his hat off with one, then two more ricocheted off the packed earth near our gate. When he started doing the do-si-do, he wasn't swinging his lady partner. His dance mate was my old cedar fence post. I feel pretty sure I could have shot his little toe off if I'd wanted. My aim is that good. But that would've put me in the poky, sleeping on a hard, smelly cot—I've done that. I prefer my feather mattress.

I didn't get locked up for it, but I got a lecture from the sheriff when that salesman complained about me.

"Maybe you was just protecting yourself, but you can't be shooting at folks unless they come in your house. Understand?"

"He was damn close," I said.

"Close ain't the law, Miss Abbott. And let's face it, you're in a precarious position with your history. Watch yourself."

I didn't like the tone of his lecture, particularly because it came from the arrogant mouth of a man who was young enough to be my grandson, but I held my tongue and said, "Good day, Sheriff."

Despite my annoyance, I didn't let that sheriff get me down. After he pulled away and drove off, I smiled, thinking about that salesman's face. I still had it in me—*sure shot*—just like the old days.

~

It's been a while since I unloaded on that salesman, and word must have gotten around that I was not to be toyed with because I haven't seen anyone in months—except for a few linesmen.

On our side of town, houses are miles apart, and because of the dust, most are abandoned—with no one to shovel, they look more like burial mounds than places of former habitation.

Our life is mostly quiet with just the three of us—me, Juan Esteban, and our chihuahua Pico. We had to sell our horses, which was tough on Juan Esteban, so that's why I got Pico. Juan Esteban carries Pico wherever he goes, cradling him in one arm like he's a baby. Pico likes me okay, but for such a little thing, he can really put up a fuss if anyone comes close to Juan Esteban.

Juan Esteban loves Pico, but horses have always had a special place in his heart. Back when we had our fields, Juan Esteban, with his big hands and strong back, handled the plowing. He'd get after a row behind our horse, Moses, and stay straight and steady for hours on end. To get him to stop for lunch, I'd have to grab Moses by the reins and lead them both back. And I've never seen a person who could coax more out of a horse than Juan Esteban—all it took was a *phoot* here or a *hup* there. And he took care of Moses like he was his child—holding the bucket while he ate his oats, making sure his bedding hay was turned and fluffed for the night, and rubbing his muzzle with the same number of strokes each evening—it was always ten, not more, not less, at exactly 6:00 p.m.

Occasionally, he'd fall asleep in the shed next to Moses and come in the house the next morning with hay scraps sticking out of his black hair like a porcupine and smelling like manure.

I'd accepted most all of Juan Esteban's ways, but smelling like manure was not one of them. I still have to trick him into cleaning up because he isn't inclined to get into a tub of water. I pick a sunny day, and when he isn't expecting it, I sling a couple of buckets of water on him—clothes and all—and he does the soap part.

Sometimes, he gets so focused on soaping up that he'll go through a whole bar of Ivory in one washing. Usually after his splash bath, he sits on the porch in the sun, dries out, and draws.

As for how we manage day to day, Juan Esteban does the cooking, I haul buckets of water from the well, tend to our garden, and wring a chicken's neck every now and then—out of Juan Esteban's sight so as not to upset him. But mostly, I spend my time wiping dust from our windowsills and sweeping thin layers of grime that have blown through the cracks in the siding.

We get along fine when people leave us alone. It's when they don't that I get edgy. My wariness all started when the professor reappeared in my life. It had been five years since I had seen him in Galveston, five years since I had been intrigued with his scientific pursuits, and five years since I had overheard his conversation with the gravelly voiced man under the boardwalk. And it was just months after my big victory at the Schützenfest.

CHAPTER 8
STRAWBERRY ROAN

1873

It was in the spring of '73—I was fifteen—when he rode into Cedar Bend on a strawberry roan.

I was in town with Cora, Marie Isabel, and Juan Esteban when I heard his voice. We were sitting on a warped bench outside the dry goods store in our dusty town dresses, sucking on peppermint sticks, when he started yelling on the opposite side of Main Street.

"You worthless mule, get your goddamned hoof off my boot!" When I looked up, the professor was switching the mule's rump with a willow stick. Juan Esteban was sitting next to me, and he crisscrossed his arms over his chest like he was hugging himself.

When the mule finally released his trapped foot, the professor gave him one last lick that made the mule rear up, almost uprooting the post where he was tied.

Before the professor could walk away, the mule flared his rubbery lips and grabbed the professor's coat tail with his teeth. Cursing again and trying to wrench free, the professor tugged on his jacket, but the mule held tight.

By then, the incident had our full attention and that of a few towns-people. Cora giggled, and though I tried to contain myself, I couldn't help but smile when I heard a rip and saw the mule triumphantly chewing on a mouthful of wool. Recognizing that he was a spectacle, the professor changed tactics. He brushed off his jacket, straightened his hat and made a beeline toward the general store with an air of importance that seemed out of place in the lazy atmosphere of Cedar Bend's dusty streets.

His mustache was no longer waxen but had the company of a scruffy beard that draped down to his second buttonhole. The lavender waistcoat also appeared the worse for wear with ripped stitching at the pockets and sleeve cuffs.

Spotting us on the bench he said, *"Excusez moi."* With a serious expression, he tipped his top hat that looked as if it had been sat on a time or two.

"Y a-t-il une hotel ici?"

I knew for sure that he didn't remember me, as I had changed in appearance. My brown hair that had been clipped short for the sea voyage was now in a long braid that reached to my waist. Easily ten inches taller, a teenager's gangly frame had replaced my youthful pudginess.

I shook my head. "No hotel, Sir."

A disgusted look crossed his face as he glanced from one end of town to the other—one hundred feet in each direction at most.

"Another miserable town," he said. The pheasant feather in his hat band quivered in the breeze like it was ready to take flight.

"Where does *un homme gentile* stay in such a place. Surely, there's a hostel?"

"There aren't any of those either," I said.

Cora, now seven, chirped in, seemingly charmed by his colorful jacket and foreign accent. "Mrs. Vivian has a room, but she has fleas. She lives just down there."

"Vraiment, non," he said and chuckled. "A woman with fleas?"

Cora giggled. "No, her cats!"

Not to be left out, Marie Isabel with her elfin five-year-old trill said, "We have a free bed, but you'll have to share the room with Juan Esteban. Our pop's a preacher—we take everybody in—are you an orphan too?"

"Aren't you charming, *ma petite fille*," he said. He scanned the rest of us on the bench—Juan Esteban's matted dark hair and bushy eyebrows, Cora's wide face and sticky lips, and my lanky self; then he tapped Marie Isabel gently on the head with the tip of his cane as if she were the chosen one.

"A petite rose in a bed of thorns," he muttered.

Marie Isabel beamed and pushed her blond hair away from her face, awaiting another compliment. She was a beauty compared to the rest of us, and though barely five, she knew it.

Instead of indulging her, the professor looked up with a pensive expression, rubbed his chin between his thumb and forefinger and mumbled, "A preacher you say . . ."

Even though I elbowed Marie Isabel and gave her a look for offering our home without permission, she kept chattering like an innkeeper trying to sell a weary traveler on her less-than-ideal accommodations.

"Juan Esteban doesn't snore like Pop, and he smells okay most of the time except for when he spends the night in the barn with Doris, our donkey. We get our baths on Sunday, so if he goes to the barn Monday, then it's a long week," she said, pinching her nose and rolling her eyes as she spoke. "And he's not loud unless Cora and I do something like fight over who gets to feed the chickens. That gets on his nerves, and he makes strange noises, so better keep your voice low if you're his roommate."

"I'll be quiet as a mouse," the professor said.

Marie Isabel hopped up from her seat and clapped her hands. "We saw a mouse just yesterday . . ."

"More like a fat rat," Cora interrupted, jealous of the attention Marie Isabel was getting and mindful of her life's purpose to correct Marie Isabel's every move. "It squeezed through a crack in the siding looking for crumbs, then skittered into Juan Esteban's room. He likes to stash breadcrumbs mixed with pan drippings under his bed to feed the little creatures. Celia gets mad but doesn't yell at him because it wouldn't change his ways."

I didn't stop either of them from rattling on about the realities of our homelife, because I hoped that their descriptions would deter the professor's interest. Though I had enjoyed the idea of his adventures, I didn't want him under our roof.

"The room sounds *parfait!*" he said quickly.

Perfect? I thought. Hardly.

"*Je m'appelle* Dr. Pierre Duvalier. I will oblige your kind invitation and follow on my horse."

"Is that your mule too?" I asked as I looked across the street and saw Juan Esteban giving the mule the last inch of his peppermint stick.

"Yes—a menace. If I wasn't in need of a hauler, I'd shoot him dead and leave him for the coyotes."

Unlike when I was on the ship and chose to be silent during the professor's tongue-lashing of the mate, this time I decided to say what was on my mind. "Perhaps if you treated him better, he might . . ." but before I could finish, Marie Isabel interrupted.

"What's your horse's name?" she asked.

"Geneviève."

"That's a pretty name," Cora said.

"Indeed, unlike the mule, Geneviève is a bright creature—and my only companion after the loss of my . . ." he tapped his lip and looked up as if he were thinking, ". . . Caroline."

"You had another horse named Caroline?" Marie Isabel said.

He shook his head. "No, my beloved wife was named Caroline."

As if sorrowful, he rubbed his eyes with his thumb and middle finger, though I noticed no tears were visible. My own eyes were drawn to his hand, which lacked a wedding ring.

"The poor thing passed of the fever, just a month hence," he said. "In just three days."

I looked down at my feet.

"I'm sorry for your loss," I said, mimicking the words Pop used when he comforted his parishioners, though my voice carried less empathy due to a general wariness regarding the professor's intentions.

"Was she pretty?" Marie Isabel said.

"A beauty and *charmant!*" the professor said. "I begged God not to take her, but alas . . ."

With a loud *honk,* he blew his nose in his handkerchief and shook his head, then slumped his shoulders and sighed. "But one must carry on . . . with the good Lord's help."

Marie Isabel pooched out her lower lip, and her mouth turned down at the corners like a diva in despair.

Recovering quickly from his momentary sadness, he raised his cane and said, "Let me gather Geneviève and the mule, and we shall follow you."

Cora, Marie Isabel, Juan Esteban, and I strolled west from the dry goods store past four one-story log buildings along Main Street: our post office, Pop's one-room Methodist church, which was also our school, and the blacksmith and livery. Nearing the edge of town, the road narrowed and wove between dipping live oak branches, then opened upon a bluestem prairie where grasses were taking on their fall fronds. Wispy fleurets collected on Cora and Marie Isabel's dresses, adding a fanciful flair to their appearance.

When he caught up with us, the professor lifted Marie Isabel into his lap on Geneviève. He offered the mule for Cora and me, even though there was little room with all his packs.

"We'll walk," I said.

"Why can't I ride?" Cora said. "Marie Isabel gets to ride."

"You want to ride the mule?"

"Yes!" she said in a triumphant voice, like riding among the odorous knapsacks and clanking pans and utensils was the highest honor.

Cora hollered to the professor. "What's your mule's name?"

"Mule," he said. "She doesn't deserve a name."

I stayed in front of Mule to avoid the stench and let Juan Esteban hold the reins as we walked. When I handed them to him, his mouth twitched like he was trying to smile but couldn't, and he stared at the worn leather straps like I had handed him the gift of eternal happiness.

Not far from our house, which sat on a rise above Cedar Bend, Cora jumped off Mule and started skipping and yelling, "Pop, Celia, we have a visitor—a Frenchman, a doctor—coming to stay with us!"

Pop and John Joseph came from around the shed where they were repairing a gap in the fence that our hogs had pushed through, and Celia rose up from our garden wiping her brow and displaying her usual "now what?" expression.

"*Bonjour!*" the professor shouted and raised his hand and waved. "What a glorious day the Lord hath made!"

With a mystified look, John Joseph stared as sweat dribbled down his bare muscular chest. "With all due respect, Mister, I'd say it's more like Hades than heaven."

I could tell by John Joseph's face that he was wary of the professor. Hustlers were rampant in our parts, and no one was going to pull the wool over his eyes.

"Believe as you will, young man," the professor said, "but in my good book, every day that the Lord has made is fine."

It was clear that the professor's enthusiasm for the Lord had risen along our way from town to home as suddenly as Paul's conversion along the road to Damascus. And to top it off, a wedding ring was now on his finger.

The professor held Marie Isabel's hand and lowered her to the ground, then gave her a tickling that sent her squealing with delight toward Pop's outstretched arms.

Pop walked up and gave the professor a hearty handshake, "Welcome."

Celia came from across the yard wiping her hands on her skirt. Her face glowed with perspiration, and dirt streaks marked her forehead. "My apologies, Sir...for my appearance."

"Think nothing of it, *madame*," the professor said. "I've caught you at chore time."

The professor tapped his finger against his chin. "Let me see . . . is it Proverbs? He that tilleth his land shall be satisfied with bread."

He looked at Pop, "Am I right, Reverend?"

Pop smiled, "Indeed."

I glanced at Celia and her shoulders relaxed, but John Joseph still stood like a ramrod—his knuckles were white as he gripped his shovel.

The professor removed his hat. "I was looking for a place to stay, and your kind children said you might have a room."

Celia raised her eyebrows, but Pop said, "Of course we do, if you don't mind sharing."

The professor stretched out his arms as if he were embracing all of us. "I came from a big family like yours, sharing is no sacrifice, it keeps things interesting."

Pop laughed. "That's a good word for it."

The professor glanced at Celia as if he sensed her reticence, then clapped his hands together.

"But I must do my share," he said. "I'll go on a hunt and find something for our meal. I'm used to such hunting, you see, as I am a university professor and doing research on your country's wild animals. I save the skins and send them to the university for further research as teaching specimens."

"A professor," Celia said as she smoothed her dress and pushed loose hair strands behind her ears. "I don't believe we have ever had such educated company." Then she turned to John Joseph. "Take the gentleman's horse and mule to the barn for hay and water, and when you're done, accompany the professor on his hunt."

Pop added, "Frannie should go along too. She's the one that can hit a squirrel on the run from a hundred yards out."

"You don't say," the professor said. "*Une fille?*"

"Yes," John Joseph said somewhat impatiently. "She can out-shoot most anybody, even you probably." Then he winked at me.

"John," Pop said. "Your manners . . ."

I smiled at John Joseph, proud that he stood up for me.

"I'm just speaking the truth, Pop, and you know it. She's the county champion."

"My, my . . ." the professor said, "how many in your county?"

"'Bout a hundred, but only ten dare to take her on," John Joseph said.

"The best of ten . . . quite a crowd." His voice had an edge of condescension. "Most definitely an excellent shooter. Perhaps I'll get to see her perform another time."

John Joseph sensed the professor's disingenuous tone. "Get your things, Frannie, you're coming along."

As I went to the house to fetch my Jaeger rifle and cartridge pack, John Joseph followed.

"This is going to be fun, Frannie. Show him what you got."

∼

We set out walking toward the willow stands near the creek as the sun was hanging just above the treetops. The professor had a rifle in one hand and a pistol strapped around his waist. John Joseph carried nothing but a knife, and I had my Jaeger slung over my shoulder. Juan Esteban walked behind us with his head bent down, looking for grasshoppers and other insects.

"That's quite a rifle," the professor said. "Does that old thing shoot straight?"

"Shoots better than most guns," I said.

"It's one of the best military rifles in Europe," John Joseph added.

The professor bristled, "And what makes you a European war specialist growing up in these backwoods?"

"I can read," John Joseph said.

The professor looked at me. "You can read too?"

"Yes," I said. "All of us can except Juan Esteban. He has his own skills."

"But reading's the mainstay of intellectual growth," the professor said. He shook his head, "But that's adoption for you—don't know what you're getting. Mixed bag—shiny apples mixed with bruised ones."

John Joseph narrowed his eyes. "Just what are you trying to say, Mister Professor?" I could see his arms tensing up and was worried that our hunting expedition might turn into a brawl.

I looked over my shoulder at Juan Esteban, who had a handful of grasshoppers wrapped in his wool cap. His bushy eyebrows were extra dark in the shadowy light, and his mouth hung open like it usually did when he was concentrating.

I turned around and said, "Come on, Juan Esteban, stick close to us. There are skunks out there." Then I said just loud enough for John Joseph to hear, "And the biggest stinker is in our midst."

John Joseph let out a belly laugh that stirred a flock of buzzards from their roosts, but once we got near the creek, the banter stopped.

"What are we looking for?" the professor whispered.

"A whitetail if we're lucky," I said, "or rabbit if we're not."

John Joseph pointed. "Get behind that pile of branches. Deer come down here in the evening to drink. If you see one, go for it. Frannie, Juan Esteban, and I will set up about fifty yards downstream."

A breeze kicked up that blew our scent over our heads and to the north—away from fields where deer were grazing on swaths of waving grasses. When I looked back toward the professor, his pheasant feather was sticking out of a web of tangled vines.

We waited for a time but saw nothing. The sun was just a sliver of orange, and wispy pink streaks raked the sky when we heard a *BAM!*

There was a thrashing and splashing of hooves as a doe came roaring down the creek at full speed. A spritz of blood streamed down her back, but it looked like a nick—not a clean shot.

"Take it, Frannie," John Joseph said as he reached out to cover Juan Esteban's ears. "Let's show this pompous ass how to do it."

I stood and took a ten-foot lead, then fired. The deer stumbled, then fell with a heavy splash. I lowered the gun and looked back at John Joseph. He was dusting off his hands and with a satisfied smile gave me a "well done" nod.

The professor ambled toward us with a jovial expression. "Looks like venison tonight."

"Does indeed," John Joseph said. "Juan Esteban will cook her up."

"The boy cooks?"

"Yep, he's pretty good," I said.

John Joseph carried the doe on his shoulders as we hurried to get home before dark. Juan Esteban led the way at a fast clip about thirty paces ahead of us, and I knew why—he couldn't bear the sight of the dead deer with its tongue hanging out and John Joseph's bloodstained shirt.

The sky was mostly gray when we entered our back field, and the only visible light was a lantern that hung on our porch post.

When Pop heard twigs snapping underfoot near our fence line, he greeted us with a hoot.

"That you out there?"

John Joseph was out of breath from the heavy load, so I hollered. "Yes, it's us."

When we entered the light, Pop slapped the professor on the back. "Well done, Doctor. What happened? I heard two shots."

"I hit her dead-center with the first one," the professor said, "then your girl finished her off."

I heard John Joseph blow air through his lips in disgust. I decided to let it ride, because if I had tried to set the record straight, Pop would have disapproved.

~

The professor spent enough days with us to amply butter up Pop with his religious ways and build confidence in the sincerity and importance of his intellectual pursuits. He and Pop talked about the Bible after the younger girls went to bed and while Celia and I cleaned up after dinner. John Joseph never participated—he preferred the barn and the company of Juan Esteban and our donkey over the professor and would sit in the hay and read under lantern light.

One evening, Pop and Celia showed the professor several of Juan Esteban's drawings—a hummingbird, sparrow, and what I thought was his best—a wood duck that he spotted down by the creek.

Before Pop pulled them out, he made sure Juan Esteban wasn't around, then whispered to the professor, "Juan Esteban gets anxious if his drawings are out of order or too many fingers touch them."

Pop laid them gently on the table for the professor to examine.

The professor pulled the lantern closer, then rooted through his jacket pockets and brought out a small magnifying glass. Taking his time, he dusted off the lens on his coat tail, cleared his throat, then leaned over the drawings with his nose about an inch from the paper. He scanned the hummingbird first.

I stood in the kitchen and watched Celia and Pop's expressions.

For a while the professor said nothing. Then he raised his head, stretched his neck, let out a *hmmmm*, and started examining the drawings again, paying particular attention to the wood duck.

Celia wrung her hands on her apron—I could tell she was getting impatient.

"We know they may not be valuable," she said, "but we think they're quite good, though we certainly aren't knowledgeable about such things."

"Yes, yes," the professor said, "of course. How could you be . . ."

Pop wasn't deterred by his haughty tone, but Celia was. She moved around the professor and reached out to gather the drawings.

"We just thought . . . no need to spend any more time," she said.

Pop jumped in, "You must admit he has a way with capturing their nature—their feathers, the detail and all."

The professor raised up, stroked his beard, tilted his head, then looked directly at Celia.

"I do say, Madame, his drawings have similarities, though a bit crude, to none other than Mr. John James Audubon."

Celia and Pop looked at each other with questioning expressions.

"You know of him, right?" the professor said with a chuckle.

Pop pushed his glasses up on his nose. "Well, of course, we know a bit of him, but . . ."

The professor didn't wait for his full response. "One of your country's most famous," he said. "And of course, you know that John James was French originally? We have our strengths—the biological sciences, painting, music, philosophy, mathematics . . ."

He rattled off so many that I wondered what was left? Clearly, in the professor's opinion, the rest of the world was left with nothing more than the less desirables—like woodchopping and ax throwing.

Not to be completely outdone, Pop jumped in, "Well, there was Benjamin Franklin, of course—"

The professor threw his head back and interjected, "Ah yes," he said, "but the French have Rousseau, Chateaubriand, and, of course, Renoir—the list goes on, you see."

Celia returned to the kitchen and started putting away cups and plates then said with a frown, "He's a bit of a know-it-all."

I nodded. "He was the same on the hunt."

Before re-stowing Juan Esteban's drawings, Pop said, "So our boy has talent?"

The professor flipped his hand in the air. "*Vraiment oui!*"

"Really?" Pop said. Pop took a long tug on his pipe, smiled, and nodded with satisfaction.

"Potential, most certainly," the professor tacked on, "but of course, talent needs nurturing, training you know."

Pop's smile flattened. "We don't have the means for training," he said.

The professor furrowed his brows. "Ah yes . . . a problem indeed." For a moment, all was silent except the sound of wind gusts and tree branches scraping against our roof.

The professor raised one finger. "I have *une bonne idee*! How about if I take him along on my adventure west. I'll be his drawing tutor, and he can help me with my work . . ." then he coughed, "along with the cooking."

I walked over to the fireplace where the professor and Pop were now seated. "Pop, I don't think that's a good idea. You know how Juan Esteban is—he needs to be with someone he knows."

The professor turned his attention to me. "How about you join us too, Frances? You could assist with shooting and cataloguing specimens. A good opportunity, don't you think—and you could help your brother?"

Celia walked over to the fireplace with an urgency in her step.

"I don't know, John," she said. "We'll need to talk about this."

The professor quickly responded, "Yes, of course, I understand. Losing their help around your place to be under my tutelage is a lot to ask. But it will only be for a few months. We will go northwest towards San Saba and explore the Colorado River, then return. I have a guide to protect us with years of experience among Indians—he's part Apache and is an expert at picking the safe routes. He will keep us away from trouble—we are to meet up with him in Austin."

I was immediately reminded of the red-headed scout that I had heard about many years back in Galveston and wondered what trials a *scoundrel* might pose during such an expedition. Clearly, the professor had decided that the scout's skills and knowledge of the country were more advantageous than the risk.

Pop lowered his pipe and looked at Celia. "We must consider it, Celia—it's an opportunity for them both to learn." Then he lowered his voice and added, "and if there's money, we could certainly use . . ."

The professor interrupted, "But of course, I will pay them a stipend for the services to make up for their absence and duties. And when they return, you'll have a small amount with which to celebrate their achievements."

Then he looked at me again. "Frances, you could go on to greater things after some time as my apprentice."

I had to admit, I was interested. Any doubts about the professor's character were outweighed by my own desires to be more than just the county's best shot. Perhaps he wasn't that big of a lout—perhaps I could tolerate him and the scout for a few months. And then, of course, there was the money— I could imagine the sweet sound of it jingling in my pocket. And what would I be doing around here if I stayed? Stuck in the same ole rut. It wasn't a terrible rut, but I could feel something driving me from inside. There had to be more to life than just Cedar Bend.

I looked at Pop and Celia. "I *want* to go," I said. "Juan Esteban will be with me. Together we'll be okay."

Pop looked at Celia. "Well?"

Celia stood near the hearth and stared at the flames for a minute, then turned around and nodded but didn't smile.

Pop stood up, walked over to the professor, and gave him a vigorous handshake.

"Professor Duvalier, looks like we have a deal!"

~

After the professor and Celia had gone to bed, Pop, John Joseph, Juan Esteban, and I gathered on the porch. While Pop smoked his pipe, John Joseph and I lay on the floorboards and stared into a moonless sky. Light from inside spilled from a window near the porch corner. There Juan Esteban sat, clenching his knees with his arms and rocking restlessly.

Whatever was agitating him didn't bother me, because I was too busy thinking about our upcoming adventure and the thrill of the unknown.

With a dose of adrenaline, I broke the exciting news to John Joseph. He sat bolt upright like someone had touched him with a hot poker.

"What?" He grabbed my arm then scanned the darkness to find Pop's face.

"How could you let Frannie and Juan Esteban go away with *that man*?"

Pop tried to calm him and tell him about their conversation—the opportunity for Juan Esteban and me, and how the extra money could help out, but John Joseph would have none of it.

"What if he takes advantage of Frannie—or both of them?"

Pop calmly rocked two times and took a long pull on his pipe. "You must trust more, John Joseph. I feel sure he's a man of integrity. Things will be fine."

John Joseph marched to the corner of the porch where Juan Esteban sat, and the glow from inside illuminated his anger.

He raised his arms in the air. "Frannie, are you crazy? He's an ass and maybe worse! It's too risky."

Though I thought of the scout and what he might add to the uncertainty, I said nothing about it for fear that this extra information would put an end to everything—definitely with John Joseph and perhaps with Pop too.

To tamp down the tension, I tried my soft approach with John Joseph. "I can take care of both of us," I said. "You know me, John Joseph. I can handle myself in any circumstance."

John Joseph stood up, turned in circles and pounded his fist into his hand. "I will not allow it," he said.

Suddenly my soft tone turned to anger. "It's not your choice, John Joseph," I said. "It's mine, and Pop has given his permission."

"I repeat, I won't allow it," John Joseph said.

Pop stood up abruptly, and in the blackness of that night, he spoke. "You will allow it!" he said, "And you will respect my decision."

～

The next morning, I was still smarting from John Joseph's angry outburst as I packed our things in the barn and loaded up the professor's mule and

Doris. Juan Esteban stood rubbing Doris's nose while I cinched her girth extra tight.

What irked me the most had been John Joseph's attitude. After all we had been through, he had reverted to treating me like a girl. Not only was I outraged, but I was hurt.

When I saw him standing in the barn doorway wringing his cap in his hands, I was ready to unleash another round of anger starting with, "You have no right . . ." but before I could collect my thoughts, he spoke.

"I'm sorry," he said. "I trust you."

My shoulders collapsed, and I took a deep breath and ran my fingers through my hair in a state of exasperation with my own stubbornness.

He held out his palms in a conciliatory way. "You know me," he said. "I'm protective and I worry. I love you and Juan Esteban and don't want anything to happen to you, but since you've decided to go, just listen to me for a second."

"Okay," I said, and I raised my eyes and met his.

His intensity returned, but it no longer bore judgment. "Be on the watch, Frannie, and you and Juan Esteban stick together at all times—and keep your distance from the professor like we do with the rattlesnakes. He has that snaky side to him."

I thought he was about to lose his temper again, but instead he took a deep breath and regained his composure. "The last thing I'm going to say is this: if anything, I mean *anything* seems odd or out of sorts, don't hesitate. Head home like your pants are on fire."

I couldn't be angry at him any longer, and since I knew nothing would change his mind, I hugged him, then reached for the mule's reins, and walked out of the barn into the sunlight. Juan Esteban followed with Doris.

When Juan Esteban and I approached Celia, Pop, Cora, and Marie Isabel, the professor was already in the saddle. His load was heavier than when we saw him in town, and Geneviève's back swayed under the weight.

He tipped his hat. "Thank you, Reverend and Madame for your hospitality, and I'll shepherd them back to you in short order." There was a clip to his tone that was different from before.

Marie Isabel pushed her hair back from her eyes, then swished her dress.

"Goodbye, Genevievè, goodbye Doris, goodbye Mule." Then Cora joined the chorus, "Goodbye Mr. Professor, goodbye Juan Esteban and Frannie."

The professor cleared his throat as if the long goodbye was grating on his nerves and gave Genevievè a kick. He said nothing more as he rode away.

When I glanced at Pop, he appeared less confident than the previous night. By his expression, I felt sure he and Celia had talked and that she had managed to chip away at his certainty. As for me, I felt a surge of excitement for what lay ahead.

I hugged Pop, then kissed Celia and whispered, "Don't worry."

She squeezed my arm and nodded in a way that showed her confidence in me, then reached out and lifted the rim of Juan Esteban's black felt hat and grazed his face with her finger. "Stay close to Frannie."

We loaded up and trotted to catch up with the professor. When I turned in my saddle to give my family one last wave goodbye, they didn't see me. A wind-witch had kicked up a swirl of dust, and they had covered their faces with their hands. John Joseph was nowhere in sight.

As we approached the hedgerow that defined the edge of our property and passed through the brushy thicket where rabbits hid, I wondered why I felt so strongly about leaving. Who was I, and how was I different from the family I was leaving behind? I had been shaped by all of them but was related—by blood—to none.

I remembered my real father's sturdy face, his strong will, his stubbornness, and his eagerness to shed our family's comfortable life in England for something new.

I blinked, then swallowed to clear the lump in my throat, realizing that this part of me came from him.

Then I shuddered at my next thought. Father had lost *everything*.

What had I set in motion?

~

By noon, a fleeting downpour had transformed the airiness of the May morning into a steamy afternoon. As we worked our way toward Austin, the whole countryside was bursting with green, and the ground was soggy under hoof. We rode across grassy plains, then dipped downward into spring-fed creek beds laced with ferns and moss. We emerged from gulches and plodded our way up eroded hillsides with slick clay embankments. Our rides' bellies and rumps were splattered with mud as were our boots, pants legs, and the hem of my skirt. And the flies were unbearable.

The professor's horse was edgy—jumping when a rabbit streaked across our path or bucking when a horsefly buzzed around its ears. The professor seemed to have little control over the mare's skittish nature.

Juan Esteban and I gave Geneviève a wide berth and trailed several paces behind to keep the mare's spookiness from alarming Mule or Doris. About a mile from Austin, the professor brought Geneviève to a halt.

"Stay here," he said. "I have some business to take care of. I'll be back this evening."

Juan Esteban and I found a grassy spot near the river and lazed around under a cottonwood tree waiting for him to come back. After a nap, I walked out onto a gravelly shoal and passed the time skipping stones, while Juan Esteban lifted rocks to examine the creatures underneath. Though he found lots of spiders, he was most intrigued with a slippery-looking salamander that wiggled its way across the rounded rocks, then disappeared into a stagnant pool covered with green algae.

I was beginning to get bored with all the waiting when I heard the professor's voice in the distance and that of another man who rode beside him. As they approached, the man held Mule's reins, and every now and then gave them a jerk, urging Mule to move faster. Mule was laden with sacks of provisions which I assumed were flour and beans and, I hoped, a slab of meat as well.

As they splashed through a wet spot, I squinted to get a better look at the man. He rode a dark brown horse with a black mane, and as they neared, I couldn't believe my eyes—brown jacket, hat, chaps, and a carrot-colored mustache.

When they pulled their horses to a stop in front of us, the professor swung his leg over Geneviève and dismounted, then he pointed toward the other man.

"This is Jasper O'Brien—he's going to be our scout."

The mustached man wore a beat-up felt hat that sagged over his ears and curled up at the front brim, and his long red hair stuck out like straw. He nodded in my direction and gave me that same yellow-toothed grin I had witnessed at the Schützenfest, but this time brown oozed from his snuff-filled lower lip.

He jerked his head back and blinked. "Well, well, well," he said, "look what we got here?" Then his eyes grew wide as he turned to face the professor.

He smoothed his mustache with his thumb and index finger. "You didn't tell me about this here girl. Just said we had an extra shooter."

"Yes, well, here she is," he said. "Thought you might have second thoughts if I said I brought a girl along."

Jasper laughed. "I'm surprised all right, but having no second thoughts. We're good friends. Shooting pals! Right girlie?"

"What do you mean?" the professor said.

Jasper leaned back in his saddle and put both hands on his horse's rump. "Darned if she didn't kick my ass back at that German festival." Then he winked at me like he had done before. "And don't worry, girlie. I've licked my wounds and picked myself back up. Ole Jasper don't stay down for long."

"My name's not girlie," I said. "It's Frannie, and this is my brother Juan Esteban."

Jasper chuckled and shook his head. "Still sassy."

I glared at him, and then he turned his gaze to Juan Esteban and gave him a long look-over.

"Big fella ain't he? Yeah, the professor told me about your brother. Said he could cook, but that he's dumb as a board." Jasper cleared his throat. "No offence, girlie—I mean, Miss Frannie. I just say it like it is."

I heard the professor laugh as he tied Geneviève to a tree several yards away.

"If that's the way you see it, then keep your thoughts to yourself," I said.

Jasper leaned on his saddle horn, and his long hair draped over the horse's mane.

"Fiery as a branding iron. I like that about you," he said.

"I don't take to people insulting my brother—that's all," I said.

Jasper gave his horse a kick and rode over to the grove where the professor had tied Geneviève. I heard the professor and Jasper mumbling, then they both looked in my direction and laughed.

The thought of Jasper being in the mix for months was unsettling, but I had a hunch that Jasper was nothing but a big talker, and since he knew I was a good shot, maybe he wouldn't give us any serious trouble. After all, that man back in Galveston had described him as a "scoundrel"—a card cheater—*not* a murderer.

Instead of breaking and running, my plan would be to remain *watchful*—as John Joseph had advised. Juan Esteban and I would stick together, and keep our distance, and I would keep my powder dry and my Jaeger rifle handy.

CHAPTER 9

DOM

1934

Keeping my powder dry would be the least of my concerns if I wanted to fire my Jaeger rifle for old times' sake. We haven't had enough rain to wet your tongue in months.

For three days now, the wind has battered our home with fifty-mile-an-hour gusts and about tore the roof off our chicken coop. Juan Esteban, Pico, and I stayed inside because it was impossible to breathe without having a coughing fit.

Last night, when the wind finally died, I peered out my window. The moon was full, and everything appeared eerie and ashen, as if the world had come to an end. I figured even the ghosts were hunkered down—too scared to make their usual rounds.

March days will whiplash you—one day you're slapped with a bone-chilling blue norther, and the next day you're sweating. This morning, I couldn't get our door open, so my only choice was to climb out my south-facing window. While doing so, I took a spill and got a goose-egg where my head met a rock.

Juan Esteban and I spent a good two hours shoveling away dust drifts nearly four feet high. Then we re-nailed the chicken coop.

After the morning activity, I was pretty worn down—my head throbbed, and my arms ached from all the heavy lifting. When my cough wouldn't quit, I had to lie down. As I looked up at the ceiling feeling old and frustrated, I started to wonder if I could keep doing my part with the household chores—my fortitude has never been shaken, but today felt different.

Even Juan Esteban seemed worn down. I heard him snoring in his room, and when he didn't get up and start cooking like he usually did around noon, I checked on him and placed my hand on his forehead to see if he had a fever.

His head was cool, but he still slept another hour. Juan Esteban has always been strong as an ox, but today he appeared limp and drained. Sometimes, I forget that it's not just me; we're both getting old.

In the early afternoon, I heard the Carson County bulldozers clearing away the drifts, so I figured I better take advantage of the situation.

With Juan Esteban riding shotgun and Pico in his lap, I cranked up our old blue Ford and headed to town. The sky was mostly clear, and lots of folks were outside chatting across their fences and waving to each other as if they'd survived a trip to hell and back.

A group of kids were playing in the street, but when their mothers saw my car coming, they waved their arms and shouted, "Out of the street, hurry!" then stared and frowned as I drove past.

I turned left on Swenson and took the side streets to avoid the unwanted attention, then parked in front of the grocery store. Juan Esteban and Pico stayed in the car while I went inside.

Mr. Wesner stood at the checkout counter.

"Good day," I said. Wesner nodded hello but didn't smile.

His shelf stocker, a young man named Tom said, "Miss Abbott—you survive okay out there last night? That black cloud dropped three inches of farming dirt in our tank—looked more like a pig waller than a drinking hole."

I nodded and replied, "We're fine, thanks." I gave Wesner a look to emphasize my appreciation for Tom's kind words. Despite my desire to ditch it, my reputation had managed to worm its way into Leilo's gossip, and I felt certain the sheriff's wife had something to do with it—after my pistol-shooting event with that slimy salesman.

I found the bulletin board and pushed a thumbtack into an index card. There were lots of notices for lost pets, but none for jobs, so I hoped mine might get some attention.

Help wanted; handyman; 3 days a week; 2 hours a day; fair pay. If interested, come by. Knock hard. 1254 S. Laurel St.

I paid for a loaf of bread, condensed milk, and cornmeal, then got on my way.

Next stop was the post office—pinned another card up there.

At around four o'clock, when Juan Esteban and I were sitting on the porch, I saw somebody coming.

It was a boy riding a beat-up bike, and though the dust was slowing him some, he seemed determined.

Juan Esteban glanced up the road, and I noticed that he tightened his hold on Pico.

The boy passed what was left of our scraggly hedgerow that used to be a solid row of green locusts but now was snaggle-toothed like me—nothing but twigs with a few brown leaves hanging on for dear life.

I continued to track him, and as he got closer, I could see that he was skinny, maybe nine or ten, and had on a blue shirt, pants, and was barefooted. He reminded me of Juan Esteban when he was little with his dark hair—shiny and black like a crow.

When he got close to the gate, the chickens stirred up. The roosters took off in all directions, fending for themselves, but our red hen did her job. She herded her chicks to the barbed wire fence—for protection—where tumbleweeds were mounded up nearly six feet high. Though she's just a chicken, I've decided she has more sense than most folks I know.

The boy slowed down and gave us a hard look-over.

"Hey, boy, if you're going to stare, say something. You afraid of us?"

"No."

"I'm just an old lady rocking on my porch minding my own business. This is my brother. We won't bite."

He shoved his hands into his pockets. "I said, I'm *not* afraid."

"Then why do you keep looking us up and down like we're an exhibit in a wax museum?"

He kicked the ground. "I don't know."

I cleared my throat. "Well, last I heard, it's polite to say hi to folks."

"Hi," he said, and looked at his feet.

"That's more like it. Now, what's your name?"

"Dominik."

"Dominik what?"

He raised his head and squinted looking into the sun. "Rostenkowski."

I chuckled. "That's a hellava mouthful. A Pole, are you?"

"Yes, half."

"What's the other half?"

"Comanche."

"You've got company," I said. "We're mutts too—English, French, and who knows what else for me. Juan Esteban's Mexican, but I think he has a little Indian in him like you. Frannie Abbott's my name. Call me Miss Abbott and you can call my brother Mr. Slocum—he doesn't talk much, so you're not gonna get much out of him even if—"

Dominik interrupted before I could finish my explanation. "My mama said you have a pistol—and you use it."

"Direct little fellow, aren't you? Well, there's some truth to what your mama said, but don't worry, my pistol's stowed away, plus I don't use it anymore."

"She said you're a crackpot too, but you don't look *that* crazy."

I shook my head and smiled. "You can be the judge of that."

"How old are you anyway? A hundred?"

I leaned forward in my rocker and gave him a steady look. "Dominik, a few gray hairs don't make you ancient."

"How old then?"

I pushed my hair behind my ears. "Seventy-three, and as long as we're sizing each other up, how old are you?"

"Ten."

"I thought you were close to that—got those big ole teeth poking out your mouth."

He turned his gaze to Juan Esteban. "What kind of dog is that your brother's holding?"

"Chihuahua—name's Pico."

"Looks like a rat—or a squirrel maybe, without the bushy tail."

"You're full of compliments, aren't you, Dominik?"

"You told me I got big teeth and that my name's a mouthful. That's not so nice."

I leaned back and took two rocks while contemplating the man-sized temperament within his small frame.

"You're a straight shooter aren't you, Dom. I like that. I'll take a straight shooter over a bull-shitter any day. You don't mind if I call you Dom?"

"Yes, my name's Dominik, not Dom, and I gotta go."

"Well, do what you gotta do," I said, ". . . adios."

Juan Esteban and I watched as he pedalled fast and left a spray of dust behind him. I guessed it was probably his suppertime. Though he was skinny, he looked decently fed. Must not be a farmer's kid. Those kids look like you could blow 'em over with a whistle.

After he passed our far gate, I noticed him turn around. Then he lowered his head over the handlebars, pedalled back, then started doing circles by our mailbox—like a buzzard over a dead possum.

"Forget something?" I said.

He balanced his bike between his legs and put his hands on his hips. "Your pistol . . . what kind?"

I whispered, "Boy's got a curiosity, Juan Esteban. Not sure what to make of it."

I hesitated, rocked a few more times, then decided to respond. "Smith and Wesson. Heard of it?"

"Of course."

"Any more questions?"

"No," he said, and then he turned and took off again.

I looked up at the sky and wondered what had motivated this boy to ride all the way out here to ask me questions, then I glanced at Juan Esteban.

"I'll bet you a nickel, he'll be back," I said.

With Pico in his arms, Juan Esteban got up, opened the front door, and disappeared inside. A few minutes later, I found him in his room sorting through his drawings.

I had a hunch about his thoughts. "You worried he might come back and take Pico?"

He furrowed his brow, and I knew what that meant. Just like me, he wasn't big on strangers, but I figured the boy was harmless.

"Don't worry. He's not gonna take Pico. He's just interested in my gun. Just like John Joseph used to be. Lots of boys are like that."

I knew that Juan Esteban was nervous that Pico might disappear some-day—just like Abel did when I sold him—the horse that came after Moses. I felt bad about that—really bad—but we needed the money. Nearly tore me apart when Juan Esteban slept in the barn for a week after that. His empathy for animals runs as deep as his caution with people.

~

I was right that Dom would be back, and I was also right that Juan Esteban was nervous about him coming 'round. Dom showed up the next day at about four o'clock.

When Juan Esteban spotted him, he gathered his drawings and held them tight against his chest, scooped up Pico, then walked inside.

I eyed Dom as he got closer. When he passed the tenth utility pole, I could see he wasn't barefooted this time and his shirt was tucked in and buttoned at the top—like he was dressed for church.

When he came to a stop at our gate, I said, "I was wondering if you might drop by again. Come to ask me more about my pistol?"

"No."

"Hmmm . . ." I said, "what's on your mind?"

He got off his bike, lowered the kick stand, and stood up straight with both hands by his side. "I've come about the job."

I chuckled. "How'd you know about that?"

"Saw it at the post office, next to the wanted posters."

"You peruse those posters often?"

"I look sometimes, when I pick up the mail for Mama."

"I was expecting somebody taller and stronger."

"I'm strong. See?"

I watched as he flexed—a muscle the size of a lime popped up.

I waved him over. "Let's talk. Come a little closer, so I don't have to yell—I got a raw throat. Take a seat on that rock under my pear tree. It hasn't given me a single pear this year, despite my watering efforts, but—"

"How much you gonna pay me?"

I pushed my glasses up on my nose. "Wanna get down to business, eh? Hold on a minute, I got a few questions."

"Okay."

"Had any jobs before?"

He hesitated and looked up at a sole puffy cloud as if it might inspire the right answer.

"No. But I do chores . . . where I live at the hotel."

"Like what?"

"Sweeping mostly—Mr. Jeffrey gives me a butter sandwich for it."

"Do you get between the cracks with a whisk broom, brush it into a dustpan and haul it outside? I need somebody who does a good job."

"Yes."

"What else you do?"

His eyes rolled upward like he was thinking. "Haul trash, wipe windows, polish furniture."

"You do all of that for a butter sandwich?"

"Yes."

"Sounds like Old Jeffrey is getting a good deal."

"I'm usually hungry, so I do what he asks."

"Do you think you're strong enough to haul water from the well and not slosh it on the way to my garden?"

"Yes."

I leaned forward. "I don't accept sloppy work. You hear?"

"I hear," he said, then he tried again. "Whata ya gonna pay me?"

I drummed my fingers on the rocker arm. "Let's see . . . how about a penny a day?"

Dom squinted like he was staring me down in a duel.

"How about two pennies a day?"

"Look at you," I said. "A miniature businessman—making deals. I'll think about it."

"You hungry now?" I added.

"Yes."

I got up and headed toward the screen door. "Come on inside and I'll make us both a butter sandwich."

When I waved him toward the kitchen table, I heard the latch on Juan Esteban's door turn and click.

Dom sat down, and I laid the sandwich in front of him.

"Where's your brother?" he said.

"In his room."

"How come he doesn't talk?"

"He's different in the mind, and speaking isn't his thing. We communicate in other ways."

"Like how?"

"When he's not happy, he scrunches his face up, and when he's agreeable he spreads his mouth wide sort of like a smile, but his lower lip drops sideways and down. I don't *always* know what he's thinking, but that's okay."

Dom shoved the last bit of sandwich into his mouth, chewed, and swallowed. "There's a girl at my school who has a messed-up brain. Kids tease her, but I don't. Mama says teasin's wrong. Julia is her name, and sometimes she screams, and we can hear her down the hall in my classroom. I think she's frustrated that she can't talk."

"Maybe," I said. "Hard to say."

I pulled a chair out, sat across from him, and took a bite of my own sandwich.

Dom looked over his shoulder toward Juan Esteban's room. "What's he do all day?"

"Helps me with the cooking, does a few chores, and draws a lot."

"How come you posted a sign for help if you got him?"

"We're both getting old and tired."

"Hmmm . . ." Dom said, like being tired was inconceivable. Then he twisted his mouth, "What's he draw?"

"Creatures mostly . . . everything he sees. Birds, bugs, rabbits, foxes— you name it. Does it all from memory."

"Maybe drawing's his way of talking."

I stared at him a moment, then pushed my chair back and smiled. "All right, two pennies a day. And a butter sandwich."

"Thought you wanted to think about it."

"Done thinking. Long as you're regular—no shows get fired. Agreed?"

"Yes, Ma'am."

"Let's give it a handshake to make it official."

Dom put his hand loosely into mine. His palm was smooth and clammy.

"What kind of limp shake is that? Grip it firm and look me in the eye. That's how you make a deal."

He squeezed my hand, but instead of looking at me, his eyes wandered around the room.

"What's that gun hanging on the wall?"

"My Jaeger rifle. Bavarian military rifle."

"Where's Bavaria?"

"Part of Germany now."

"Girls aren't soldiers—why do you have it?"

"It was my father's—he bought it from a soldier because it was the best rifle at the time. He gave it to me when he died, just after we came over from England."

He walked to get a closer look. "Does it still shoot?"

"Yes."

"Can I hold it?"

"Not today. Maybe another time."

I looked at the clock, and it was near 5:00 p.m. I needed to check on Juan Esteban and didn't want Dom to be in the house too long. I didn't know how Juan Esteban would react to Dom being around, so I was inclined to take things slowly.

"You better get on home. Getting close to supper time."

CHAPTER 10
UNWANTED VISITOR

1934

The next day when Dom arrived, he was out of breath like he had sprinted from the gate to where I stood in the backyard. I looked at my watch.

"You're early. It's 3:30."

"Came straight from school."

I pointed to the well. "Give me a hand, would you? Turn that crank. My back's killing me. Gotta water those seeds."

"What'd you plant?"

"Radishes, carrots, rhubarb, and beets. We'll see what takes. This morning, I wired that tarpaper to the fence to keep the dust out. Hope it works."

Dom turned the crank with both hands until the bucket surfaced at the top of the well. I grabbed it by the handle and headed toward the garden, but after a few steps, my cough set in.

"I'll carry it," Dom said.

"Thank you. Remember, don't slosh it. Makes for more trips."

He bent his knees and walked slow as a tortoise.

I followed behind, and when I pointed to my newly planted rows I said, "Dribble a little here. Not too much."

More came out than a dribble, and he looked up to see if I was mad.

"It's all right. Try to stay steady."

That day he must have made twenty trips to the well and swept both porches while I wiped off the counters inside. I noticed that Juan Esteban was keeping tabs on him from his bedroom window.

When I didn't hear any more sweeping, I poked my head out the door. "You want a drink and some food now?"

"Yes."

"Come on in."

As I spread butter between two slices of cornbread and drizzled it with honey, I glanced over my shoulder and caught him eying my Jaeger rifle again.

"What kind of shooting have you done?"

"Target shooting. I was the champion of Bastrop County back when I was thirteen."

"Hmm . . . but I mean animals. Hunting."

"I've shot a fair amount in my time. Lots of deer. They were plentiful, but you had to watch out for the Indians when you were out. Even a snap of a twig would send a shiver up your spine. My brother John Joseph always came with me—along with Juan Esteban. John Joseph was older and strong, but Juan Esteban was an even better hunting companion. If you ever got lost, Juan Esteban could get you out of a fix—he has a memory as detailed as a map. John Joseph and I would be walking in circles, then Juan Esteban would shake his head and take off. We'd follow like lost sheep, and every single time, he'd get us back on track."

"Did you ever see a Comanche?"

"I've seen you, haven't I?"

"No, I mean back then when you were growing up."

"Yeah, they'd come to town, to trade stuff, but I never saw any fights, or anybody get killed."

I laid the cornbread on the table. "No white bread today, just cornbread."

He took a bite then licked his fingers. "Mama said we were proud people—fierce when we had to be—to protect each other."

"I get that. My brother, John Joseph, made sure I understood that family was worth fighting for. If he caught anybody saying unkind things about us, he'd take 'em out—he was as bold as a cornered cat when it came to that. Loyalty was top in his book."

"Who'd he fight with?"

"Mostly kids who teased Juan Esteban for being different. I'll never forget the walk home after Juan Esteban's last day at school. He got kicked out 'cause he had trouble learning book stuff. Me, John Joseph, Juan Esteban, the Lawson girls, and Chester Johnson were headed up our dirt road, and when Juan Esteban bent over to examine a carpenter ant, Chester kicked him in the ass and knocked him over.

"The Lawson girls laughed, but John Joseph didn't. He tackled Chester, wrestled him to the ground and said, 'If you ever touch my brother again, you'll wish you hadn't.'"

I started fixing my own cornbread and smiled, thinking about Chester eating a mouthful of dirt.

"But listen, Dom. Fighting's mostly bad. One fight leads to another, and then there's no end to it."

"You've been in fights?"

"Dom, Dom, Dom. You sure ask lots of questions. You could wear out your own shadow."

"Our teacher says if you don't ask anything, you don't learn anything. And I figure, since you're old and all, you probably know a fair amount."

"I guess I'll take that as a compliment," I said and laughed.

When Dom heard barking coming from Juan Esteban's room, he looked out the window. "Uh, Miss Abbott? There's somebody out by the mailbox."

My fingers were sticky with honey, so I rinsed them in the sink. "Somebody passing?"

"No, he's just standing there."

"Is it one of those utility men checking the lines?"

"No, he's not wearing a uniform. He's wearing an old suit."

As I dried my hands, Dom squinted and said, "It's an old man—got reddish gray hair sticking out of his hat and lots of wrinkles."

I dropped the towel like it was on fire.

"Dom, you scoot out the back door, and go on home. I'll finish up the chores."

"But today's payday."

"Right, here you go. Take this nickel. I'll see you next time."

"But that's more than we agreed on."

"It's all right, just take it and shoo."

He pursed his lips. "Something worrying you, Miss Abbott?"

"No, everything's fine."

I made sure he got out the back door and down the road before I ventured outside. A hot breeze suddenly kicked up, and sweat pearled on my upper lip as I stepped onto the porch.

"Got any food for a poor ole man?" he said. A few of Jasper's top teeth were gone, and he was skinny as a bean pole.

"Looks like you can't eat anything but oatmeal these days."

He laughed. "You've always had a way with words."

"Why're you here?" I said.

"Surprised I found you? I'm just stopping to say hi—been awhile. Can't go too long without saying hi to my sweet Frannie." He had a sickening smile on his face.

"Well, you said it, now get on your way."

"Frannie, come on now. No reason to be impolite."

"What do you really want?"

"Just a little money, that's all. I'm on my way to El Paso. Heard they got pretty girls out there with big tits like you. Oops—I mean like you used to—a bit saggy now?"

"Shut up, you bastard. I ain't afraid to use my gun on you."

"Enjoyed the pokey that much huh?"

"I don't mind going to jail again for your hide."

"Oh, come on. Dying in jail ain't no fun. Just give me some money. I'll be on my way and singing 'Puttin' on the Ritz.'"

"I give you two dollars—that's all."

"I believe five will do. The Ritz is expensive."

I shook my head in disgust.

"Ain't worth it to ya?" he said, then cackled.

I walked into the kitchen and pulled out a mason jar and counted out five one-dollar bills, then wadded each one up and threw it in the yard about ten feet from my front steps. "Come and get it, but if you take another step toward my porch, I'll blow your head off."

"Oh Frannie, your sweet talk sends me over the moon." He blew me a kiss, then scampered like a squirrel to pick up the bills. When he finished, he tipped his hat, showing a mat of greasy hair.

He started toward the gate with a quick step and sang:

If you're blue and you don't know where to go to
Why don't you go where fashion sits?
Puttin' on the . . .

He suddenly stopped mid-verse and turned around. "How rude of me. I almost forgot to ask. How's that simple-minded brother of yours?"

My face heated up like a stove. "None of your business."

"You tell him I said, 'Hello.'"

"Get out of here, goddammit. And don't come back!"

I could tell by his smirk that this wasn't the last I'd see of him, because he had a history of messing with me even after I had been released from jail.

CHAPTER 11
BEAR STORY

1934

It's been two days since Jasper showed up hassling me for money. It wasn't the money that got under my skin; it was his threat to expose the truth and put Juan Esteban's life in jeopardy. To put it out of my mind, I decided to focus on a chore that I knew Dom could help me with.

When he showed up dragging his feet like he was tired, I didn't play into his game.

"Got a big job for us today," I said. "Cleaning the chicken coop."

Dom sighed like he was on the brink of dying.

"When you're getting paid, you don't get to choose your chores—you just do what the boss says."

Dom groaned, "Okay."

I looked over my shoulder and saw Juan Esteban come out of the house with his drawing paper and pencil. He sat on the far end of the porch and watched us with Pico in his arms.

"Now let's get these chickens out of here," I said. "Shoo 'em out into the yard so we can get busy. We've got to remove the nesting hay, then scrape the crap, sweep it up, then haul it to the fertilizer pile next to the garden. Chicken droppings are good for vegetables."

I watched as Dom herded the chickens. Most of them scattered quickly, but my red hen pecked him on the foot. I chuckled to myself.

"Ouch!" he said. "Dang chicken. I oughta give you a swift kick!"

I raised my voice loud enough so Juan Esteban could hear.

"Don't you lay a hand on my hen," I said. "She's my number-one egg layer—never takes a day off."

I handed him a scraper. "Ok, let's get to work."

Dom put his elbow over his nose. "Smells awful," he said.

"Yep, but I try to think of something else while I'm working and imagine pleasant things. Like taking a walk along a river, in the cool shade of towering pecan trees . . . when the air is sweet with honeysuckle, and the grass is thick and green under my feet . . ."

I looked at Dom. "Take the story from here."

Dom pooched out his lips and thought. I could see his mind moving far away. "Yeah, I'm out there by that river, around dusk, with my rifle, searching for squirrels or something bigger to shoot. I have my gun loaded and ready . . ."

I shook my head and chuckled—that boy's got guns and hunting on the brain, just like John Joseph did. As I listened to his boy story, I noticed Juan Esteban had taken an interest too and had inched his way to the edge of the porch about fifteen feet away. His head was down, and he was drawing, but I knew he was listening.

Dom's eyes grew wide, and he stopped scraping. "Then I hear something rustling in the bushes! *Scratch, scratch*, moving slow and easy . . ."

"What is it?" I said, like I was there with him.

"Don't know. Listen, it's over there?"

"Maybe it's an armadillo."

"No, sounds bigger than that."

"Can you see anything?"

"No but can you hear that? *Grrrrr.*"

"A coyote?"

"No, bigger, furry . . ."

I gasped to add drama. "What is it?"

Dom shouted, "A bear! Run for your life, Frannie, and I'll . . ."

I waved my hands and shook my head. "Wait, wait, time out. Stop the story for a second."

"Why?"

"I'm no idiot. If I run, the bear will chase me, and then I'm done for—can't outrun a bear."

"How do you know?"

"Let's just say I have experience."

"You tangled with a bear?"

"Not me, another fellow." I didn't tell him that it was Jasper O'Brien—the fellow that showed up just two days earlier.

"What happened?"

"I was hired by a professor, a zoologist, because of my shooting expertise to help him hunt for animals like wolves, bears, bobcats, and mountain lions. He planned to use their skins and stuff them—for museum exhibits.

"He was a crappy shot himself, so he figured I'd come in handy. Juan Esteban was with us along with a scout.

"We were camped near the Llano River. The man at the trading post told us that black bears were on the move, and that one had gotten into his chicken coop and taken three hens.

"The professor was hell-bent on shooting one, so we stayed there a few days with the hopes of getting a chance. On the third night, I awoke before daylight. The moon was a big yellow ball, and the river was shimmering gold. I stayed under my blanket and watched as the moon danced in and out of puffy clouds until I heard a rustling and saw our scout's skinny body, in nothing but his long johns, headed for the trees to do his business.

"It wasn't long before I heard a *holy shit!* and a thrashing of branches then a splash. The professor was snoring, so I grabbed my Jaeger rifle and headed toward the noise, and Juan Esteban woke up and followed. When I got to the water's edge, I saw that fellow on the opposite bank running. He was buck naked, and in the yellowy moonlight, he looked like a streaking comet. There was something big and black barreling down behind him—about twenty yards back.

"'Help!' he yelled.

"His voice was shrill like a squealing piglet. I ran along the edge of the bank trying to keep up. My nightgown got tangled in a wood drift laced with cat claw, and while I floundered to untangle myself, Juan Esteban started clearing a path ahead of us, pulling at the thorny vine with his bare hands and shoving dead limbs to the side like they were toothpicks. Across the river on a gravelly shoal, I saw our scout climbing a bald cypress tree.

"I knew enough about bears to know that wasn't the smartest move, but I guess he didn't have a lot of choice.

"He was weaving his way through the branches and was about ten feet up when the bear caught up to him and stood at the base of the trunk, then reared up on his hind legs and gripped the tree trunk with his claws.

"When he heard bear's claws ripping against bark, that fellow started hollering even louder.

"'Help, somebody help!'

"By then the sky was starting to glow as the sun came up, and I could see both of them clearly. Out of desperation, that scout started waving his arms and making growling noises, but he wasn't fooling the bear. And when the bear began to crawl up the tree, he started chucking cypress cones and whatever twigs he could find.

"I shouted from across the river. 'I'm here—got my gun.'

"'What took you so damn long,' he yelled. 'Shoot it, dammit! It's getting close.'

"By then the bear was sitting on a limb about six feet below him considering its next move. Our scout climbed another ten feet, but the branches got skinnier, and the one he sat on bent under his weight. He clung to the trunk and shimmied up as far as he could until there was nowhere else to go.

"The bear headed upward again and moved through the tree like it was climbing a ladder. Then there was a noise in the Carrizo cane at the edge of the shoal."

"What?" Dom said. His eyes were wide.

"Out ambled two cubs with their heads raised, sniffing the air."

"Whoa," Dom said. "What'd you do?"

"I knew right then I couldn't shoot that bear, because of her cubs, unless there was no other choice. I needed another plan to scare her off, so I fired a shot about three feet to the right of her into the tree. The cubs reared up, but she didn't budge from her perch. Instead, she climbed higher until she was within three feet of that fellow and raking her paw against the tree trunk.

"He screamed and let out a sob. 'Shoot! Shoot!'

"I held my rifle tight against my shoulder, leaned in, and fired another shot, aiming at the branch the bear was standing on. It hit the bark with a solid thud, so I reloaded and fired again at the same spot.

"*Schoom! Thwack!*

"Bark splintered into pieces, and there was a faint *pop*. I was out of ammo and that fellow was howling and clinging to that tree for dear life.

"A gust of wind swept down the canyon and swished through the trees.

"*Crack!*

"The limb snapped like a fractured bone, and the bear tumbled and crashed through the tree branches like a cannonball. She must have dropped fifteen feet before she found a branch to hold onto for a split second. It was enough to break her fall. Then she hit the ground with a thud and rolled. Within seconds, she and her cubs were gone—into the carrizo cane.

"When our scout climbed down and swam to my side of the river, his eyes were wide as big as that moon and he shouted, 'Don't look!'

"He scrounged around and broke off a sycamore branch and used its wide leaves to cover his parts. 'That was a helluva job, Frannie,' he said. His legs were still shaking. 'But you should have taken her out. How come you didn't?'

"'She had cubs,' I said.

"'Who the hell cares?'

"'I do. You don't shoot a bear with cubs.'"

After I finished my tale, Dom looked at me. "Dang, Miss Abbott. That's some story."

"Yep," I said, and reached for the whisk broom and started sweeping the hen boxes. A few minutes later, I felt a headache coming on, and I teetered and fell against the wire fence.

"You okay?" Dom said.

"Just a little faint from the heat," I said. "I better go inside, get a drink and lie down."

Dom held my elbow as we walked toward the porch. "Steady, Miss Abbott, take it slow."

When we got inside Dom said, "I'll get you some water. You head to your room."

I sat on the edge of my bed, and Dom came scampering back with a tall glass filled to the brim. "You sure you're okay?"

"Yes," I said. "I'll be fine."

"Okay then. I'll finish up, then check on you before I head home."

For about thirty minutes, I lay on my bed. The window was half open, and I could hear the broom swishing and Dom's footsteps as he trod back and forth from the chicken coop to the garden. After a while, I got up and parted the curtains to take a look. Dom had finished cleaning, and Juan Esteban was tending to the nests, taking extra care to provide the same amount of hay for each nest, like he was counting each piece of straw, while Dom tried to herd the chickens back.

"Go on, shoo!" Dom said. "Get back in there," but the chickens spread in every direction with necks bobbing and wings flapping, and the more he tried to herd them the more they fled to the far corners of our fenced yard.

Finally, he stopped, put his hands on his hips, and sat down on a stump. "Damn chickens!" he said.

I smiled because I knew what was coming next. Juan Esteban put the last handful of straw in our red hen's box, then stepped outside the coop and squatted down and pursed his lips and blew—*hooo*. I knew the sound well—more like a mourning dove than a whistle. The chickens slowly strutted back and formed a loose ring around Juan Esteban while they pecked at the ground. Juan Esteban gently picked each one up and stroked its feathers. Then holding it like a fragile object, he lay it in its proper box. He backed out of the coop, carefully closed the gate, then went back to the porch and started drawing again.

Dom sat back and shook his head. "Dang, Mr. Slocum, how'd you do that?"

Not long after, I heard the door open, and Dom poked his head into my room. "You okay now?"

"Yes," I said. "Much better."

"We got the job done."

I turned from the window and smiled. "I see you did."

"Your brother's something else with those chickens. They were running from me like the sky was falling, but they came to him like they were friends. I ain't never seen a chicken do that."

"If it makes you feel any better, they run from me too, but they follow Juan Esteban around the yard wherever he goes."

Dom laughed. "A chicken train."

I chuckled and sat back down on the edge of the bed. "You're a funny boy."

Dom rubbed his hands on the back of his pants to clean off the dirt. "Guess I'll be on my way then," he said.

"See you next time," I said, and before he was out of earshot I added, "Thank you, Dom."

I heard the screen door shut, then heard Dom holler, "Bye, Mr. Slocum."

~

I lay back down on my bed and stared at the ceiling. I thought back on that day of the bear incident and remembered the events that followed, along with the fury and the shock.

CHAPTER 12

THE BROOCH

1873

After I shot the bear out of the tree but didn't fire directly at either the mother or cubs, I witnessed a side of the professor that I hadn't seen before. When we got back to camp, Jasper told him the whole story, and the professor's eyes narrowed with rage. He reached down, picked up a rock, and hurled it my way. I jumped aside just as it whipped past my knee, then he picked up another and rolled it in his palm like he was ready to throw.

Knowing Jasper's character, I was surprised that he came to my aid, but I guess at that point, he owed me his life.

"Cut it out!" he yelled. "We'll get another chance at that bear."

The professor frowned and stared straight at me. "I didn't hire you to pick and choose your shots, you hear?"

I nodded. Instead of dropping the rock, he slung it at Juan Esteban, and the rock grazed the rim of Juan Esteban's hat.

The professor shouted at Juan Esteban. "Get a fire going and cook some breakfast."

My body stiffened. "Don't talk to my brother like that!"

The professor took on a mocking tone. "Oh, the little protector. Bravo, *ma fille.*"

I was seething but held my tongue as the professor walked over to Geneviève, saddled her up, and told Jasper to do the same.

"Going to town for supplies," he said. "We'll be back in a few hours for breakfast."

While Jasper and the professor were gone, I helped Juan Esteban. We searched for kindling, then dragged three drift logs back to our campsite. The fire was popping as I lay on my pallet and listened to a white-winged dove calling across the canyon. Juan Esteban filled a pot with water, beans, and perfect cubes of fatback, then sat in a grassy area, pulled out paper and charcoal pencil, and began to sketch.

After drawing a few short broad strokes, he smeared his markings with his index finger, then opened his pocketknife, sharpened his pencil to a neat point, and drew more refined lines over the smudges.

Intrigued by what he was rendering, I slid closer and peered over his shoulder. It was an exquisite depiction of two cubs standing among cypress knees.

$\sim$

When Jasper and the professor returned, the professor was still in a foul mood. Juan Esteban was stirring the simmering pot of fatback and beans when Jasper held out five eggs.

"Throw these in," he said.

Juan Esteban cracked each one like it was a treasure, then stirred them into the bean mix. No one talked while we ate. Jasper slurped and licked his plate, and bean juice smeared across his cheeks.

The professor's face flushed red. "You're a brute! Don't you have any etiquette?"

Jasper looked up. "What's that mean?"

"Manners, stupid. You're disgusting."

Jasper wiped his mouth on his sleeve, leaving a brown smear. "Guess I ain't as fancy as you are, but I don't intend to take any lip from a Frenchie."

Jasper scooped a spoonful of beans from the pot and flipped it at the professor, then cackled. The beans hit the professor's chin, then dribbled down his shirt.

"See how fancy you look now," Jasper said. "Same as ole Jasper with stains on your clothes—you're in America, hombre. Nobody's special."

The professor was fuming but didn't say anything. He got up, reached for his pistol, raised it, and pointed it directly at Jasper's forehead.

"I ain't afraid of you," Jasper said. "You need me too much."

"Oh, yeah?" the professor said, then cocked the hammer.

Jasper was squatting on the ground and started to inch his way backwards. "Come on," he said, ". . . I was just having a little fun with you."

The professor held his aim, and I was afraid Juan Esteban and I were going to witness a murder.

I abruptly stood up. "Stop, enough," I said.

The professor looked at me, then back at Jasper as he held the gun in position. His mouth opened into a wide grin, he squinted, and squeezed the trigger.

Click

Jasper fell back against the dirt with his hands over his head, and for a moment there was complete silence.

Then Jasper jumped up and pointed his finger at the professor. "You're a lunatic!"

The professor lowered the gun and bared his teeth, then mumbled under his breath, "Dimwit."

I swallowed hard and remembered the professor's words back in Galveston when I was under the boardwalk and listening to him speak to that man about Jasper.

"Dimwits are easy to outsmart," the professor had said, and I knew then that this was the professor's first attempt to keep Jasper in line.

Over the next several minutes, I was watchful to see if things would settle. Jasper sharpened a knife in long slow strokes and eyed the professor as if he were thinking about where to plunge it—the heart or the back—while the professor put his gun back in its holster, hung it from a tree, and took off his shirt.

"Let's go wash the pots and pans," I said to Juan Esteban, and when we moved toward the river and crouched at the water's edge scouring the pots with handfuls of gravel bits, the professor followed and washed his face and shirt beside us.

"Don't worry," he said. "O'Brien's not going to give us any more trouble."

"Just don't mess with my brother," I said. "I swear we'll leave, and then you'll be out of a good shot and a cook."

He waved his hand at me as if he were pushing my words aside and didn't respond to my threat. Instead, he wrung out his shirt, then said, "When you're done with the washing, pack up, let's find that bear. She'll bring me a mint if we can get her."

"I thought you said the skins were going back to the university for research?" I said.

The professor blinked. "Of course—that's what I mean. It will be treasure in our museum collection—*a mint*, just like I said."

Back at camp, Jasper had his shirt sleeves rolled up and was whistling as he shoved his jacket in his saddle bag and strapped on his pistol. He saw me watching and grinned, then nodded in the professor's direction. The professor had his back to us and was slipping his arms into the sleeves of a dry shirt.

Jasper adjusted his hat, gave his pistol a pat, then held up his finger and thumb like a gun, pointed in the professor's direction, and curled his index finger as if he were pulling a trigger. He gave me an exaggerated wink.

I realized that both he and the professor were intent on letting me know who was in charge—as if they were roosters fluffing their feathers and trying to impress me with their masculine prowess.

Shaking my head in disgust, I hauled our bags and bedrolls over to where Doris and Mule stood chewing on mouthfuls of grass. We dumped our duffels at our rides' hooves, then Juan Esteban carefully stowed his drawing implements in an envelope and tucked them inside his jacket pocket. He knelt and slid the drawing of the bears between two boards and cinched a bow knot.

The professor came over and tapped Juan Esteban's shoulder, and Juan Esteban jerked away like he had been pricked with a knife.

"Let me see," the professor said.

The professor reached for the wood press, but Juan Esteban took three steps back.

"It's okay," I said. "Show him."

Juan Esteban slowly removed the bow, took another step back, then held up the drawing close to his chest.

"Hmmm . . ." the professor said, "not bad, but you need to work on the shadows." He pulled a small leather-bound sketchbook from his pocket and drew what looked like an apple.

"See, it's floating." Then he put a dark line on the apple's left edge and drew a shadow at its base. "Now, it's grounded. Do the same for your bears."

Strangely, the professor seemed almost kind. Then he turned to me and said, "Come here."

He reached into his saddle bag, pulled out a book, and thumbed to a page near the end. "Read this later—*Ursus Americanus*—that's the Latin name for American black bear. Ursus is the genus, Americanus is the species. It's an encyclopedia of western mammals—you can hang onto it."

~

We hunted bears for two more days, skirting the river in the evening where sunfish rose and flipped at the water's surface, sucking in water bugs and minnows. In the mornings, Juan Esteban stayed with the horses, Mule, and Doris while the professor, Jasper, and I climbed stony canyons searching for openings in the cliffs that might serve as dens, but there was no *Ursus Americanus* to be found.

I could sense the professor's agitation increasing each time we came back with nothing. He threw his hat, barked orders about fixing food, and grumbled about how slow we were. Adding to his ill humor were the sounds that kept us up at night—most of all, the chorus of coyote howls echoing among the limestone cliffs. After several nights of high-pitched yelps mixed with rough barks, the bags under the professor's eyes turned into a double layer of overlapping skin.

One night, he jumped from his bedding, ran barefooted towards the edge of the woods, and cursed the "bloody beasts." And on the night of a full moon, the professor took it one step further.

That evening, as the sun set behind the hills, the crickets seemed especially loud, and shortly after, several full-throated bullfrogs chimed in with
their baritone croaks. But it wasn't until the howls resumed about fifty yards
from our campsite that I awoke from my fitful sleep to a *BAM*.

Startled, I sat up, looked around the campsite, and saw the professor's
pistol smoking at the tip. Juan Esteban pulled his blanket over his head and
curled up in a ball.

Jasper, wild-eyed and frantic yelled, "What the hell?"

A reddish gray creature flailed, then fell about three feet away from
Jasper's head. Jasper stared at the dying coyote and then turned toward the
professor.

"Son of a bitch—you could have killed me!"

The professor muttered, "Don't think I haven't thought about it."

Jasper sat up, leaned on his hands, and glared at the professor. "Well,
I got news for you, mister . . . you ain't the only one's been thinking along
those lines. I've about had enough of you with your insults and pushing me
around. This ain't no pleasure trip for me."

The professor drew his knife, then tossed it at Jasper's feet. "Just shut up
and skin it," the professor said.

Jasper growled. "See? That's exactly what I'm talking about. And why
the hell are we skinning a coyote anyway? It's worse than a mangy old dog."

"Coyote pelts are better than nothing. Now get after it," the professor
said.

After the professor gathered his clothes and started toward the river,
Jasper yelled after him.

"I'll get to it when I feel like it!"

After a few more minutes of stewing, Jasper looked at me with cow eyes.

"How about fixing me some coffee, Frannie. This morning's off to bad
start." Then he pointed at Juan Esteban. "And tell your brother in whatever
language you two speak to make something decent to eat. All we've had is
beans, beans, beans."

As I made coffee, Juan Esteban patted out eight Johnny cakes and fried
them in a cast-iron skillet.

As the corn patties popped and spurted in the sizzling lard, Jasper flopped down next to the fire and warmed his feet, then turned on his side and leaned on his elbow. He pointed his finger in the direction of the river.

"Imbecile," he said, then raised his thumb and index finger like he was showing me a measurement. "I'm this close to ditching this guy. If I didn't need the money, I'd be out of here. Look at the way he treats all of us. Like he's a king or something."

I nodded but didn't feel like fanning Jasper's flame.

After downing the Johnny cakes and grumbling about everything imaginable, Jasper got down to the dirty work of skinning the coyote. He took the professor's knife, thrust it into the coyote's neck, then slid it across its underbelly and toward its tail.

When a rank smell soured the air, Juan Esteban stopped eating and moved about twenty paces away to a hackberry tree where he hid behind its trunk.

Jasper yelled after him. "Don't like blood and guts?" Then he held up a strip of intestines and stretched it like a rubber band.

"Leave him alone," I said.

"Ah come on, Frannie," Jasper said. "Can't a fella have a little fun around here? The professor's got his underwear up his crack, and you don't do nothing but dote over that brother of yours like he's a big ole baby."

I could see Juan Esteban rocking back and forth, so I walked over, handed him a cup of coffee, and sat cross-legged next to him. His hair was getting long and hung like a curtain over his eyes, and he cradled the cup in his hands and let the steam curl around his face. After a few minutes, his rocking began to slow and eventually subside. We sat within a bed of grasses, and there was cluster of bluish-purple flowers that reminded me of the forget-me-nots in Mother's botanicals and the color of her favorite dress.

I reached out and plucked one and spun the stem between my fingers, watching the yellow center transform into a tiny sun-like form, and I thought of Mother and her admiration for beautiful things—her botanicals, her dress, her brooch. At the time, it seemed only to be a sweet memory, but later I would believe it was more—a hint of her presence and perhaps a warning for me to be vigilant.

~

After skinning the coyote, Jasper washed up in the river while the professor spread the coyote skin over a log and lathered on turpentine.

He glanced my way. "Get some tacks out of my pack . . . about seven," he said. "I'm going to hang it up and let it dry."

I knelt beside his saddlebag and dug around, pulling out a handkerchief, matches, extra ammunition, a spare horseshoe, a curry comb, and near the bottom, I came to two small tin boxes. I shook both, listening for what sounded like tacks. The first clanked inside like a collection of metal objects, so I opened it and found nails.

I held one nail up, "These?" I said.

"No, too big," he said. "The box with the shorter brass tacks. They're under the sock."

I opened the second box and on top was a silk sock folded over several times with something small but weighty inside. I took the sock and rested it on the handkerchief, then counted out seven tacks and carried them over to the professor.

One by one, I handed them to him as he spread the skin between two tree trunks and hammered the tacks.

After he had used five, I held out my palm offering the last two.

"Don't need them," he said. "Put them back."

When I got back to his pack, stowed the tacks, and was ready to put the sock on top, there was a swarm of wings around my head, and I jumped and swatted as something zoomed past my ear, then circled back toward my nostrils. I frantically flapped both hands, but when the stinging creature grazed my cheek, I whipped the sock to shoo it away and sent whatever was inside flying.

In a panic, I searched for what had fallen out, hoping that the professor didn't notice. Before long, I spotted a shiny object flickering in the sunlight within a pile of dead leaves. As I crept closer, I could see that it was about two inches long, oval shaped, and had a silver backing with a pin. I leaned over and saw a date inscribed on the back. When I picked it up and held it in my palm, I almost fainted.

I blinked. Was I hallucinating? Then I refocused on the date—May 15, 1836—my parents' anniversary.

My mind swirled as I remembered the details, from just five years before, on our overseas journey, and what happened that last day came back with clarity: the professor, the cigars, the fire, Mother's bag, her dress, the brooch, and worst of all mother's panicked expression when she thought the dress and brooch had been thrown overboard.

For a moment, I stood there not knowing what to do. Then I had an overwhelming impulse to snatch my mother's brooch, grab Juan Esteban, and *run* from the thief!

Suddenly, I felt the professor's presence behind me. "What are you doing?" he said in a loud voice.

I jumped as if he had read my thoughts and caught me red-handed.

As I held the brooch in my palm, my hand was trembling. "It fell out of the sock. I didn't mean to drop it . . ."

He interrupted, "Be more careful, for God's sake!" then he held out his hand and motioned for me to hand it over.

"I'm sorry," I said, but I didn't mean a word of it—inside I was raging with anger, and when I saw his expression, I could almost see the wheels turning in his head.

He took a deep breath. "It was my wife's . . . a gift from me to her." Then he held it up to the light, examining the craft of its iris carving. He rubbed his chin and nodded. "Beautiful, isn't it, but I now see that I must stow it in a safer place."

He slid the brooch back into the sock, tucked the sock in his inside jacket pocket, then patted his chest. "Close to my heart."

I was repulsed by his words, and my stomach churned with disgust as I walked back toward Juan Esteban. I collapsed on the ground next to him and put my head in my hands as I wracked my brain over what to do.

CHAPTER 13
THE COUGAR

1873

The opportunities to get my hands on the brooch were next to none—the professor mostly slept on his stomach, tucking his arms under his chest, making it impossible to reach into his pocket without waking him. And since he slept lightly—because of the "bloody beasts"—my timing had to be precise.

"Patience," I thought. "Wait for the moment when either he takes off his jacket or moves the brooch to another hiding place."

While I waited and watched, we continued our hunts and tracked a cougar in a rocky draw along the Colorado, just south of San Saba. It was midafternoon, and I told Juan Esteban to stay in camp to fix supper rather than join our troupe, so as not to witness another animal skinning.

On horseback, Jasper led the way through a cragged crevice towards what he believed to be a cougar's den. Water, trickling down fern-covered rock faces, dampened our path, and Jasper's horse kept slipping and stutter-stepping, making Geneviève—the professor's horse— skittish.

"Give us some goddammed room," Jasper whispered over his shoulder. "Geneviève's nose is up Jake's ass."

The professor pulled back on his reins and Geneviève slowed.

"And let Frannie pass, she's the one that's making the shot," Jasper said.

As Mule and I slid by, Mule gave Geneviève a shove with her oversized belly that pinned the professor's leg against the rocky embankment. He let out a groan like a bawling bull.

Jasper turned around and slapped his leg in disgust. "Well, you've ruined it. There's no way in hell we'll find that cat now. He's probably crept back in that cave so far that we'd have to crawl to find him."

"Then get off your damned horse and crawl," the professor said.

"I ain't that stupid," Jasper said. "For what you pay me you expect me to risk my life?"

The professor looked at me. "Since we have a damn lily-liver on our hands, get back in there and see if you can get a shot."

Jasper said, "Now look who's the sissy. You're sending a girl back in there 'cause you're too scared."

I was tired of their stupid antics, so I hopped off Mule, pulled my rifle out of the scabbard, and crept toward the cave's opening.

"If you get him backed in a corner, shoot him in the chest," Jasper whispered.

"Utter genius," the professor said shaking his head. "What do you think she's going to do, shoot it in the tail?"

The cave was south facing, so the sun lit the first ten feet, and I could easily stand up for a few more steps, but after that, I had to bend my knees to keep my head from hitting rock. Cat prints were everywhere in the soft dust of the cave floor, but when the surface changed to damp compacted clay, they were no longer visible. As I crept forward, light rays pierced through cracks overhead, creating small patches of brightness, and I was able to see my way for another seven paces.

The smell of guano was oppressive, and I knew I had come across a bat haven because I could hear their squeaks in the distance. Then, *eek—flutter.* A bat swooped past my head, circled, then disappeared farther back into the blackness.

With my rifle steady against my shoulder, I considered my options. If I took a blind shot into the cave, I might hit something, but it would be risky. The shot could lead to a charge, and if it was a cougar, I knew I'd only get one shot. If I missed, I'd be on my back, and the thought of what might happen next gave me a shiver. I had to spot it before it pounced.

I picked up a stone and threw it into the darkness, then immediately raised my rifle. I thought I heard something—not a bat—but wasn't sure what. I threw another rock as hard as I could and heard it clatter against the cave walls. The darkness of the cave had turned into sort of a twilight, as if a lantern had been lit. There was another rustle.

My heart throbbed in my ears like a beating drum.

I took five more steps forward and saw light pouring in—about twenty feet up—from a hole in the cave's ceiling. Water was dribbling in from a limestone ledge above and created a blurry veil between me and what appeared to be the end of the cave. I cocked my rifle and held it against my shoulder while I adjusted my eyes to what lay beyond.

I blinked to make sure what I saw was real. Staring at me were two yellow eyes about six inches apart. I couldn't tell if it was a cougar, but whatever it was didn't move a muscle. This was my chance.

My finger was on the trigger, and I was ready to squeeze, when behind me I heard a growl, then *a whoosh* of air, but before I could turn around someone grabbed me, and my gun went flying.

I twisted my shoulders trying to wrench free, but whoever held me tightened their grip and started cackling in my ear and dragging me away. Then a shadowy figure ran toward my gun, scooped it up, and sprinted off.

"Let me go," I yelled.

"Grrrr," he said in my ear and cackled again.

"Who are you? Let go!"

I was kicking and yelling as someone dragged me toward the cave opening, and when we hit the light, he released his grip. I spun around with knees bent, ready to run.

Before me were two men. The cackler was still laughing—he was tall, thin as a corn stalk, and had a buck-toothed grin. The other—the swooping shadow—stood stone faced staring at me with my gun in his hands. He was shorter but more muscular and had black hair in a long braid.

The muscular one reached for my wrist and pulled me outside into the open air. His calloused hands felt like leather against my skin, and in the sunlight, I could see that even though his complexion was dark and weather worn, he was young.

"What do you want?" I said.

The tall one made a hissing sound and held his hands with bent fingers as if they were claws, then roared with laughter.

"Meet the cougar," he said.

"There was one," I said. "I had in my sights but then you jumped me."

"Right," the skinny one said. "Anything you say . . ."

The young one wasn't laughing.

"Who are you?" I said. I felt a shake in my voice, so I clenched my teeth to regain composure.

The tall one—who had suddenly stopped laughing— poked me in the back. "Never mind that. Let's take a little walk—follow that Injun."

The young man turned around and glared at the tall one. "I told you, call me Karuk."

The tall one smirked. "Yeah, yeah, whatever."

"Where are we going?" I said.

"Just keep your mouth shut; you'll see," the tall one growled.

I followed Karuk as we weaved through boulders and along rocky ledges. His long braid swished between his shoulder blades, and his body smelled like a mixture of earth and sweat. My mind raced—where were Jasper and the professor? Were these men kidnapping me?

After a long silence, I got up my nerve. "What do you want with me?" I said. "I don't know you and have done nothing to harm you."

The tall one pointed his finger at me. "You ain't, but your pal has. My buddy Sam's got a bone to pick with that red-headed squirrely thief. He led us out past Fort Concho to hunt buffalo, then ran off with the skins in the night—sold 'em and took off with the money. Sam hired this here— what's-his-name Karuk—to help find him. We knew he'd be somewhere in these parts. Too much money to be had with the buffalo—draws rats like him."

Though I wanted to say, "Where there's one rat, there's a cluster," I didn't, because my situation was too precarious.

"Slick's my name," he said, "and I'd like to say it's a pleasure to meet you, Missy, but it ain't."

"The feeling is mutual," I said.

"Don't you sass me, girl," Slick said. "You're in a tight spot, if you haven't figured it out."

Before long, we entered a grassy area near the river where squirrels scurried, digging for hidden nuts.

I thought of making a dash for it but knew I wouldn't get far. I looked up and saw Jasper and the professor leaning against a sheer rock outcrop. Jasper was bare naked except for his socks, and the professor only had on his underwear and boots.

To my right, another man stood dressed in the professor's lavender waistcoat with no shirt. He had the professor's green necktie draped around his neck and was smiling from ear to ear.

Slick burst out laughing. "Sam, ain't you a dandy!"

Sam walked toward Jasper, then said, "Take off them socks."

"Come on," Jasper whimpered. "Give our clothes back. You can take my horse. That should be enough pay-back."

I could hear Jasper's knees knocking like two stones tapping together, and I knew that I had been right about him. He was all talk, and when things got bad, he crumbled.

"Don't think that's going to cover it," Sam said. "Seventy-five dollars in skins for your scraggly horse? No deal."

"Why're you holding me captive?" the professor said. "I've done nothing."

Sam sneered. "You're a partner to this bastard. That's reason enough for me."

The professor glared at Jasper and snarled through his teeth. "Now look what you've done. We're all dead."

"That's where you're wrong," Sam said. "Not *all* of you."

Sam looked over his shoulder at me, then nodded to Karuk. Karuk walked away and returned, leading Mule by the reins. Using my gun, he gestured for me to saddle up and then led me and Mule in the direction of the river's flow.

I looked back at Jasper and the professor but knew I could do nothing without my gun. My thoughts turned to Juan Esteban at camp several miles downstream, and I was frantic to know if he was all right.

We waded quietly through knee-deep grasses in the shade of pecan groves and stirred a turkey gobbler and hen into a quick-stepped retreat for cover. As we rounded the bend, the wind made ripples against the water, as if the river had reversed course. I could smell smoke in the distance—maybe Juan Esteban's fire. We must have walked a mile when the young Indian stopped.

When he turned to me, the sky reflected in his dark eyes. "Your friends are cowards—leaving you to face the cougar while they sit and watch. And I know you saw the cat, because I heard it too, but who knows if you would have survived. That's an old cougar, but experienced and lethal. I've seen him many times and once watched as he took down a ten-point buck with a single pounce. So maybe you're lucky. I convinced Sam to release you because of your bravery. He told me to keep the gun, but you'll need it."

He handed it to me.

I blinked and was about to thank him, but before I could say anything, he slapped Mule on the rump, and Mule took off at a steady trot. I didn't look back.

I needed to find Juan Esteban.

～

By the time Mule and I rode into camp it was dark. The fire was crackling, but as I looked around in the yellowy light, I could see that *everything*—our bedrolls, pots, plates, Juan Esteban's saddle bag and duffel—was strewn about. I panicked.

"Juan Esteban," I yelled.

I heard nothing. I yelled louder, and my shouts bounced off the canyon walls and stirred a wide-winged creature into flight. I got off Mule, lit a lantern, and scoured the wooded areas, thinking that he might be hiding. Maybe the men had come through.

"Juan Esteban," I shouted. "Where are you?"

I raised the lantern and surveyed the area where Doris was usually tied. Amongst hoof indentations were a swirl of deep scrapes and thick padded paw prints, as if there had been a violent scuffle. Then I saw Juan Esteban's boot prints in the middle of it all. I spun around trying to find their trail and saw that all three had turned in the direction of the river.

I took off running and shouting, "Juan Esteban, Juan Esteban . . ." through brambles and across soggy ground that felt thick as pudding. The lantern light didn't extend far, and it blinded my view of the distance. I put it down and stood flat footed and blinking, trying to adjust my eyes to the darkness. It took a moment, but I began to see the tops of the cliffs in shadow and behind a starlit sky. In the riverbed and to my left, I heard water trickling over rocks, and to my right, the water was a glowing flat surface.

Then I heard a splashing sound.

I whispered. "Juan Esteban, is that you?"

I heard a snort, but nothing else. As I crept closer, I realized that I hadn't brought my rifle, and I swore under my breath for being so careless.

"Juan Esteban," I said quietly, and saw someone behind a horse's body leaning against it with an arm draped over its back. Both were in the middle of the river—water was above the horse's belly, and all I could see was its withers, neck, and head.

As I drew closer, I heard a moan, and I knew by its familiar tone that it was Juan Esteban. I splashed my way into the water and waded toward him until I was waist deep and about fifteen feet away. Immediately, I recognized that it wasn't a horse, it was Doris.

"Come where it's shallower," I said and waved him my way. For a moment he just stared at me. Though I couldn't see his expression, I knew he was scared.

"It's okay," I said, "the bear is gone, and I'm here."

He led Doris through the water by her reins, and when he was just a few feet away, I could see that his shirt was torn at the shoulder, and his sleeves were covered in blood.

"Oh, my God! Are you hurt?" I said, but he pulled away as if he were still afraid. I looked at Doris's rump, and her hindquarters were raked with claw marks. Juan Esteban held a bloody rag in his hand, then reached down, dipped it in the water, and gently dabbed Doris's wounds.

Juan Esteban still wouldn't let me touch him, but he followed me back toward camp and to the fire. We were both cold and shivering, and I looked him up and down while he held Doris's reins and rubbed her chest.

In the firelight, I saw that he had small scrapes on his arms and a bigger scrape on his shoulder where his shirt was torn, but his wounds appeared to be from brambles and not from a bear. Doris had clearly taken a swipe, but I figured that Juan Esteban must have gotten to her before the bear caused severe injury.

After changing into dry clothes, we huddled near the fire and stared into its flickering light with heavy eyes, and I wondered what had happened with the bear. Had it attacked Doris while Juan Esteban was sleeping? Perhaps it had chased them into the water, and that's why Juan Esteban and Doris went deeper—if so, it was a miracle that the bear gave up.

Everything about the day felt like a bad dream, and I wondered what had happened to Jasper and the professor. Had they made it out alive? And if so, would they come looking for us?

~

We got a few hours of sleep, but that was all. Just before daylight, Juan Esteban whipped up a pot of grits while I quickly packed our belongings. When I heard approaching footsteps, my heart began to pound. The professor and Jasper appeared, looking bent-over and bedraggled, like beaten dogs.

Both had scratches all over their bodies, and their feet were bloody, but despite their sorry state, Jasper ran toward the pot of grits and scooped up globs with his fingers, and even though he was still naked, my presence didn't concern him.

The professor reached for the pot. "Give me that," he shouted. He pushed Jasper away, held the pot near his mouth and spooned in five large mouthfuls, then growled at Jasper, "Put on some pants!"

When the professor noticed that Juan Esteban and I were packing, his eyes turned into slits. "Where are *you* going?" he said.

I straightened my back. "We're going home," I said.

The professor chuckled behind a smirk. "Oh, no you don't. Your work isn't done."

When I didn't stop packing, he approached with his arms outstretched and palms up. "We need to talk. I got a proposition for you." But before he could say anything else, Jasper interrupted.

"Hand over that pot," he said.

The professor looked at me. "We'll talk later," he said, then he shoved the pot into Jasper's chest.

Jasper's eyes grew wide. "There's hardly anything left."

"It's all you deserve," the professor said, "with all the damn trouble you've caused."

Jasper huffed, then scooped out the remains and licked his fingers in a way that made my stomach turn. He had grits all over his face and in his long hair.

"They took our horses and guns," he said. "I thought we were goners."

"Oh," I said, only feeling bad for Jake and Geneviève.

The professor walked over to his pack that hung from a tree, pulled out a bottle of whiskey, and took a long swig.

Jasper shouted. "Gimme a nip of that."

"Get your own damn whiskey," the professor said.

Jasper moved toward the professor and in a begging tone said, "Come on, I got us back in the middle of the night. That's gotta be worth at least one slug."

The professor reluctantly handed him the bottle. Jasper turned his back and guzzled a third of its contents.

"You son of a bitch!" the professor yelled.

Jasper cackled like a hyena, then thrust the bottle back into the professor's hands. "Serves you right for eating all the grub."

The professor gave Jasper a disgusted look. "If I had my pistol, I'd take you out right now."

"Ain't it my lucky day!" Jasper hooted. "The great professor has spared my life." He bowed, "Bless you, your royal highness."

The professor didn't respond but turned and walked down to the river, waded in up to his waist, and cradled his whisky bottle like it was his only friend.

I followed and stood on a boulder nearby. "What do you want to talk about?" I said.

With his back to me, he pointed his thumb toward camp. "I'm gonna get rid of that bastard—then we'll talk."

I wanted to ask him if he still had the brooch so I could consider my next move, but given his mood, the time wasn't right. Instead, I took the deer trail back and found Juan Esteban sitting at the base of a cottonwood with his pencil and paper in hand. He looked up into the canopy and stared, but I couldn't see what held his attention. After several minutes he started drawing.

It had turned into a pleasantly cool morning. I sat cross-legged by the fire in a spot where I could keep my eyes on Juan Esteban and cleaned my gun, hoping that Jasper might pass out and give me some peace, but I wasn't that lucky. Instead, he flopped down nearby.

"How'd you get free?" I said.

"They talked among themselves about whether they should kill us, but Sam had the last word and said we weren't worth wasting a bullet on. He said, 'Let 'em wander around like plucked chickens.' Then they mounted up and disappeared into the hills. The bastards. The professor cussed my ass all night."

"What happened to you?" Jasper said.

"The young one let me go—gave my gun back too." I didn't tell Jasper what he said about him and the professor being cowards because I didn't want to stir up more trouble. And I didn't mention the bear event with Juan Esteban for fear that Jasper and the professor would want to go after it again and rope me in to help.

Jasper picked at his teeth with dirty nails. "I knew once they'd let us go that they'd probably let you go, too."

As Jasper mumbled on about what a bitcher and moaner the professor had been all night, my thoughts drifted back to the young Indian and his expression before he gave Mule a swat. I felt like he understood things that the rest of us didn't—maybe like Juan Esteban.

After a few minutes, Jasper's voice turned into a slur, and he started singing.

"*Oh, my darlin', oh my darlin', oh my darlin', Clementine, you are lost and gone forever . . .*" But before he could finish the song he was snoring.

I looked toward the river. The professor was asleep with his mouth open in the shade of a willow, his whiskey bottle still in his grip.

Juan Esteban was still at work, so I joined him and watched as he drew the breast feathers of a bald eagle with such precision that I could feel their softness in the tips of my fingers. Then he detailed the wings—outstretched, V-shaped, with splayed feathers reaching upward. With the scratch of his pencil, he captured the wispy texture of each feather. Next, the talons and legs emerged—leaning forward, pushing off a branch that bent from the weight and power of the eagle's take-off.

I watched in amazement. I wanted to tell him how much I loved and admired him, but I didn't dare break the spell. I thought of Celia, Pop, Marie Isabel, Cora, and John Joseph. and how much I missed them, and was almost certain John Joseph had been right. My decision to join the professor had been a huge mistake. But if we hadn't, I would never have discovered the brooch.

About an hour later, the professor and Jasper awoke, and both were still drunk. The professor stumbled back to his bedding and flopped down, while Jasper lay on his side with his head braced against his elbow, eyeing Juan Esteban's every move.

Over by Doris and Mule, Juan Esteban was organizing his drawing materials and had loosened the screws on his press to put the eagle away.

Jasper jumped to his feet and shouted. "Hang on, Da Vinci," Jasper said. "Let me get a look at the masterpiece."

"Leave him be," I said.

"I ain't gonna leave him be," Jasper said. "I want a look!" He stumbled toward Juan Esteban with a wretched smile on his face, and I got up to follow.

John Esteban hugged his drawing and turned his back to Jasper.

"Come on . . ." Jasper said, "just a little peek?" Then quick as a cat, Jasper snatched the drawing, ran toward the fire, and dangled it above the flames.

"How much is it worth to you, Juannie boy? Are you man enough to fight for it, or are you just a weakling?"

The edge of the paper turned tan and curled from the heat. Panic stricken, Juan Esteban whipped his head my way and stared wide-eyed at me.

Like a bullet, I ran full speed, lunged, and hit Jasper in the gut with my shoulder. Jasper stumbled and fell backwards against a boulder, hitting it square against his back. He gasped for breath and tried to speak, but no words came out.

The drawing flew in the air and landed just a few feet from the flame.

The professor let out a roaring laugh—like it had come from some barbaric place. "Cat got your tongue, Jasper? For once, Fat Mouth can't speak!"

The professor picked up Juan Esteban's drawing, gave it a long look, then handed it to me. "Keep it somewhere safe."

I gave it to Juan Esteban, and he scurried off to put it away. The professor wobbled over to my bedding, picked up my gun, then looked at me.

"Loaded?" he said.

I nodded.

He pointed the gun at Jasper. "Get out of my sight." His eyes bulged. "Instead of leading us to a cougar, you led us into a trap. And they took Geneviève and everything I had that's worth anything—except for . . ." then his mouth shut like a snapping turtle's.

I swallowed hard. Did he still have the brooch?

He pulled back the flintlock on my gun. "If you don't get out of here by the time I count to ten, I'll shoot you dead."

Jasper hiccupped and straightened his back. "I'm leaving on my own. I'm sick of your pompous ass and everything about this stupid expedition. And as for Frannie, good luck. She could have helped us, but she didn't. And her stupid brother can't cook worth shit!"

I wanted to flatten him again—but I didn't. I was ready to be rid of Jasper. And though I was interested in the professor's "proposition," I mostly wanted to figure out if the brooch was still around, so I could plan my next move.

An hour after Jasper stumbled out of camp on foot and after the professor had sobered up, he approached, clenching something in his fist. My first thought was maybe it was the brooch, but that made no sense. Why would he voluntarily let me know that he still had it?

He opened his fingers, and three coins lay in his palm.

"This is incentive for you to help me. It was going to be Jasper's pay, but he's such an idiot that now it's yours. And if you stick with me and do as I say, there'll be more."

"What are we going to do?" I asked.

"We'll stay here tonight, then break camp in the morning and head to town. I've got to find another horse. After that, I'll fill you in on the rest."

"I thought all your money was stolen," I said.

He wore a wry expression. "A lot of it was, but I know how to manage my risks."

When I took the coins from him, I knew I was taking yet another risk of my own. There was still a chance that the professor might have the brooch. If he did, I vowed to find it, but I needed a plan.

CHAPTER 14

WOLVES

1873

With Jasper gone, I slept less fitfully and awoke to a cardinal singing. The sun was rising, and clouds just above the canyon's narrows were brushed in a glowing orange.

I heard the professor moving around, and I sat up.

"You and your brother get up, get some coffee, then let's head out," he said.

"Coffee?" I said.

"Yeah, it's ready," he said. I was shocked when I saw the coffee pot hissing over the flame and wondered what this change in temperament was all about. Was he trying to butter me up for his "proposition?"

Mule seemed to understand that something was up, too, when the professor approached him using a calm voice.

"There, there Mule . . . we're going to have a nice little ride."

He threw the saddle blanket over Mule's back, then heaved the saddle into place.

Mule took two steps back, then tipped his rear hoof downward in the kicking position. When the professor tried to tighten the girth, Mule took a deep breath and swelled his belly with air.

"He's bloating," I said. "He'll have you off him before you can get your feet in the stirrups. Let me see if Juan Esteban can settle him."

I turned to Juan Esteban, who was organizing his satchel and drawings.

"Come rub his nose," I said.

Juan Esteban came over and gently caressed Mule's muzzle. Mule didn't release at first, but after a few strokes and some scratches behind his oversized ears, his belly decompressed.

"That's a mule," I said and glanced back. "Maybe Juan Esteban and I should ride Mule. Doris won't give you any trouble."

"She's too short for me," the professor said.

"Would you rather ride or get tossed?" I said.

The professor blew air through his lips, like riding a donkey was beneath him.

"Jesus rode a donkey," I said, "but not good enough you?"

Ignoring my words, the professor looked Doris over. "What are those scrapes on her rear?" the professor said.

"Dunno," I said giving him my best blank look. I wasn't about to tell him about the bear. Getting away from this camp and all the terrible things that had happened was all I could think about.

"Whatever it was, Juan Esteban has fixed her up. She'll be fine."

Regarding Doris, I will admit that the professor had a point. He was a sight as we ambled along for several miles with his feet scraping the ground. Several times I heard him curse as catclaw vine snagged his leg and ripped his long johns.

Juan Esteban was serious-faced most of the ride. I knew he wasn't happy about the professor riding Doris. He gripped my waist extra tight and kept looking back at the professor with furrowed eyebrows. To ease his anxiety, I searched along the river for wildlife and pointed when I saw something. We watched as a gray heron took flight. It flew upstream and landed on a shoal, then waded into a shallow pool, dipping its neck between slow-moving strides. When the heron came up with a finger-long flapping fish and raised and extended its slender throat to swallow, Juan Esteban gently pinched the back of my arm to let me know he had seen it.

At the edge of town, the professor made us stop near a thicket that was overgrown with climbing vines.

"Dismount, and I'll walk between Mule and Doris until we get to the general store. I'm not going to be a laughingstock."

We walked along in a tight cluster and headed straight toward the general store.

The streets were bustling with all types: soldiers, cowboys, women in bonnets and dresses, Mexican families, Indians, and gentlemen in dusty top hats. I looked down at my shabby dress and Juan Esteban's ripped pants and was embarrassed by our appearance, but no one paid us any attention—there were too many other things going on.

It was a Saturday morning, and the market square was buzzing with selling and buying. San Saba, the county seat, had more buildings than I had ever seen—some even made from stone. The courthouse was two stories high and had a bell at the top. Juan Esteban and I both craned our necks and squinted into an overcast sky when the bell rang out nine dongs.

Main Street was a sea of dust as cowboys drove herds of cattle through the middle of town and pushed clusters of Mexican boys with their sheep to the street's edges. I hadn't seen so many people in one place since my vague memories of Galveston. Juan Esteban walked behind me so close that he kept kicking the backs of my feet with the toes of his shoes.

After we tied up Mule and Doris, the professor said, "Do as you wish—I have business and will meet you back at the river—set up camp in that pecan grove we passed. Get a fire going—I'll bring supper. Mule and Doris will stay with me, because I have to load up on supplies and need Mule to haul them."

Juan Esteban looked at me—I knew he was worried.

Trying to redirect his attention, I said, "Come on, Juan Esteban. Let's see what's for sale."

We bought a few corn dodgers to put in our pockets for later, and as we weaved through the crowd, we came upon tables full of jellies and jams, honey, smoked meats, pickled pigs' snouts, but most of all smoked pecans.

Children were running everywhere. A boy with sweaty curls ran by me and grazed my arm as he tried to tag another boy.

He had a peppermint stick hanging from his mouth, and I called after him, "Where'd you get that?"

"There," he said, and pointed toward a table in the shade of a mesquite tree.

Two girls about the age of Marie Isabel and Cora were sitting on a log with baskets in their laps and shouting, "Candy here, get your candy."

I waved for Juan Esteban to follow, and when we got near, I said, "We'll take some. How much?"

"Six for a penny."

Juan Esteban stuck his nose close to the basket.

"Hey, get back," the girl with blond curls said. "Nobody wants your grubby nose in their candy." I pulled Juan Esteban's shirt and tugged him back a few steps. He stared at the girls with a flat expression.

"What's wrong with him?" the little girl said.

"Nothing's wrong with him. He's just different," I said.

She looked at me, then back at Juan Esteban, and twisted her mouth to the side like she wasn't so sure.

I handed a penny to the older girl, and she counted out six peppermint sticks, rolled them in a piece of paper, then tied a loose knot with a string. Juan Esteban watched her every move, and when she handed him the package, he dropped to his knees, then retied the string into a bow that looked like a perfect four-leaf clover.

The little girl smiled.

"What's your name?" I said.

"Jenny."

"Thanks for the candy, Jenny," I said. The older girl didn't seem as enchanted with Juan Esteban's talents, but she still waved goodbye.

We found a shady spot on the boardwalk, sucked on our peppermints, and watched people walk by. A boy pulled a wagon filled with overstuffed gunnysacks jammed with wool; a soldier rode a long-legged stallion and shared the saddle with a pink-cheeked woman; an old lady carrying a cane poked at every child in her path— "Out of my way . . . ain't you kids got manners?"

I looked back to where we had tied Mule and Doris, but they were gone. At the same hitching post, a coal-colored horse stood, and an older man sat on a stump and fed the horse a carrot. The man's posture was crooked, like he'd been broken and put back together more than once. He scanned the street with a wary eye, then squinted and tightened his lips when he saw a group of five rugged-looking men on horseback coming his way.

As they got closer, I could see their sun-scorched faces and shaggy hair. Following behind was a mule with a stack of wolf pelts tied to its back. The lead rider, a man with a long gray beard that brushed his protruding belly, tipped his hat, and mockingly said, "Good day, Sheriff."

As the others snickered, the sheriff spat and sent a stream of brown juice their direction. "Boys . . ." he said, then pointed his finger towards the edge of town.

The old man laughed. "We won't be long, Sheriff—just a shave and a little pleasure for some weary travelers—that's all."

Across the street I heard a familiar booming laugh and saw the professor arm in arm with a middle-aged woman in a flouncy dress with a low neckline. Her hair was tied up in an orange ribbon, and she twirled a daisy between her fingers as she tottered at the professor's side. The professor, in new woolen pants and a white shirt with a stiff collar, chattered the whole time. *"Mais oui ma petite oiseau, je suis un professor and . . . how do you say . . . a descendent of the throne—the House of Orleans."*

The woman batted her eyes.

My instinct was to race across the street and warn her. "Watch out, lady!" but I didn't—the day was turning out to be a nice one, and I didn't want to spoil it, plus I had plans to make.

The professor gave her a pat on the rear end as they entered a two-story wood-frame building with three women fanning themselves on the upper balcony. As they opened the front door, I could hear the faint notes of a fiddle and accordion mixed with raucous laughter and singing. Before long, the five wolf hunters swaggered toward the building gawking and whistling at the women above.

I knew it would be a while before we saw the professor again. Meanwhile, I pondered my plan. That night, I would search for the brooch again.

If I found it, we'd be gone. If I didn't, I'd wait to hear about the proposition and decide my next move.

~

We set up camp just under the soaring branches of a pecan tree and spent what was left of the afternoon gathering sticks and fallen limbs for the fire. At the river's edge, our footsteps stirred a cluster of snapping turtles from their log, and they slipped into the green water with barely a splash.

When we heard the crunch of hooves coming our way, it was nearly dark, and the fire was popping, spraying sparks upward like fireflies.

Emerging from the shadows and into the firelight, the professor rode toward us straddling a boney white horse and leaning over the saddle horn like he was about to topple over.

"There you are!" he shouted. "Why'd you have to camp so damned far away. I've been riding forever."

I threw up my hands. "It's where you told us to camp."

He ignored me. "I'm famished. What's for dinner?" he said.

"Dinner?" I said. "You have the supplies. We've been waiting for you."

He looked at me incredulously. "What? I gave you money."

"That was my wages—you're responsible for the food."

He swung his legs over his horse, dropped to the ground, and stumbled toward me reeking of whiskey. "Must I do *everything*? Surely you and your half-wit brother could do *something* for a change."

I narrowed my eyes. "Where's Mule and Doris?"

He looked over his shoulder and put his hand to his ear. "Shush, listen I hear her." He waited for a moment, then shouted, "Dor-ass, get your dumb ass over here," and then he buckled over in laughter.

I had to concentrate on keeping my fist at my side, so I wouldn't use it. When I glanced at Juan Esteban his dark eyes flashed red with the fire flames, and then he abruptly stood up, started turning in circles with his arms covering his head.

"Where's Mule?" I said.

"Sold her, for this one… but she was so worthless that it wasn't enough. Had to sell some other things too."

"Like what?"

He plopped down beside the fire. "The drawings…got a package deal… from some guy at the livery stable. He was headed out of town on Mule last I saw him."

"What?" My voice was shrill. "You sold Juan Esteban's drawings?"

"Yep," the professor said and burped. "*Pardonez moi*!"

"Those weren't yours to sell! They belong to Juan Esteban!"

He glared at me. "Look, Missy, I don't give a rat's ass about who they belong to. I needed a horse and that's that."

Juan Esteban started moaning.

"Shut up!" the professor yelled.

I couldn't take it anymore. I had to know. "Did you sell the ivory brooch too?"

He eyed me.

"What's it to you?"

"Nothing . . ." I said, "I just wondered because I know it means a lot to you and . . ."

He growled, "Of course I didn't—got to have some assets besides a washed-up horse."

I was incredulous—uncertain whether to be happy the brooch was still in his possession or angry that he had saved the brooch and sold Juan Esteban's drawings instead. And that something that meant so much to me—the brooch—was nothing but an asset to him. I paced back and forth and noticed Juan Esteban doing the same in the shadows.

"Sit, for Christ's sake," he said. "Just like a female to make a mountain out of a molehill."

I wanted to kick him or something worse, but right now I needed to keep my wits about me.

I walked over to Juan Esteban and whispered. "It's okay . . . we'll get them back. Tonight." I touched his elbow ever so slightly to reassure him, even though my own confidence was on shaky ground.

My next move was to settle things down so the professor would fall asleep. I handed him two of the six corn dodgers in my possession and sat with him while he popped them in his mouth and chewed. When he was finished, he pulled out a whisky bottle and washed them down.

"That all you got?" he said.

I lied and nodded my head.

His face squinched up tight. "Next time don't be so stupid and buy more." Then the additional liquor started to set in, and his voice calmed.

"I'm beat," he said. "That whore was feisty as a wild mare."

He put his hat over his eyes and sighed. "Go to bed, because early tomorrow, we're hunting wolves. Fellow told me how to do it—bought him some whiskey for his tip."

"So, what's the proposition?" I said.

"That's the proposition," he said. "You help me, you get more money. And if you help with the skinning, you'll get Jasper's pay, too."

"How much?" I said.

"Depends on how many wolves you shoot." Then he covered his eyes with his hat.

Once again, I felt bamboozled by this good-for-nothing thief, and I felt my face flush with anger. Though he was offering more money, it was only what we'd be due—nothing more.

At that moment, I knew exactly what I had to do.

~

Before I could get my bedroll spread out, the professor was snoring. I tried to convince Juan Esteban to lay his blanket near me, but he wouldn't. He lay on the bare ground close to where Doris was grazing and tied her reins around his wrist. His hair and eyebrows were covered in dust and his eyes were wide as an owl's. I went over and knelt by his side, and I whispered, "I'm going to look for the brooch, and we'll go. We'll head back to town, speak to the livery boy, then track down that fellow and Mule. We'll get your drawings back."

I walked over to where the professor lay. He was using his saddle pack for a pillow. When I tugged on the pack, he jerked his head and mumbled, then chuckled and rolled over, but the pack was still snug under his head.

I tugged again.

Like he'd been hit by lightning, the professor suddenly sat bolt upright.

"What the hell are you doing?"

My heart raced. "Well, uh . . ."

I noticed his eyes were open, but his eyeballs had rolled back under his lids.

I stayed still as a rabbit.

After a few seconds of leaning on his hands, the professor flopped back down and started babbling nonsense.

I crept over to Juan Esteban. "He's too restless," I said. "Tonight won't work, but don't worry. Tomorrow."

⌒

I lay awake much of the night thinking about where the professor might have hidden the brooch and didn't realize I'd fallen asleep until the professor nudged me with the toe of his boot.

He was fully dressed and had his pistol strapped to his hip.

"Wake up. We've got work to do."

It was still pitch black, and I could hear the frogs croaking in the distance and the gurgle of the river rapids.

"What time is it?"

"About two hours before sunrise. We have to get out there now—shoot some deer. I know where they're bedded down."

I rubbed my eyes. "I thought you wanted wolves?"

He stared at me with an impatient expression. "Just tell the boy we'll be back after daylight and to have breakfast ready."

⌒

The night was mostly overcast, but there was a three-quarter waxing moon behind the clouds, and the sky glowed.

"Follow me," he said, and I stayed behind him as we crept through a willow thicket near the water.

The professor stepped on a branch, and it snapped. He stopped in his tracks.

There was a snort across the water. The professor pointed toward a mass of carrizo cane. "In there," he whispered. "Get as close as you can without scaring them . . . then fire fast, as many shots as you have. I'll unload a round with my new pistol too."

"What about the skins?" I said. "I thought you wanted them?"

"Not this time."

I hunkered down and crawled on my hands and knees, careful to stay hidden in the brush. Something about what I was doing didn't feel right, but I did it anyway. When my knees and palms squished into soft sand, I found a spot where I could rest my rifle on a log.

I knelt and pulled back the flintlock— another snort, then a rustle. I hesitated and looked back at the professor. He had his hands raised in the air like *come-on, shoot!*

I squeezed the trigger. *BAM!*

There was thrashing in the cane, then the professor fired six shots while I reloaded and fired again. *BAM.*

More thrashing.

Adrenaline raced as I jammed another slug in.

Breaking through the cane, a deer dashed across the sandy beach, so I steadied the gun against my shoulder, led it by six feet, and *BAM!*

The deer stumbled, pitched, then raked the sand with its front hooves and with panic-stricken eyes dragged his rear legs toward the water. Blood was streaming from its haunches.

"Dammit!" I pounded the sand with my fist, realizing I had hit the buttocks, not the shoulder, and had no more ammunition.

The professor ran out of the thicket toward water. He waded across the river with long strides while gripping a knife in one hand and a burlap bag in the other. When he got to the carrizo cane, he slashed through the reeds, slinging his arms in every direction. Then I lost sight of him and saw nothing but the quivering heads of cane stalks.

"We got two here!" he yelled. His voice was wild and greedy.

I took off my shoes and started across the river toward the deer that lay on the beach. My feet squished deep into sediment pockets and my skirt dragged behind me, waterlogged and heavy. As I neared shore, I saw the deer's front legs twitch, but the back legs were limp and covered in blood that oozed into the sand. Her flesh was stretched tight around her belly, and I could see veins just below her white fur. There was more life inside her than just her own. I dropped my gun and knelt by her side. I felt an overwhelming stillness, and everything peripheral disappeared into a foggy nothingness. The only thing I could hear was the doe's breath and mine.

I touched her neck. Her skin rippled. A red droplet hung from the tip of her nostril. In the light, it looked like a shining ruby. I blinked, then swallowed hard, recognizing it for what it really was.

I jumped when his voice pierced the calm.

"Drag it over here," the professor yelled.

"She's not dead yet," I said.

"Who cares," he said.

"I do," I whispered.

I felt a wetness on my cheek like water trickling from a dry spring after a long drought. I wiped my face with my sleeve, but the tears kept flowing. For the first time, I understood how Juan Esteban felt.

It took all the strength I had to pull the deer to the water's edge until half of her body was in the sand, and half was floating.

The professor was yelling at me the whole time. "Hurry, goddammit— no time to spare."

I knelt and wrapped my arms around her neck and with a firm embrace, dipped her head under water. For a second her front legs thrashed, then her muscles loosened, and the weight of her neck and head weighed upon my arms like a heavy stone.

I looked over my shoulder, and the professor was standing there with an incredulous expression—his hands were covered in blood. "What are you doing? I've been working my ass off to drag these deer onto the beach, and you're just sitting here."

He grabbed the doe's legs with a roughness that sent a shiver down my spine, then dragged it through the sand and positioned it next to the other two. The burlap bag sat next to the deer, and he kneeled, dug inside, and pulled out a handful of powdery white substance.

"This will do the trick," he said. "Strychnine."

He threw fistful after fistful of the poison over the deers' bodies, then rubbed it in with furious circular motions making sure it was stuck to skin and fur. I wanted to scream *stop*! I wanted to shove him aside and kick him with all the energy I had to defend the dignity of the lifeless mound—to protect the creatures that would come to feed. But I didn't.

Instead, I watched and felt my heart plummet like it was tied to an anvil sinking into depths I had never known.

After he was finished, he stood up, then walked to the river and washed his hands. I could hear his splashing as I stared at the three lifeless lumps. The fur's tan color was transformed into a ghostly white.

The professor walked toward me drying his hands on his shirt.

"We're setting a trap," he said. "Now we'll hide in the brush and wait for the wolves." He rubbed his hands together. "We'll be lucky if we get four or five. That's what the wolf hunters told me. They don't die immediately. They stagger around, then walk toward the water because they're thirsty. We'll have to watch so we don't lose sight of them. He grinned. "The tails bring the big money—the skins next."

I turned and waded back into the water.

The professor yelled, "Where you going? I'll need your help."

"Do it yourself." I yelled back. "You're a bastard!"

When I got back to camp, I pulled my bedroll next to Juan Esteban's. He was lying on his side, and I could feel the warmth off his back. I put my hand over his left hand that lay on his hip. I didn't dare wake him. He wouldn't have wanted me to hold his hand.

$\sim$

Juan Esteban was hunting for wild onions and I was drinking coffee when the professor rode in with five wolf pelts loaded on his white horse. Juan Esteban glanced over his shoulder, but when he saw the skins and their gore smeared across the horse's boney haunches, he turned away.

The professor walked over in blood-stained clothes and threw his hat at me. "Thanks for nothing," he said. "Next time you'll do as you're told, and if you don't help me today with preparing these skins, you'll get none of your wages. And forget the extra money!"

Something surged inside me like an erupting volcano. "I don't care!" I shouted. "Juan Esteban and I are leaving!"

The professor laughed, then he wagged his finger at me as if he were scolding a child. "You better care, Miss Frannie. How are you two going to make it home with no money? Do you and your brother like eating dirt?"

"We'll manage," I said. "We'll shoot something and get by."

"What will you shoot with?" he said. "Ammunition for your gun is in my possession—not yours. I paid for it. I own it.

He stared at me with raised eyebrows. "And without ammunition, how will you protect yourself if you meet up with thugs like the ones we met on the cougar hunt? Or worse yet, Indians," and he winced as if considering a gory ending.

"And just in case you think you might steal some plugs and powder from me, you're out of luck. We used it all up with the wolves."

"I'm not a thief!" I said, and I wanted to add, "Not like you!" but I didn't. I needed to hide what I knew.

He clapped his hands as if everything was settled. "I only see one possible scenario here—you stick with me, we spend another two weeks shooting wolves, you finish the job, I pay you, and you go home."

I couldn't stand his demeaning tone another moment. I bolted to the river. My head was spinning—he was right; we were trapped like hostages until he was ready to release us. I was stupid to think we could just take off and ride the 150 miles home with no money, no food, and no protection. I had a small pouch of powder, and maybe three more slugs hidden away, but that was it.

And the more time we wasted with the professor, the more our chances of finding Juan Esteban's drawings dwindled. Most likely, the man who bought them would continue to ride further west—how would we catch up? And what if he had already sold them by the time we caught up? And if even if he did have them, how could I buy them back with no money?

Angrily, I threw rocks, hurling them against the embankment on the opposite side until my arm was sore. Then I dropped down and sat on a sandy shoal. I raked my finger across the sand and wracked my brain about what to do.

I had only one option to turn things my way. It was risky, but it was the only shot I had.

~

I helped the professor with the skins all morning. The smell was awful, and by afternoon, the cool of the morning had evaporated, and the air was hot and thick with humidity. Sweat streamed down my neck and dampened the front of my dress as I brushed the loose flesh from the skins. Each skin took over an hour, and since we had no food except for four more corn dodgers, my stomach was growling and pitching. I didn't dare eat the corn dodgers though—I needed to ration them and save them for later.

"We won't go out tonight," the professor said. "We'll ride into town tomorrow, get some food, sell the skins, then ride ten miles upstream the next day and do it again."

I listened but made no comment. My only objective was to finish the day's job and go to bed. And in the middle of the night when the professor was snoring, I would get back to work.

~

When I heard his first snore, I pushed off my covers and whispered to Juan Esteban, "Pack up. I'm going to find it now."

I had narrowed down the possibilities of where the brooch might be. I doubted it was in the clothes he wore. He no longer had a coat, and if he kept it in his pants pockets, there'd be a lump. I hadn't seen one. Perhaps his duffel— that would be easy to search while he was sleeping. But if it was in the saddle pack like I expected, my work could be precarious—if he continued to use the pack like a pillow.

I checked the duffel first. Most of the objects were large and heavy—his skinning tools, jars of turpentine, brushes, a small shovel, a hammer—not a safe place for a delicate brooch. As I reloaded its contents, the hammer slipped from my hand and clanked against the shovel.

The professor rustled and let out a snort, then mumbled something indecipherable in French.

Next the saddlebag. I put an extra log on the fire so I could see more clearly. Not only was he cradling it, but his arm was looped through a buckled strap.

Removing it without waking him seemed nearly impossible. Slowly, I pulled back the strap, trying to release the buckle. The leather was stiff, and I gave it a quick yank to free the prong from the hole. The professor stirred, rolled on his side, and hugged the bag tighter. I held my breath a moment—how could I loosen his grip?

I looked toward the river where a willow tree lay low against an embankment and had an idea. With my pocketknife in hand, I searched the willow for the best branch, found a long thin one, cut it clean from the trunk, and then sheared off its leaves except for three at the end. I left one sturdy offshoot and cut it down to a five-inch prong, making a crude hook.

After creeping back to where the professor was sleeping, I crouched behind his head where he couldn't see me if he opened his eyes. Very gently, I raked the leaf across his arm with barely a tickle. At first, he didn't move. Then he grumbled, jerked his elbow, and slapped his arm with his left hand. Then he settled in on his back.

The saddle bag was loose from his chest, but he still held the strap with his fist. I tried again, and this time I grazed the tip of his right ear ever so lightly as if a mosquito had landed. Suddenly, he sat up and roared, "Goddammit!" then whipped his arms around his head and fell back into his bedroll and pulled the covers over his head.

The bag was free. I used the willow stem again, hooking the leather strap on the prong, and slid the saddle bag away from the professor's body, then moved behind some brush where Juan Esteban had the lantern hanging from a tree and was packing.

I needed to work fast in case the professor stirred again, so I opened the flap and unloaded its contents: a handkerchief, a pocketknife, socks, his pistol, bullets, pencil, coins. I dug deeper but couldn't find the brooch. I took a deep breath—where could it be?

After reloading the saddle bag, I scanned the campsite, then tiptoed back to where the professor was sleeping and lay the saddle bag next to him. I was beginning to lose hope, when I remembered my mother's hiding place. Sewn in somewhere—but where? A log popped in the fire, and the light flared bright for a split second. I could see the professor's blanket clearly. I knelt and ran my fingers down the blanket's edges, then swallowed hard when I came to a lump near his neck. I rubbed it between my fingers, feeling its oval shape. With the tip of my knife blade, I loosened the threads that fastened a pocket. My hand was shaking when I removed the brooch and held it in my palm, and I quickly raised my skirt and tucked it into my slip pocket.

Within minutes, Juan Esteban and I were saddled up on Doris and riding through shadows and light. Hanging just above the cliffs, the moon was bright as a giant lantern. The beauty of it made me think of Mother. Had it been luck? I didn't think so, and I pictured Mother smiling as wide as the moon before us.

As we rode toward San Saba, I *hoped* that whatever had led us to the brooch would lead us to Juan Esteban's drawings—and that we would never see the professor again.

CHAPTER 15

LEILO—THE VASE

1934

My experiences with the professor and Jasper taught me to be wary of hope. Though I could hope for this or hope for that, most times hope has let me down.

A few days ago, when I was in town picking up my mail, the postmaster said, "I sure hope we don't get another duster like the last one."

I shook my head and thought, "Mister, you've just jinxed us. Now, we're guaranteed to have a storm like none other." And I was right.

A few days after Dom and Juan Esteban had finished cleaning the chicken coop, I awoke at 7:00 a.m. to a dull eastern light and Juan Esteban's footfalls as he paced the floor between the front door and kitchen. He had Pico under his arm, and Pico was shaking.

"What is it?" I said.

I knew it was going to be bad when I looked to the northwest, and the sky was pitch black. I put the car in the shed, and Juan Esteban and I covered our garden and moved the hens inside. Then it hit. Juan Esteban seemed to calm down with the hens inside, but I was the opposite. When one-inch-round hail pellets slammed against our roof, sending the chickens into a frenzy, I started pacing myself.

I thought of Dom. *Damn chickens!*

Juan Esteban sensed my raw nerves, gathered up the hens and carried them to a closet and closed the door behind him.

I looked out the window and watched as every tree in sight was stripped of its leaves. Then I heard glass shatter at our back windows. That's when I took to my bed.

~

The next morning was dusty and dry. The storm had brought no rain, just a cloud of soil from somewhere out west. When I touched my bedroom doorknob, a spark flew. And when I pulled out a pot to heat some water, another shock lit me up.

"Dammit!"

As the water heated, I surveyed the house. A thin layer of dust covered everything, but it wasn't tan like our own soil. It was dark, like someone had scraped it from a riverbed and sprayed it around. When I heard the water boiling, I poured it over coffee grounds and then into a cup. I took a big slug, then ran to the sink and spat. Coffee and black earth don't mix.

Juan Esteban came into the kitchen with chicken crap all over his clothes, and the smell was something awful. He had deep bags under his eyes and was yawning.

"You okay?" I said.

He looked at me with a flat expression, then proceeded to carry the chickens outside, shovel dust from the coop, shake out the straw, and return the chickens to their boxes.

That morning, I mostly puttered too—wiping down bookcases, tables, and shelves with a wet cloth. When I got to my oak chest of drawers, I circled the dust cloth around the few items that meant something to me.

There was a necklace of buckeyes from my sister Cora, and a bracelet of woven string from Marie Isabel, both gifts for my thirteenth birthday. Then I blew a film of dust off the winning slug from my Jaeger rifle that Pop had dug out of the target with his penknife the day I was hailed King.

And there was Pop's pipe next to it. I held the bowl up to my nose, closed my eyes, breathed in the aroma, and savored its essence. It reminded me of home and the leafy scent that filled the air after a rain, in the post oak thickets that surrounded our property in Cedar Bend.

The pipe brought back memories of Pop and his gentle nature, and I cherished it for that. He passed about a year after Juan Esteban and I moved to Leilo, but we were unable to attend the funeral because it was harvest time. As a keepsake, John Joseph sent me the pipe, along with a note that recounted the night he died. His note said,

Pop died on a cold night in his rocking chair in front of a warm fire. As usual, he stayed up after everyone had gone to bed to smoke and rock. I can't say why, but I awoke around midnight and walked into the living area where a few embers still glowed in the hearth. Pop was slumped in his chair, and a spray of tiny holes were seared into his shirt from where the pipe had fallen from his lips and spilled tobacco ashes across his chest. His skin was the color of a dull moon, but there was a look of satisfaction on his face, as if he had taken one last deep inhale of sweet-scented peace, then passed.

In that note, John Joseph captured a feeling that gives me comfort, and when I'm in my own rocking chair holding Pop's pipe, I feel as if the space between heaven and earth is like a thin veil—as if I can feel Pop in the room with me.

When I'm not using it, I keep it next to a turkey feather set in a wren's nest.

The nest and feather were a gift that John Joseph and Juan Esteban brought to adorn the small table in my jail cell. They had walked all morning and most of the afternoon to visit on a rare warm January day.

It was the sixth visit for John Joseph and Juan Esteban. Pop, Celia, and the girls had come three times. I understood that it was difficult for them to visit more often, because keeping food on the table required hard work every day.

The first time John Joseph and Juan Esteban visited, I wore the dress the sheriff's wife had made for me. She had taken care to insert wool within the pockets.

"For your hands," she said. "These winter days can get chilly if you ain't got a fire."

The day she gave me the dress, I wanted to hug her, not only in thanks, but to feel the warmth of another body. She laid the soft cotton fabric across my outstretched arms.

"Doing okay?" she said. "Got enough blankets?"

"Yes," I said.

She crossed her plump arms over her chest and looked at her feet like she was embarrassed by her work. "The pattern ain't all that pretty, but it's all I had."

I ran my fingers over tiny white stars on navy blue cotton.

"Looks like the view I see at night," I said, but when I looked up to say, "Thank you," she had already turned away as if her act of kindness was breaking a rule.

Counting stars was one pleasure I experienced in my cell. On clear nights, I pulled one end of my cot outside into the three-foot-wide courtyard and lay on my back and counted. In August, when Venus with its dazzling beams crossed my view within a lasso of stars, I was amazed. My view was narrow, so I rarely saw the moon, but when I did, I felt as if I was receiving a visit from a long-lost friend.

When family came the sheriff let me walk free outside the jail. We sat on the packed earth with our backs against the limestone block wall in the shade of a sycamore tree and talked about the weather, news at Pop's church, Celia's quilting endeavors, how Marie Isabel and Cora were doing in school, the barn animals, and Juan Esteban's drawings. When we ran out of things to say, we sat in silence, closed our eyes, and listened to sycamore leaves rustling above in the breeze—the sound was soothing, like a gentle rain.

During their last visit, John Joseph and Juan Esteban gave me the nest and feather.

"Juan Esteban found the wren's nest, and I found the turkey feather, so it's a gift from both of us," John Joseph said. While he spoke, Juan Esteban drew in the dirt with a twig.

"I found the feather down by the creek, just at the water's edge. There were tracks everywhere—looked like about six turkeys had come to drink. When you're home, we'll go hunting and find us a tom—dinner to celebrate your homecoming."

He looked at me with an expression that was somewhere between happy and sad—he was eighteen by then; his formerly full face had thinned, and chiseled cheekbones emerged.

"How are the girls?" I said.

"Marie Isabel is fine—chatty as usual. I thought when she got a little older, she'd stop gabbing so much, but she can still talk the ear off a corn stalk."

I laughed.

"Cora had her eleventh birthday, and Celia made her a rhubarb pie—just like she did for you on your eleventh."

"Was it delicious?"

"It was. Juan Esteban had red juice all over his face—I think he enjoyed it the most."

John Joseph put his hand in his pocket. "I've got something else," he said. "It's from Celia and Pop. Celia bought it in town. Came all the way from China, the merchant said."

He handed me a tiny vase, no more than an inch tall, and I examined its elegant form and color—deep blues with thin spirals of inset brass.

"It's beautiful," I said.

As we continued to talk, Juan Esteban got up and walked to the edge of the jail yard and picked a tiny yellow daisy, then came back and laid it at my feet. I put the flower in the vase and smiled.

"Thank you, Juan Esteban."

He turned his head to the side and looked away. I could see the profile of his nose and mouth in the shadow of his thick bangs. His jaw was wide and strong, and his hands looked like a man's, not a boy's.

After a few hours, we said goodbye, and I watched them walk away. When Juan Esteban turned to come back, John Joseph gently tugged on his shirt tail. I felt a lump rise in my throat, and tears welled up in my eyes.

~

After gently squishing the nest to shore up the feather, I looked for the vase that I kept in a wooden box with a glass face. It was missing. I wondered if Juan Esteban had moved it, but that seemed unlikely. He never touched anything on my chest of drawers.

No one else had been in our house for months except Dom, and suddenly my distrustful side kicked in.

When he showed up for work, he rubbed his hands together to warm up and chirped, "Miss Abbott, you feeling better?"

I didn't have the patience for chitchat.

"Dom, you got something to tell me?"

"What do you mean?"

"You know what I mean."

He looked at his feet. "Miss Abbott, I don't know what you're talking about."

"You better not be lying, Dom. My china vase is missing—did you take it?"

He didn't say anything.

"Should I take that as a yes?"

He nodded.

My cheeks were red hot, and I was about to give Dom a blistering lecture on stealing and the bad things that come from it when he said, "I gave it to Mama for her birthday."

My anger turned limp, and it took me a minute to collect my thoughts. Dom was looking at his feet with his shoulders slumped and hands stuffed into his pockets.

"Dom, if you had told me I would have given it to you, but stealing is wrong—it'll land you in jail, and that's no way to live."

"I didn't think you'd miss it."

"That's not the point. Stealing is stealing, no matter how big or small."

He shuffled his feet. "Is that why you were sent to jail?"

I jerked my head around and stared straight at him. "How did you know about that?"

"Kids at school told me when they heard I was working for you—they said I was a dumbass for setting foot on your property."

I swallowed hard. "Don't want to talk about it."

Dom wiped his forehead with his sleeve and stared through me with his piercing black eyes.

"I was honest with you, why can't you be honest with me?" he said.

I turned, walked to the window, and gazed silently into a dusty blue sky. A red-tailed hawk circled, then swooped downward and emerged from a spray of dust with a squirrel hanging in its talons. I felt a shiver as the squirrel's tail wiggled with spastic fear.

I didn't turn around when I spoke. "I killed a man—that professor I told you about. He stole Juan Esteban's drawings, and when I confronted him, there was a tussle. I was scared, and . . ." I paused for a second and took a deep breath, "so I shot him."

I could hear Dom breathing. We stood in silence for a moment, then Dom cleared his throat, "Did you feel bad afterwards?"

The empathy in his tone made my knees weak. No one had ever asked me this question, and I wasn't sure if I had ever asked myself.

"Yes," I said. ". . . even though he was a sorry son-of-a-bitch."

Dom didn't say anything as I continued to stare out the window. I tried to collect myself and sound confident, but my voice came out raspy and weak.

"I wouldn't blame you if you want to quit. You'll get your pay for the full week. We'll be fine on our own."

I was expecting to hear the screen door slam, then the solemn squeak of our front gate, but when I turned around, Dom was still standing there. He didn't look like the wiry ten-year-old boy I had hired two months ago—he looked stronger and taller.

"No," he said. "I'm staying. I'll start cleaning around the yard—there's a lot of sticks and debris lying around."

After Dom went outside, I checked on Juan Esteban. He had started his morning routine. He spread the window curtains, filling his room with morning light, then opened his trunk and neatly laid out stacks of drawings on his bed. He held each one up to the light, inspecting every detail, then used a soft brush to dust the surfaces, being careful not to touch his pencil lines. After he finished, he restacked them in the same order and restowed them in his trunk. By now, his collection was over two hundred drawings: big cats, deer, pronghorn, wolves, birds, butterflies, and even the tiniest of species, from doodle bugs to leaf-cutter ants.

I peered over his shoulder, careful not to disturb him.

For a moment, he lingered over one that I had never seen before—a Luna moth. The moth was clinging to the surface of a worn fence post, revealing the dark edges of its wings. I marveled at the ornate dots that he had rendered like all-seeing eyes.

I thought again about Dom—his dark eyes, his question, his understanding. *How did I feel?* he had asked.

Feeling—it was as if he had unearthed an archeological ruin. For almost sixty years, I've put all my energy into feeling for no one except Juan Esteban and my far-away family back home. And now there was Dom.

That evening after he left, it was as if the barometric pressure had plummeted—there was a heaviness in the air like a millstone around my neck. My affection for Dom was changing me, and for the first time, I felt bad about lying.

~

The next afternoon, when Dom came back, I blew off the dust-caked latch, twisted it and raised the window. "Hello, Dom."

Dom waved. "Lotta work here."

His face was serious. He leaned the shovel against the garden fence, took his shirt off, and tied it to a post. He stood bare-armed in a thin cotton undershirt with his hands on his hips, surveying the yard.

"Made some biscuits for later," I said.

"Nice."

I watched as he shoveled soil away from the shed door, dumped it into a wheelbarrow and hauled it to the edge of the fence line.

"I missed you," I whispered.

Outside, the sun was beating down, and sweat trickled down his arms. When he saw me, he stopped working and gave me a serious glance.

"Your garden took a hit, but we aren't giving up on it, Miss Abbott. I have some seeds from Mama. She said to give them to you—we need to plant them now, so you'll have turnips and cauliflower in the fall."

He pointed toward the corner of the property. "I'll shovel up some of those chicken droppings and mix them with the topsoil that blew in—see that dark dirt there? Mama said that's the good stuff—from the river flats to the west. That tan stuff is worthless. It'll be hard to separate, but I'll do my best."

He looked at me and cocked his head to the side. "You okay, Miss Abbott? You look kind of pale."

I lifted my chin and tried to straighten the slump that was becoming my usual posture. "Just worn down, I guess," I said. "These storms take a toll sometimes, but I'll be fine."

He kept looking at me and squinted. "You sure?"

"Yes," I said, "absolutely sure. I'll grab another shovel. Let's get to it."

Dom smiled. "I have to say, I was a little worried about you during those storms—just you and Mr. Slocum without me to help. I wanted to come, but Mama wouldn't let me—too dangerous, she said. 'Your lungs will get caked with dust, and within minutes you'll be nothing but buzzard food.' I don't like the idea of being pecked by a buzzard, so I told her I'd wait until it all passed."

"You're kind to care," I said, "but I'm a tough old bird. No need to worry."

We shoveled for a while in silence. Dom had sweat through his undershirt when he looked up. "Speaking of birds, if you could be any kind of bird what would you be?"

"Hmmm . . . let me think," I said. "I'd be a pretty bird of some kind. Maybe a bluebird or a painted bunting or maybe a . . ."

He interrupted my thoughts mid-sentence, "I don't even have to think. I'd be an eagle—a bald eagle, not a golden. The bald eagle has a look like he wants something and he's gonna get it."

I nodded and smiled. "That's a good choice. There's something about an eagle isn't there? Majestic."

Dom pursed his lips while he mulled over my words. "Yeah, I'd say so, and fierce—like me."

I chuckled. "We'll have biscuits and honey in an hour. That'll give us something to look forward to."

"With milk too?" he said.

"Yes," I said, "that too."

"And after that, can I hold your rifle?"

I laughed. "You're still thinking about that, huh?"

He smiled. "Of course, you said I could awhile back. Remember?"

"Well, today's the day," I said.

~

After Dom finished his biscuits and milk, I walked over to the wall where the Jaeger rifle was mounted, reached up, and took it down.

"I'll show you how to polish it," I said, "just like my pop taught me when I was about your age. Have a seat and hold the gun in your lap. I don't want you pointing it in the house. That's not good gun sense."

I handed the rifle to Dom and went to the kitchen to get a rag and a small can of bee's wax mixed with turpentine.

When I glanced back, Dom was running his index finger within the scrollwork pattern.

"It's so smooth," he said, then he moved his finger toward the firing mechanism. "How do you cock it?"

"We'll get to that after we polish it—outside in the back yard."

I returned with the bee's wax mixture, handed the rag to Dom and said, "Dip that rag in and get just a little smudge. It doesn't take much. Rub it on the wood like you're making circles. You'll see how it shines up."

I watched as Dom worked.

He looked up with an intent look in his eyes. "Looking good?"

"Darn good!" I said. "Now, let's go outside. Hold the gun and point the barrel down. You never walk with the barrel in the air. That's how accidents happen."

"But there's no ammo in it," he said.

"It's about good practice," I said. "Keep it down whether there's a slug in it or not."

"Okay," he said.

Dom walked as carefully as the day he did when he was first carrying water from the well, and when we got outside, I said, "All right, now here's how you aim it."

I went through every step, just like Pop had taught me.

Dom bit his lip and held the gun to his shoulder, spread his legs and leaned in.

"Just like that," I said.

"Ready to shoot it?" I said.

Dom's face lit up.

"You're gonna let me?"

"Just once," I said. "Don't have many slugs anymore."

I showed Dom how to load, then he raised the gun, and I stood behind him. "Ok, pull the flintlock back and squeeze the trigger nice and slow."

BAM. He rocked back a little but stood steady.

"Atta boy," I said.

Dom grinned as wide as I've ever seen him.

"Dang, Miss Abbott. That's some kick!"

I held my hand to my heart, and my breath caught in my throat. He sounded so much like John Joseph back when we had our shooting range.

After Dom left, I continued to think of John Joseph and his loyalty to Juan Esteban and me.

While I was in jail, he wrote me every week, and I wrote him back. Though he kept me up on the whole family, much of his writing was devoted to Juan Esteban, because he knew I'd be wondering how he was doing. One letter broke my heart.

Juan Esteban isn't the same without you, Frannie. I don't think he understands why you're not here. He spends most of his time in the barn with the animals— turning their bedding, filling their feed boxes and water troughs, and climbing the ladder up to the loft where he sits by himself and draws. Being around the animals and drawing seem to be the only things that give him comfort. Occasionally, he'll

let me sit with him for a spell, but you know me, I don't have the
patience to sit for very long.

He's been doing a lot of drawings that I think are memories from
the expedition— wolves, coyotes, and types of birds that don't live
around here. I caught a glimpse of a drawing with a horse rearing
up in a woody patch and another of Doris and a bear—probably the
incident you told me about.

You'll be happy to hear that he did the one of a painted bunting
just like you asked him to. I'd bring it for you to see, but he's taken to
hiding them, and no one knows where they are.

But mostly we're doing fine, and I don't mean to make you worry.
We just miss you, Frannie. It's not the same without you.

In my response letter, I didn't tell him that his words made *me* cry.
Though I miss John Joseph, there's something about having Dom around
that makes me feel better—as if a little bit of John Joseph is with me. And
the rest of the afternoon, I had a sensation that I hadn't felt in years—I
was happy. I hummed as I did the dishes, and while Juan Esteban dried
plates and put them away, I dipped my hand in the warm water, flicked my
fingertips, and spritzed his face with droplets. He blinked, and his mouth
grew wide. I laughed and spritzed him again, and he licked his lips.

$\sim$

That night, after Juan Esteban had gone to bed, I sat by the hearth, smoked
Pop's pipe, and thought about my feelings earlier in the day, and what happiness was and wasn't to me. It has never been a sustained emotion, and
perhaps it isn't for anyone.

But maybe unlike others, I'm wary not only of hope but also happiness—so often, it seemed to be followed by something bad.

CHAPTER 16

THE LIVERY

1873

With the professor behind us and the brooch in my pocket, Juan Esteban and I rode Doris toward San Saba looking for information. I was hell bent on finding Juan Esteban's drawings and would do whatever it took.

Since it was still nighttime, the town was quiet, but I scanned the moonlit structures on both sides of main street looking for signs that stated their business—I remembered from our last visit the location of the general store, the market square, the sheriff's office, but I was looking for something else. The professor had said he had traded the drawings and mule to a man at the livery, and I guessed that it would be near the edge of town, so the smell of manure would be less overwhelming.

At the north end of Main Street, I spotted a wooden building surrounded by a cedar picket fence. When Doris heard a neigh, she let out a snort, and when the scent of hay filled her nostrils, she took off at a clip until she neared the corral fence.

I looked up and was able to make out the painted white letters above the barn door. Shay's Livery, it said, so Juan Esteban and I dismounted and searched for a place to rest until the sun came up. We found a grassy spot just beyond the corral and lay on our backs while Doris browsed looking for scattered hay straws along the fence line.

I didn't realize that both of us had drifted off to sleep until I was awakened by the sound of footsteps. A lanky figure sauntered toward the stable, yawning, with a shovel in one hand and a lantern in the other. I knelt and watched as he unlocked the barn door, then slid it open. From inside, I could hear clucking chickens. I walked toward him, leaving Juan Esteban behind to sleep.

He heard me approaching and held up the lantern. His expression was wary.

"Who's there?" he called.

I stepped into the lantern light, and when he saw I was wearing a dress and had long hair, he relaxed.

"My name's Frannie."

He took a deep breath. "You scared the dickens out of me. Thought maybe I was gonna lose my scalp, or get kidnapped, or have my throat slit, or . . ."

I interrupted hoping to calm his vigorous imagination. "Sorry," I said. "I didn't mean to alarm you. I just need some information—and I thought you might help."

"It couldn't wait until the sun comes up? This ain't a time to be jumping out of dark places with questions. You're lucky I didn't smash you over the head with my shovel."

"I'm sorry, again."

He gave me a good look-over. "How old are you anyway?"

"Fifteen," I said.

"Me too."

"What's your name?" I said.

"Folks call me Pepper—'cause my last name's Culpepper. First name's Harrison but I didn't want to be called Harry. Call me Harry and you get a punch to the face."

"I'll be sure not to do that," I said. "Like I said, I'm Frannie and my brother, Juan Esteban, is napping over there."

He squinted his eyes in Juan Esteban's direction and didn't say anything, but when a horse started kicking its stall, he shouted over his shoulder, "Settle down, Shep."

He turned back toward me. "Look, I got to get to work soon," he said, "because if Mr. Shay comes in and sees that I haven't shoveled the stalls, he'll have a fit. So, what's your question?"

"Did you see a man, yesterday, leave town with a mule?"

"Saw lots of mules yesterday."

"But this mule has a list in his step," I said. "He leans to the right like his legs are shorter on that side," and I slumped my right shoulder and took a few steps to show him how Mule walked.

He snickered. "You do that well."

I felt my face flush.

He scratched a few nubby hairs on his chin. "Yeah, now that you mention it, I do remember. He was headed west—that way. Man riding him was an old fella—had all kinds of stuff hanging off that mule. Said he was a traveling salesman. It was late afternoon. Probably didn't get far before nightfall."

I took a deep breath, thinking that we had a chance. "Thank you so much." I wanted to hug Pepper, but I didn't.

He gave me a long look, and I could see his blue eyes just underneath his straight brown hair. I was immediately conscious of my ratty clothes and my own hair that looked like it'd been through a twister.

He held his lantern closer to my face. "You're kind of pretty," he said. He appeared serious, not flirtatious—like he was trying to figure out what pretty meant to him. "If you come back through town, drop by."

"Oh?" I said. "Thank you." I cleared my throat, "I guess we better get going."

"See you, Frannie," he said, and when I looked back, he was leaning on his shovel with one leg cocked at the knee.

As Juan Esteban and I rode away, I could hear Pepper singing in the stable. No one had ever told me I was pretty. I felt a strange rush and a tingle in my chest. Feeling restless, I gave Doris a little click with my tongue, and we started trotting.

When we reached a four-way junction in the road I felt my heart sink. "Which way?" I mumbled.

Juan Esteban slid off Doris and examined a cluster of hoof prints that crisscrossed a dusty pit. There was just enough moonlight to see. He put his face close to the ground and crawled from one hoof print to the next.

I shook my head. There was a good chance we'd never find Mule and the old man, *and* I'd have to break my promise to Juan Esteban. In my head, I practiced what I would say. "We'll get more paper. You can draw another eagle. It'll be even better . . ."

Juan Esteban sat back on his haunches, then popped up and sprinted as if he were running for his life.

"Hold up," I yelled.

At a V in the road, he turned left, kicking up dust in his wake. I gave Doris another *click*. "Come on, girl!"

When we caught up, I trotted by his side.

"Come on up," I said, and held out my hand, but he wouldn't take it. Instead, he grabbed Doris's bridle and kept running. We traversed open meadows, ducked into the shadows of oak motts, and ran up a rise along a washed-out gulley. Juan Esteban tripped but got back up and started sprinting again. At the top of the hill, he suddenly stopped and stared.

Even though it was cool out, sweat was streaming down his face.

In the distance was a dim glowing light. It was mostly bluish in color except for an occasional flicker of orange, followed by a curl of smoke.

Juan Esteban tugged again on Doris's bridle.

We traversed a hillside that overlooked a valley, and after a few minutes, clouds moved in and obscured the moon, the wind picked up, and I could smell dampness in the air to the south. We walked quietly and slowly until we could see firelight more clearly. A man was hunched over the coals rubbing his hands for warmth.

"Hello," I shouted.

We walked closer. I saw the man slowly reach for his holster. He raised his pistol and pointed our direction. He squinted. "Who's out there? State your business."

"Don't worry," I said. "No harm intended—we just want to talk."

"Stop where you are!" he said. "Let me get a look at you."

Through the dim light, I could see his wrinkly face. He was wearing a bowler hat, and his gray hair hung below his collar and curled under his chin. His face was worn, but he had soft features. He pushed his glasses up on his nose, and when he saw us more clearly, he lowered his gun.

We were about ten paces away when I said. "My name's Frannie, and I'm with my brother, Juan Esteban. We want to talk to you about that fellow at the livery back in San Saba—Pepper's his name. He said you bought our mule."

I heard Mule bray in the shadows, then Doris blew through her nose.

"Yeah, I know that boy. But I didn't buy that mule from him. Was an older fellow—with a French accent."

He rubbed the tip of his stringy hair between two fingers. "What brings young folks like you out here?"

I looked over at Mule. He was laden with everything imaginable—pots, pans, overstuffed gunny sacks, hats strung together and tied to the saddle horn, blankets, and a bugle. He shifted his weight, and metal objects clacked together.

"We want to buy something from you," I said.

"Come over then. I got lots to sell—maybe you'll find something that suits your fancy."

As we neared, I saw that his cheeks were chapped and red.

"We heard you bought some drawings along with the mule," I said. "We want to buy them back. They didn't belong to the man who sold them to you. They were my brother's."

"Ah yes, the drawings. That fella said they were valuable—museum quality. That I could fetch a pretty penny for them in a big town that appreciated art. I liked them, so I took him up on it—I traded my white horse for the mule and drawings. I hated to be rid of Lola, but she was getting too old to carry my load—not as sturdy as that mule."

Mule sauntered towards us when he saw Juan Esteban and gave him a nudge on the shoulder. Juan Esteban turned and scratched Mule's ears, then reached down and grabbed a handful of grass, and Mule wrapped his lips around the entire bunch.

The old man snickered. "Your brother and that mule seem to be friends."

"Yep," I said. "She's pretty stubborn, but he knows how to calm her."

"She don't seem stubborn to me," he said. "She just knows what she wants."

I laughed.

He raised one eyebrow. "So, how're you planning to pay for those drawings—'cause I'm a businessman, you see. That fella may have stolen them from you, but I bought them fair and square. No charity."

I swallowed hard, trying to build up courage to voice my next words. "We don't have much money, but I have something I can trade." Already feeling a sense of loss, I took a deep breath, reached in my pocket, and pulled out the brooch.

"It was my mother's. She brought it from England. Made of ivory."

I held it in my palm for him to examine, then he adjusted his wire rimmed glasses behind his ears. "These specs ain't worth a hoot anymore—can't see up close, can't see far away, can't see a damn thing." He lowered his head, and his nose was within an inch of my palm, and I could feel his warm breath on my fingers.

"Shouldn't you hang on to a piece like that—being that it's a family thing?"

I paused briefly considering his question. What did the brooch mean to me? Sure, it had sentimental value, but Juan Esteban's collection of drawings were beautiful representations of life itself—both story and science—and perhaps most importantly, they were *everything* to him.

I looked down and cleared my throat. "The drawings are more important."

"Hmmm," he said. "Well, I'll tell you what. This looks like a mighty fancy brooch, and if it's ivory, like you say it is, it should be worth a fair amount. Seems like a fair trade."

I smiled. "Deal."

"Now just in case you're thinking about it, I can't trade you anything for that Mule. I can tell your brother likes her, but I need her, and I like her too."

I glanced at Mule. "Yeah, she's a good mule. Juan Esteban gets pretty attached to animals, but he'll be okay—especially seeing that you treat Mule well, and at least we have Doris—our donkey."

He gave me a soft smile. "Your brother seems like a special boy. I can't put my finger on it, but I usually have good hunches about people."

His smile flattened, and he furrowed his brow. "I can't say I was too keen on handing over Lola to that professor—I had a funny feeling about him. But I can't help that now. I have to live for the day—old as I am."

"What's your name?" I said.

"Joe O'Shaughnessy."

"Mr. O'Shaughnessy, I want to thank you for your fairness. We better be on our way. We've got a long road home."

"Where's home?" he said.

"Cedar Bend, near Bastrop."

"Long trip. You don't want any coffee before you go?"

I examined his eyes. They were a soothing, soft blue-green like water—inviting me to linger and wade in.

"I guess I'll have a little," I said. "Juan Esteban will enjoy a few more minutes with Mule."

I followed him over to the fire, and he pulled over a crate for me to sit on and patted it with his hand. Mr. O'Shaughnessy and I sipped coffee for about another half hour—I mostly listened while he talked about how he was headed west toward the mountains.

"The air is nice out there—a man can breathe deeper . . . and the breeze, the endless sky . . . " His voice was melodic and peaceful. It was like a salve that soothed the raw anger that had infected my every thought after so much time with the professor and Jasper.

In a way, I hated to leave his nurturing presence, but Juan Esteban and I needed to move on. It wouldn't be long before the professor awoke and found us gone. And I was certain he'd check the seams of his blanket and figure out that the brooch was gone, too.

CHAPTER 17
RUN

1873

As we traveled eastward in the mid-morning light, I decided to spare Doris the load until we got near San Saba, when we'd really need her to pick up the pace. I walked out front with Juan Esteban close behind. He wore his hat low on his forehead to shade the sun that peeked through openings in the cloud cover. He wasn't pulling on Doris's reins—instead she kept up with his pace as if he were dangling a carrot.

While we walked along, I pondered our plan to get back home.

I had only two coins in my pocket—the ones the professor had given me as part of his so-called "proposition"—but it wasn't enough for food *and* ammunition. I'd have to pick one. Food would help us survive, but just like the professor said, it wouldn't protect us. I could probably purchase a small bag of powder and maybe ten slugs. And since I was a good shot, I felt pretty sure I could provide enough game for us to survive the week-long trip home and still have a couple of shots left for protection. But there was another problem. Going to town to buy the ammunition was risky. The chance of running into the professor gave me a chill, and what about Jasper? He might be skulking around too.

As we neared town, I heard the distant dongs from the bell tower, and we rode close to the cliffs and followed deer trails through dense woodlands to stay out of sight. When we were just below town, I had an idea.

I knew Juan Esteban wasn't going to like it, but it seemed like the only option for me to go unrecognized. We took cover within a mott of live oaks, and I rooted through my saddle bag and pulled out my pocketknife.

I had never been fond of my hair color—a dull light brown—so cutting it was no love lost. But not having scissors—just a knife—was going to result in a rough cut. Would I look like a lunatic? Despite that, I bent over and sliced through thick clumps, cropping my hair to within four inches of my scalp and watching as it dropped to the ground. My only perception of my appearance was by touch, and when it seemed to be close to boys' length, I gave it a good ruffle with my fingers.

I was expecting Juan Esteban to be stunned, but he wasn't. Instead, he watched with intrigue, then bent down and picked up the long strands and lay them out on a log like he was preparing for a new artistic endeavor. I shook my head and smiled, admiring the cleverness of my brother's ways.

The haircut was just the beginning. I'd wear Juan Esteban's hat and his extra shirt—the problem was he had only one pair of pants. I hated to do it, but we were desperate. When I pointed to his pants his eyes narrowed, and he turned away from me.

"I'm just going to borrow them," I said, "for about an hour. You'll get them back—just like I got your drawings back."

He hesitated, so I added, "I promise."

As he began to slide his boots off, I knew he trusted me, so I grabbed his shirt and hid behind a tree and started to change.

"Now toss me your hat and pants," I said, and a few moments later both came flying.

"Thank you, Juan Esteban," I said in a gentle voice, hoping to calm his nerves. When I reappeared wearing his clothes, he was standing behind Doris, and all I could see was his stocking feet, his chest and head.

I pushed his hat onto my head and didn't delay.

"I'll be back before you know it," I said, "just stay here with Doris and remain out of sight."

I zigzagged up a steep hillside, and when I got close to the buildings on Main Street, I stopped and surveyed the area for any sign of Jasper or the professor. It was a busy morning, which worked in my favor, as I ducked in and out of crowds and navigated my way toward the general store with my hat pulled low over my brow.

The sheriff was in the same position as last time, sitting on a stump eying those who passed. The saloon seemed as busy as ever, but instead of a fiddle and accordion, a piano clanked out a raucous tune.

Outside the general store, an old man sat on a bench stroking his beard, and next to him was a boy shelling peanuts. I stepped through the doorway, took a few cautious steps inside, and eyed the clientele but recognized no one. Behind a counter were floor-to-ceiling shelves, and as I scanned the rows of boxes and jars looking for gun-related items, I heard a voice with a familiar twang at the far corner of the store.

"Gimme a pair of them socks."

I darted behind a pile of flour sacks.

"You got the money?" a different voice said.

The twangy voice countered. "Now, Mister Johnson, I ain't asking for a handout, I'm telling you my credit is good."

"Mr. O'Brien," the man said in an irritated tone, "every time you come in here, you say the same thing, but I'm looking at a bill here that hasn't been paid in two weeks. My store isn't a bank."

I heard Jasper shuffle his feet. "This time is different," he said. "I got a job lined up that starts tomorrow, and I can pay the total due in three days. I just need a few items for the journey."

"And what kind of job is this? You gonna run away on your tab and leave me empty handed?"

"No, sir," he said, "I've got some tracking to do, and the man who's paying me is good for it. He spends quite a bit of money in your store, and if you force me, I'll drag him in here to vouch for me, but trust me, he's easily agitated and liable to take his business elsewhere if he's put out—you understand?"

The store owner let out a sigh, "What are your needs other than those socks?"

I didn't hear exactly what Jasper said because he lowered his voice, and a group of rowdy kids started jabbering near the candy jars. I continued to hide among stacked-up blankets and horse-related gear until I heard Jasper's footsteps heading for the door, and then I popped my head over the top of a saddle mounted on a wooden horse.

Jasper gave the store owner a wave, then with his irritating sing-songy voice said, "See you soon!" But before he reached the door, he stopped in his tracks and stared in my direction.

I ducked my chin against my chest as he pointed my way. "How much for that saddle?" he shouted.

Mr. Johnson shouted back. "You can't afford it! Just get on out of here."

Jasper mumbled something coarse under his breath, then purposefully scraped his spurs across the wooden floor, leaving deep scratch marks in his wake before swaggering out and into the street.

When everything seemed clear, I walked up to the store counter and announced my needs. "Number ten slugs and a bag of powder," and even though I was trying to capture the timbre of a trombone, the word "powder" came out like a flute.

The man laughed. "Voice changin' on you, huh? Must be about fourteen, right?"

"Yessir," I said.

He turned and eyed the shelves, then pulled down two boxes and laid them on the counter, then I pushed my two coins his way.

He raised one eyebrow. "You're a penny short, kid."

I cleared my throat trying to think of something to say, but before I could get it out, he slapped his hand on the counter as if the deal was done.

"It's okay, but here's a little piece of advice." Then he leaned in, winked, and whispered, "I wouldn't go off and join the church choir right now." Then he roared with laughter.

"No sir, and thank you . . ." I said and stuffed the boxes in my pocket, and as I was darting across the street, I could still hear him bellowing.

When I got to the woods near the hillside, my mind was racing. What was Jasper up to? I clamored down the slope, tripping because Juan Esteban's pants were too long. I stopped to roll them up, then I bolted. I didn't stop running until I reached the edge of the oak mott where Juan Esteban stood with his back to me, wearing his shirt, underwear, and boots.

I didn't want to scare him, so I whispered, "Juan Esteban, it's me," but he didn't look back. I moved toward him and saw that he had used my hair and sprigs of grass to fashion a bird's nest that he had situated in a possum haw tree.

It was perfectly shaped, and though I wanted to examine it more closely, there was no time to waste.

I spoke to him in a clear and steady voice, "We have to go," I said, and after hurriedly changing clothes, we were off.

~

We pushed all afternoon and then a few hours into the night, taking turns riding Doris, but the darkness made it difficult to follow the trail.

Juan Esteban eyed our surroundings like he was looking for something.

"Are we on the right path?" I asked, but I couldn't tell by his expression whether it was a yes or no.

"Let's rest," I said, "for a few hours. Then we'll get up and go again."

I was asleep when I felt a shove. I immediately reached for my rifle next to my pallet, looked up, and blinked.

"Dang, Juan Esteban. You scared me. Can't you wake me a little more gently next time?"

It was barely light, but I could see that Juan Esteban had already saddled up Doris and was ready to go. For the next hour, while I rode, Juan Esteban remained on foot and scoured every grassy opening and thicket. I felt sure he was looking for familiar landmarks that were imprinted in his mind. I wondered if they were like pictures, or were they moving with our steps—a stream of images overlapping and unfurling in time.

CHAPTER 18

A SHOT

1873

It was midday and had been raining for hours when we heard twigs snapping in a woody patch up ahead. I pulled Doris to a stop and surveyed the area but saw nothing.

"Maybe it was a deer," I whispered.

I gave Doris a touch with my heels, but Juan Esteban grabbed the halter and held us back.

"We can't stand here, forever," I said. "Whatever it was is gone."

Juan Esteban didn't budge.

Thunder rumbled in the distance, and the sky was a light gray to the east and a heavy dark gray to the south. I heard another snap and a whinny and out from the dense vegetation came two dark figures on horseback wearing rain tarps. The horses ambled as if they were in no hurry, and as the riders approached and their faces came into focus, I shuddered.

"Well, well, well . . . if it ain't our Frannie and her sidekick. Where are you two headed at this time of day? A little afternoon jaunt?"

The professor didn't say anything, but he was wearing the same cruel sneer I had witnessed and remembered back when I was ten—on board the ship with my parents—when he had berated the mate for his stupidity. Back when my mother knew he was an unscrupulous character before anyone else did.

Jasper stretched his neck out and examined my appearance.

"What happened to your hair? Looks like a rat got to it."

I didn't respond because I was too busy considering escape options. I slid my eyes from left to right.

"Don't even think of making a dash for it," Jasper said. "You ain't got a chance."

I stared at the professor. "What do you want from us?" I said. "We're headed home because you've done nothing that you promised—you sold the drawings—you're a thief."

The professor circled around us on Lola, examining our packs and bags. Jasper leaned into his saddle horn and chuckled.

"Speaking of thievery," the professor said, "I believe I could call you the same."

I grit my teeth. "Yeah, I took it," I said. "It was mine to begin with."

The professor shook his head and looked at Jasper. "Not only is she a thief but she's a liar."

"I was on that ship with you," I said.

The professor raised his eyebrows and pulled back on Lola's reins.

I stared straight at him. "You stole that brooch from my mother."

Jasper seemed confused, narrowed his eyes, and glanced between us.

The professor roared with laughter. "How ridiculous. What a tale!"

"What's she talking about?" Jasper said. His hat was soaked, and water dripped on his shoulders.

The professor waved his hand. "Nonsense," he said.

Jasper looked at me, then back at the professor, not sure whom to believe.

"I was just ten, on a ship from England with my parents; the professor was on board too. Years later, when I agreed to be a part of his expedition, I didn't see any point in telling him who I was—why would he care? And I didn't know he had stolen the brooch until I found it."

Jasper scratched his beard. "I gotta hunch Frannie's telling the truth."

I waved my arms at Jasper. "I am! Now let us go!"

The professor slid off Lola, then slowly and steadily walked toward Doris and me while Juan Esteban held the reins. "I've got to get what's mine first." He pointed and shouted, "Get off!"

"You won't find it," I said. "I traded it, to get the drawings back."

"You did what?" The professor's eyes bulged, and he clenched his fists. "I don't believe you," he said, then he reached up, pulled my arm and yanked me off Doris. I stumbled but regained my footing.

"Hey, easy!" Jasper said.

"Shut up!" the professor said as he rifled through the saddle bag. He threw all of its contents onto the ground. Our last four corn dodgers and Juan Esteban's drawing supplies lay in a muddy puddle, soaking up water like sponges.

I glanced at Juan Esteban. He held Doris's neck tight against his chest.

The professor turned the saddle bag upside down—nothing else fell out. He started shaking the bag in a rage. "The drawings were junk!" the professor said. "The brooch was worth money. You're a moron if you traded it."

I was spitting with anger and stepped toward the professor and pointed my finger. "They are *not* junk. They are beautiful, and they are Juan Esteban's! You're nothing but a liar. You never intended to send animal pelts back to Paris. You're collecting pelts for money—it was all a sham! You're nothing but a heartless petty criminal."

Jasper took two steps forward on his horse. "What about my wages—our partnership? If the brooch is gone, we ain't got nothing."

The professor wheeled around and faced me, then raised his eyebrows and smiled. "Ah ha!"

"What?" Jasper said.

The professor broke out laughing. "Like mother like daughter." He looked me up and down with a wicked grin. My dress was soaking wet, and my hair was matted against my head. I took two steps backward.

He waved at Jasper. "Come hold her."

"What for," Jasper said.

"Just do what I say, dammit!"

Jasper walked over, stood behind me and grabbed my shoulders. I tried to wiggle free, but he gripped tighter.

The professor stared at me. "Ah, yes. I do recognize you. Your face—less full, more cheekbone, but still the same." Then he looked down at my neckline. "You've certainly grown there—just like your mother." He took his finger and followed a water droplet from my chin down to my cleavage. "Lovely indeed."

I slapped his hand away, and Juan Esteban jumped when he heard the smack of skin against skin and started stepping backwards into the shadows.

The professor raised my chin with his finger. "But you also have her face—it's how do you say . . . possum like?" He laughed, then continued. "I had to lie through my teeth to think of something nice to say to your father. I felt bad for him—married to the ugliest of the marsupials."

I tried to kick him, but he stepped back, and my shoe left a muddy smear across the thigh of his pants.

"Hold her tight," he said to Jasper. "Pin her against your chest."

Jasper wrapped both arms around. He smelled sour and reeked of chewing tobacco. His nose was an inch from mine.

The professor bent down and started pulling at my hem. "I know it's here somewhere. Just like your mother—your hiding place."

"It's not there!" I said. "I told you. It's gone."

He got up then raised my skirt. "Your undergarments then," and he patted up and down my legs and over my buttocks.

"Get your dirty hands off me!" I yelled.

Jasper suddenly let go and raised his arms. "I ain't gonna be part of this shit," he said.

The professor took two steps back and glared at me. "Don't worry—you are of no interest to me. If you don't have the brooch, then I'll take something else."

He walked over to Doris, untied Juan Esteban's drawing press, then glanced over his shoulder. "Are you sure you don't have the brooch? All you have to do is hand it over, and we'll be on our way."

I didn't say anything.

"Then I'll take these back and sell them again—you were right. They are worth something. Your little Audubon is quite talented. If things had gone as planned, I would have taken his drawings and sold them in Galveston—along with the skins. I'd be fat and happy—sitting in a rocking chair, smoking a cigar . . ."

Then he glared at Jasper. "But you ruined everything!"

Jasper shouted, "Don't go blaming me again for all your problems."

The professor pulled out his pistol and pointed it at Jasper. "Throw me your gun."

"Hey, wait, I'm on your side," Jasper said.

"Throw me your gun, or I'll shoot your horse."

Jasper gritted his teeth. "You son of a bitch," then he tossed the gun near the professor's feet.

The professor bent down and stuffed the gun in his waistband, then pointed at Jasper. "You stay here with the girl and that dull-minded boy. I don't need you anymore. If you follow me, I'll shoot you and your horse. I'm done with all of you!"

He backed up with the drawing press under his arm and continued to point the pistol our way. He mounted on Lola, then gave her a spur in the side. She barely moved, so he gave her another kick, digging deep with his spur, and pink flesh emerged and blood trickled down her belly. She jerked her head, then reared up. The professor slapped her with the reins, "You old hag . . . settle down."

She continued to buck and wheel around. The drawing press hit the ground with a thud. I ran toward it and scrambled in the mud to pick it up.

Lola kept kicking and spinning, and the professor was now holding onto the saddle horn with both hands. Behind me, I heard a familiar *click*.

Then everything went black.

~

When I came to, water was splattering against my face, and my head was throbbing. Rain was pouring in sheets. Juan Esteban knelt over me with a frightened expression. I sat up and saw Jasper on his knees clawing at the ground with his hands. He looked up when he heard me rustling.

"You okay now?" He had mud on his face and hands.

I rubbed the lump on the back of my head and grimaced. "Yeah, I guess. What happened?

"You got kicked."

"Lola went berserk when she heard the shot."

"What shot?"

Jasper paused then stood up and walked over. "You don't remember?"

"No, I don't remember anything."

"Your crazy ass brother shot the professor with your gun. Now I'm trying to bury the son of a bitch, but I ain't making a dent in this soggy earth. The hole keeps caving in on me."

I couldn't believe my eyes when I saw the professor sprawled next to the hole. I looked at Juan Esteban. He was sitting, clutching his drawings, and rocking back and forth. His shirt was stained with blood, his eyes were wide, and a string of spit dripped from the corner of his mouth. I tried to wipe it with my shirt, but he shirked me off and rubbed his mouth with his shirt sleeve.

"It's okay, Juan Esteban, everything will be all right," I said, but my mind was racing, and nothing was all right.

I turned toward Jasper. "How do I know it wasn't you that shot him?"

"Are you crazy?" he said. "The professor had my pistol. How could I have shot him?"

I blinked, wondering if Jasper was telling the truth. "But you could have grabbed the rifle and done it yourself—you've threatened to before."

Jasper stared straight at me with cold eyes. "You're pissing me off, Frannie. I'm telling you what happened, and you ain't listening. Your brother went haywire when he saw you on the ground and the professor with the drawings. He ran after him like a wild man, then shot him in the back. When the professor hit the ground, he jumped on him and started pounding him with his fists. That's why he's all bloody. And go look, his blood's all over the gun. If you think you're going to pin this one on me, you got another thing coming."

A chill shot up my spine. "What are we going to do?" I said.

"*We* ain't gonna do nothing. Now that I see you're okay, it's in your hands. I'm out of here."

I tried to stay calm, but my voice was shrill. "Where are you going? You aren't going to turn him in, are you?"

He narrowed his eyes. "Maybe I will, maybe I won't. It depends."

"On what?"

"On what I get out of this."

"You can have it all," I said. "Take the professor's horse and his gun—you can have mine too. Just leave us and promise not to say a word."

Jasper snorted. "Do you think I'm an idiot? I don't even want to touch your smoking gun."

"Can you just promise then?"

Jasper wiped his muddy hands on his shirt and shook his head with an expression of pity. "It goes against my better instincts, but I won't say nothing for now cause you're in a real fix. I almost feel sorry for you. As long as the professor is buried and gone my lips are sealed. But mind you, if somebody finds out, I'll be looking out for ole Jasper."

Jasper didn't take long to clear out. As he rode away with Lola in tow, he looked back at me and snarled. "Remember what I said, and don't think I'm too soft to turn your brother in." Then he gave his horse a kick. "*Arriva durchee.*" I remembered those exact words like it was yesterday—the same words he shouted when he rode off from the Schützenfest.

～

Juan Esteban and I buried the professor that night. The rain subsided for a few hours, making the digging easier, but it still took until daylight to get four feet down using our hands and sharp rocks to rake the earth aside. I heard a pack of wolves howling and barking in the distance—their sound was eerie and frantic and expressed my own emotions as I lugged heavy stones down from the hillside and lowered them onto his body before we covered him up.

When I raked the first handful of dirt over his torso, I felt colder than I've ever been.

～

For two more days, we traveled in the rain. Drizzle would last for an hour or so, then there'd be a flash of lighting, a boom, and a gushing downpour.

The river was roiling and muddy, and Juan Esteban and I both walked—the ground was too soggy for Doris to carry either of us. For overnight shelter, we huddled under ledges in the limestone cliffs, but our clothes were soaked, and we shivered all night.

Because of the damp, animals were laying low, and my chances for seeing anything to shoot for food were next to nil. I was able to corner a few frogs in a pool of water, scooping them up with my skirt and then grilling them on a stick over a small fire, but that was hardly enough to fill our stomachs. On the third day, I resorted to gathering prickly pear pads. I sheared the needles off, then boiled the pads until they were soft. Though we gobbled them down, my stomach still felt like an empty pit, and I was certain Juan Esteban felt the same and probably worse. His skin color was as gray as the sky, and his eyes looked like they had disappeared into dark caves.

The next day on the trail, I knew his condition was worsening, because he wasn't looking around to find our way; he was only looking down. When I put my hand to his forehead, he was burning up, and I felt a deep-boned chill remembering the same look on my mother's face—through the window at the inn in Galveston—the day before she died.

"Tomorrow, we'll go to higher ground and find shelter," I said.

Early the next morning, we left the lowlands and climbed upward through shrubby hillsides to the rolling hills above the river, where mesquite trees dotted the prairie among sweeping vistas of tall grasses. Though our footing was better, I was nervous about leaving the river. With Juan Esteban so sick, he wouldn't be able to guide us, and I wasn't sure I knew the right trail. One thing was certain—we had at least two more days before reaching Austin.

For a few hours that afternoon, we made camp in what was left of a log home. Most of it had burned to the ground, but there was one side where the roof hadn't caved in.

I started a fire, and Juan Esteban curled up in a ball and shivered uncontrollably even though the day was mild. I was sure I had a fever too because of my own chills, but I had to get food. Too weak to track and hunt, I crouched outside our shelter to see if something might appear. My eyes were blurry from exhaustion, but I saw movement in a cactus patch about thirty yards out, then a jackrabbit's ears appeared just above a yucca's pointed tips. When the rabbit heard me pull back the flintlock, it took off at full speed. I watched its ears bouncing as it crossed the prairie, and led it by about fifteen feet, then squeezed the trigger. It flipped and rolled, then lay limp in a patch of bare ground.

There was nothing good about the meat, but I didn't care. It was stringy and tough, and I ate hurriedly, but Juan Esteban only nibbled and put it back down. Since I needed the strength, I picked at the bones and meat that Juan Esteban had left, because at least one of us needed energy to walk.

"We need to get going," I said, and got up and tied my gun and saddle bag on Doris's back. When I looked back at Juan Esteban he was on his feet, but when he attempted to walk, he stumbled and fell to the ground with a thud as if it were his last breath.

I sat down next to him and rested his heavy head in my lap and gently touched his hair. He would never have let me do that if he weren't sick, but because he did, I felt a tenderness between us that brought tears to my eyes. Doris walked over and stood over us and pushed her muzzle against Juan Esteban's limp legs as if she were encouraging him to rise and walk. I stared at her, wondering if she knew something I didn't, and all I could think of was that she was our last hope.

"Juan Esteban," I whispered, "Doris will carry you." Doris stayed steady as I gave him a leg-up, but the effort it took to get him in the saddle seemed to sap what remained of his strength.

As we walked, he lolled back and forth with Doris's strides, and my mind drifted to unanswered questions. I wondered what had driven Juan Esteban to shoot the professor? Was it about the drawings, the yelling and shouting, the professor's rough handling of me, his treatment of Lola?

I mumbled to myself. "We should have left earlier. If only I had left the brooch behind, then none of this would have happened."

For another half day we trudged on until the river started to fan out in the distance. On a rise, I could see the fertile flatlands ahead where the trees were taller and bright green, like an emerald bracelet following the curve of the river.

To encourage Juan Esteban, I pointed. "Look, we're getting close," even though I knew we had at least another hard day of traveling just to get into Austin. Though Juan Esteban raised his head and steadied himself, a split second later he was slumped over the saddle horn, limp as a homemade doll.

~

It was Doris who led the way that fifth day, as if she knew what to do. I stumbled beside her until I couldn't go any farther, then slumped to my knees. I knelt there and watched as she carried Juan Esteban away until they became a small dot in the distance. The day had heated up, and I used the last of my energy to crawl to the shade of a mesquite and leaned against its trunk praying that someone would find either Juan Esteban or me.

~

The old doctor who leaned over me with his ear against my back to check my breathing told me that a goat farmer had found us. He came across Doris as she grazed among his herd with Juan Esteban hanging over her neck.

How that man knew to come looking for me was a mystery, but he did. I wondered if Doris led him, or maybe the man just had a hunch, or maybe it was something that Juan Esteban did.

I have a vague recollection of the farmer's dark blue shirt, and the sour smell of his collar, as I rode with my head resting on his back and my arms around his waist, but I don't recall his face, nor do I have any idea how old he was.

My only clear recollection is waking up at the doctor's home on a cot with Juan Esteban lying next to me on a floor pallet. The one-room log building smelled of smoke, and I could see a pot bubbling with some kind of stew over a fire.

It took two days in the doctor's care along with a few good meals to get us back on our feet. When I said I had no money to pay him, the old man shook his head.

"It doesn't matter."

I wondered about the reason for his generosity. After so many days with Jasper and the professor, I had become wary of genuine kindness, and it felt strange to accept it without feeling like I owed him something.

We got back to Cedar Bend a day later, and I can't say why I didn't tell my family about the bad things that happened. Maybe it was pride and stubbornness—not wanting to admit a mistake—but I think it was mostly the trauma of having to relive it. For a couple of months, I kept my mouth shut about all the violence and only shared the accomplishments—like my shot saving Jasper from the bear, and of course Juan Esteban's eagle drawing.

But all the while I was thinking about the professor's death and what would I do if his body was found. It wasn't until the sheriff rode in that I fabricated my own version of the truth.

CHAPTER 19

THE SHERIFF

1873

The day the sheriff appeared at the edge of our pasture, it was warm and clear—much like the day when Juan Esteban and I left Cedar Bend with the professor.

Pop and John Joseph were in town with the girls, and I was digging post holes to put the pig pen back in place when I heard a snort across our pasture. I looked up and saw a figure on horseback headed our way. I hadn't seen him since my last time in San Saba, but I recognized his crooked form as he shifted awkwardly in the saddle.

The sheriff tied his horse to one of our newly set fence posts and walked with a limp toward the barn. Celia met him near the water trough with her hands on her hips.

"Can I help you?"

"Name's Sheriff Dick Ogden from San Saba. Looking for a Miss Frannie Abbott."

I pushed my hair back and walked toward the sheriff.

"I'm Frannie Abbott."

He took his hat off and used the brim to fan his neck. "I have a few questions to ask, may we find a shady spot? It's damn hot in the sun."

Celia threw a worried look my way. "Of course," she said, ". . . let me get you some water."

We sat around a table under our live oak tree. The day was not only hot but oppressively still, in keeping with the heaviness of the mood.

When Celia came back with a tin cup of water, the sheriff groaned as he briefly stood and waited for Celia to sit.

"My damned knees," he said, ". . . too much time in the saddle and too many times getting thrown off."

"Sorry for your pain," Celia said.

"It's okay, Ma'am," he said. "I hate to come here with trouble, but we had a little incident near San Saba. After a heavy rain, a dead fellow washed up on the riverbank about a mile out of town."

Celia shifted her position. "What does that have to do with Frannie?"

"I'm not sure yet," he said, ". . . that's why I have questions. A farmer found his body—professor Pierre Duvalier is the dead man's name."

Celia's eyes grew wide, and she gave me a nervous glance.

The sheriff looked at me. "You know him?"

"Yessir, I do. My brother and I were on a hunting expedition with him."

The sheriff scratched his head. "Do you know a fellow named Jasper O'Brien too?"

"Yes," I said. "He was with us part of the time."

"Turns out Mr. O'Brien rode into town and sold the professor's horse at our livery. A worker there—a boy named Pepper—recognized him and said the professor and that Jasper fellow knew each other."

The sheriff paused and mopped his forehead with his handkerchief.

"We found Mr. O'Brien on his way west, brought him back to town and questioned him. First, he said he didn't know the professor. After I grilled him a bit more, he said that he knew him but hadn't seen him in months. He was shifting in his seat like he had ants in his pants."

The sheriff leaned over, picked a stem of grass, and chewed on it. "Now, I'm pretty good at detecting liars, so I pressed him. That's when Miss Abbott's name came up, along with her brother . . . a Mr. Juan Esteban—Mr. O'Brien didn't know his last name."

I cleared my throat. "That's right," I said. "Juan Esteban Slocum. He's my brother."

"Well, Mr. O'Brien claimed that the last time he saw the professor, he was with you and your brother, and that the professor had fired him from his job, and he went on his way."

The sheriff looked at Celia. "Do you mind my asking where your son is?"

Celia got up and said, "I'll get him," but I grabbed her arm to stop her.

"He's inside," I said, "but he won't be able to tell you anything because he doesn't talk."

"Hmmm . . . I guess we're in a pickle here," the sheriff said. "Let me get to the point then," and he reached in his pocket and pulled out a misshapen lead slug. "We dug this here slug out of the professor's back, and when I showed it to that Jasper fellow, he acted mighty surprised but said you would have a gun to match it."

He looked me in the eye. "Is that true, Miss Abbott?"

Under the table, my hands were shaking, so I intertwined my fingers and held them tight together.

I nodded. "Yessir, I have a Jaeger rifle. It shoots a slug like that."

"Can I see it?" he said.

I went inside, pulled it down from the wall, walked back out, and laid it on the table.

He examined it, cleared his throat, then pulled out a piece of paper. "I know this is going to be more bad news, but I got a warrant for Mr. Juan Esteban's arrest. Mr. O'Brien said the professor and Juan Esteban had bad blood."

The sheriff gave me a long look. His expression gave no hint of emotion, as if it had been carved from stone.

When I didn't say anything, Celia jumped in.

"Bad blood?" she said. "Juan Esteban doesn't have bad blood with any-one. He's gentle as a lamb."

"That's right," I said, and at that moment, I knew it was time to reveal my lie.

Celia laid her palm on my clasped hands as I spoke.

"The professor took my brother's possessions—his drawings—said he was going to sell them. Juan Esteban's drawings are everything to him. Juan Esteban lunged for him to get them back. The professor tried to push Juan

Esteban away, but Juan Esteban kept coming at him with his arms—clawing on him—trying grab the drawings and take what was his. I tried to pull them apart, but the professor was too strong. He grabbed Juan Esteban by the neck and pushed him up against a tree trunk. I could hear Juan Esteban choking like he wasn't getting air . . . and . . . " I swallowed hard, "so I shot the professor—in the back—to save Juan Esteban."

No one said anything—the only sound was the piercing screech of blue jay's call.

The sheriff cleared his throat, stared at his feet, then raised his head, and narrowed his eyes. "Miss Abbott, is that an official confession?"

I nodded.

The sheriff twisted his lips and shook his head. "I wish I could say things looked brighter for you, Miss Abbott, but shooting a man in the back is murder."

Celia was frantic. "She was protecting her brother. For God's sake, have some mercy!"

"The law is the law, Ma'am. I'm afraid I'm going to have to take your daughter into custody. The judge will have to sort this one out."

"No, wait! Please, Sir, my husband will be home later, and John Joseph. We'll need to talk. You can't just take her!"

He stood up wincing, then sighed. "There'll be no waiting, Ma'am. I have to get on my way."

Celia's face grew red, and she lunged for the sheriff and grabbed his vest, "Don't touch my daughter!"

I reached for her arm, gently pulled her away, and whispered in her ear.

"I did it, Celia. I'll go with the sheriff."

After spilling my words, did I regret my lie? Absolutely not. It was my fault that we were in this mess, and I took the blame so Juan Esteban wouldn't be hanged—he didn't deserve it, but no one would believe him. I felt certain no one could fathom the professor's cruelty unless they had been there.

I supposed they might not hang a girl, but they were sure to hang a boy who shot someone in the back.

My trial—my day of reckoning as I've called it—was a month later. August 19, 1873. That was the day I heard the judge's gavel slam, and the day I walked in front of the sheriff down the dusty road and into the walled prison yard and to my cell. It was the day that I heard the metal key turn and click inside a rust-speckled lock. I remember the sound and moment distinctly—as if the *click* was defining the end of one life and the beginning of another.

CHAPTER 20

RELEASED

1875

I heard that *click* for the last time one year and nine months later.

I was eighteen and had survived incarceration with an assortment of cell neighbors ranging from the foul-mouthed types who whispered obscenities at night to overly friendly drunks who talked incessantly. Because of it, I learned who to be wary of and who was harmless.

The day the sheriff approached my cell wearing his Sunday clothes and carrying a brown paper sack, I was expecting lunch, not freedom.

"We're letting you out early," he said, " because we need your cell for a wanted outlaw." Then he looked at me with a weary face as if the responsibility of having a girl in jail had worn him thin.

"You're free to go," he said, then he handed me the sack. "My wife made you another dress."

I swallowed hard. Not only was I thankful for the sheriff and his wife's thoughtfulness, but I was elated with the thought of surprising my family.

"Please tell her how much her kindness has meant to me," I said, and we stood facing each other for an awkward moment. I had an impulse to hug him, but as if he sensed my desire and was uncomfortable, he held out his hand for a shake.

"Now go on, scat," he said like he was shooing away a cat. Then he gave me a tired smile.

Did I linger? Absolutely not. I ran as fast as I could for as far as I could, then walked until I was about an hour outside of Cedar Bend. Being an early spring day, the Mexican plums and redbud trees were emerging within the understory at the trail's edge, showing off their pinks and whites within a tangle of gray twigs.

I left the path and traipsed through a brushy thicket, then bathed in a creek that wound through a grove of sycamore trees. As I lay on my back in a pool of frigid water gazing at the trees' soaring white branches against a blue sky, my skin tingled and turned a rosy pink, and I felt renewed and fresh for the first time in two years. I changed into my new dress and abandoned my old one, relieved to be rid of anything that smelled of jail.

In that last hour of my walk, I tried to remember what home was like on an early spring morning—the smell of smoke from the chimney wafting across our field, the woodsy scent of dry leaves under foot, Cora and Marie Isabel's chatter, the sound of Celia's broom whisking across the wooden floor, Pop's whispers of morning prayers from his bedroom, Juan Esteban's figure over a cast-iron skillet as he poked at slivers of pork, John Joseph scraping his spoon across a metal plate of biscuits and gravy.

And when everyone greeted me with surprised expressions, long embraces, and both relief and joy, I assumed that most everything would be the same.

It wasn't until I saw a new face on the porch that I realized things were different.

"This is Hannah," John Joseph said, ". . . my wife." His smile was as broad as I've ever seen, and he stared at her as if she were a cherished object of art, then turned to me with an excited expression. "I waited to tell you because I wanted you to meet her in person."

And when I saw Hannah's swollen belly, I could see that even more change was on the way.

"That's wonderful news," I said, but I couldn't help but feel a hint of jealousy as I realized I'd have to share John Joseph's affection with another.

Plus, that wasn't the only new development.

Though John Joseph and Pop still managed the fields together, John Joseph had taken the lead role in choosing the crops and doing the heavy lifting of plowing and harvesting. Celia had taken up quilting. She sold her wares at Pop's church and was now leading the church choir –a surprising notion because I had never considered her to be musically talented. Pop spent more time at church, too, as his parish had grown from twenty to fifty members, requiring more of his time to lead bible study, visit the sick, and oversee a building expansion.

And though I liked Hannah a great deal, she had taken on the duties that had previously been mine. What's more, she seemed to do everything better. No longer did Cora and Marie Isabel need my help with their handwriting. Instead, Hannah hovered over them and kept them on task as if it were fun—not the burden I had felt. Without ever raising her voice, she did an excellent job of managing their constant chattering and sisterly bickering. And they were crazy about her—you could see it in their faces when she took special care brushing and braiding their hair, or when she mended their frayed hems or read to them at night. And to my complete surprise they didn't mope when she asked for their help with the dishes.

After I thought about it, the only person who seemed to need me was Juan Esteban. And I was gratified that after my return, he fully resumed his explorations of everything creeping and crawling.

Feeling borderline replaced by Hannah on the home front, and a bit bored with little to do, I decided to contribute to my family's welfare by seeking work. It didn't take me long to realize that my reputation as a convicted criminal presented limited options. So I started doing odd jobs that no one cared about who you were—like washing other folks' dirty clothes and mucking out stables. Invisible work, I called it, and I plodded along for a full year working and saving money.

But at the end of the day, it was getting me nowhere, and I didn't feel good about anything. Yes, I had my family, but all I had to show for myself was a jar full of coins and blistered, chapped hands.

And the scorn—as the town's social pariah—had taken its toll like a festering sore. I couldn't go anywhere in Cedar Bend without feeling shame—the finger pointing and whispering, the name-calling and ubiquitous sneers weighed on me like an anvil. But the most unbearable was the look of fear in children's eyes when they met my gaze.

"Don't pay attention to them," John Joseph said. "Your family knows who you really are, we love you, and that's all that matters."

But to me, that wasn't enough. I felt an urge for change.

"I need a place where I'm not an outcast," I told John Joseph. "A place where I can live and grow and leave the past behind."

"It will just take time," is all he said, ". . . be patient," and I was struck that the most impatient person I knew—John Joseph—was asking me to be patient.

~

I was patient for a few more months, but that came to an end the day I was cleaning aprons for the butcher in a shed between his shop and the dry goods store. While I stood over a hot fire and swirled blood-stained clothes in a large kettle of boiling water, I heard someone sucking their teeth behind me. I turned, squinted, and saw his lanky bow-legged figure standing there. He had on a long black coat, and I instantly recognized him by his long stringy red hair.

"Well, there you are," he said. ". . . been searching all over."

He eyed me in a chilling way, then circled around and whistled. "Look at you all aglow—a real woman now. Ain't no bean pole anymore—rosy cheeked, filled out with a curve or two. Just the sight of you makes me frisky."

When he reached out to touch my arm, I jerked it away. "Don't you dare touch me!"

My voice was loud enough to catch the attention of a woman passing by, and when she saw me, she tugged hard on the hand of a fair-haired child and dragged her out of sight as if she was running from a brush fire.

"How come you're so feisty?" he said. "Ain't you glad to see your ole pal Jasper? Haven't laid eyes on you since the day of your trial."

When I didn't answer, he chuckled.

"Yeah, I was pretty liquored up that day, and I bet I gave you shudder when I yelled out that you was a liar." He gave me wink and a fake smile. "Remember?"

I remembered all right, but I didn't give him the satisfaction of a response.

Jasper kicked a log, then rubbed his chin with his fingers and gave me a squinty-eyed look. "Still hanging on to your secret, eh? After all this time . . . what is it? 'Bout three years since Duvalier's been dead? Ain't you a martyr."

"What do you want?" I said.

He shook his head. "Not sure yet. Obviously, you ain't got a cent to your name if you're a butcher's maid."

He sucked his teeth some more and looked around. "How come that brother of yours ain't here? As I recall, he was always tracking in your footsteps like an ole blind dog."

"Shut up," I said.

Jasper raised a finger. "Hey . . . I got an idea. How about I drop by your place, maybe Juan Esteban could cook me up something good just like the old days?"

I tried to sound strong, but inside I was petrified. "Leave us be."

He shook his head and chuckled. "Don't know if I can do that, Miss Frannie, cause secrets have value—and being the one person who could set the story straight has its benefits. I could march right down to that sheriff's office and strike up a very interesting conversation."

He took two steps toward me, then poked his finger my direction. "Understand?"

I glared at him but didn't say a word.

"I ain't asking for nothing today, but that don't mean I won't be back tomorrow, or the day after." Then he spat at my feet. "Maybe your pa has a little money he might be willing to chip in on your behalf. There are options you see?"

That was the last straw. I gave him a stout kick in the shin with my boot, and he hollered, cursed, and hopped, making such a racket that people outside the dry goods store turned their heads, and I could see that my already massacred reputation among townspeople had bottomed out.

The butcher appeared in the doorway with a long knife in his hand. "What's going on?" he said.

"He's keeping me from my work," I said.

The butcher pointed a finger at Jasper. "Get the hell out of here—no loitering around these premises."

"I was just having a friendly conversation," Jasper said.

The butcher cleaned his knife on his apron and left a bloody smear. "No loitering, I said!"

Jasper shook his head, snickered, then spun on his heel and tipped his hat in the butcher's direction. "Mighty fine day to you too, Mister." Then he looked over his shoulder at me. "I'll be back for more and don't you forget, I can expose your *charaaaade!*"

He said it with a hiss that made my flesh crawl.

~

My family didn't want me to go, but I knew I didn't have a choice. Jasper's visit made my situation clear—I needed a plan for Juan Esteban and me, so when I saw that poster for cheap land in the panhandle, I took notice.

When I announced my intent to move north, those at the family dinner table were suddenly silent.

John Joseph was seated at one head of the table, and Pop at the other. Celia was on John Joseph's right, Hannah on his left, and Juan Esteban, the girls, and I filled the spaces in between. I didn't look at John Joseph, but I knew his mouth was flattening into a tight line like Celia's.

Hannah reacted as if the room were closing in on her and quickly stood up, braced her palm under her growing belly, then waved for Cora and Marie Isabel to join her outside.

Pop didn't speak as John Joseph hung his head over his plate. Then he stared at Pop out of the corner of his eye and clenched his jaw.

"So, you're going to let her do it again, I suppose?" John Joseph said.

Pop pushed at the food with his spoon but said nothing.

"So?" John Joseph said again, then stabbed his meat with his fork and released his hand, leaving the fork to stand upright as if it were another witness to the insanity of my proposal.

"Pop's not letting me do anything," I said. "Besides, this is different. I'm grown now. I make my own choices."

It was as if John Joseph didn't hear me, and he started shaking his head back and forth like a pendulum. Then suddenly he stopped and stared at Pop. "Frannie went through hell because of you," John Joseph said. "Because you couldn't see beyond the nose on your face."

"That's not true, John Joseph" I said. "It wasn't Pop's fault. I convinced him. I was determined, you remember."

He turned his head my way and eyed me with an intensity that I had never seen before. "He could have stopped it!" John Joseph said.

"You're wrong!" I said forcefully.

Pop dropped his forehead and cradled it in his palms. "He's right, Frannie. I will never forgive myself. And I won't do it twice."

I could feel the stubbornness—inherited from my real father—settling into my own frame like bricks in mortar. "No," I said. "That's where you're both wrong."

Determined not to relent, I stood there ramrod straight. And I didn't dare tell them about Jasper's visit for fear that John Joseph would track him down or maybe go so far as to kill him. John Joseph had reached a boiling rage—greater than I had ever seen before—and I didn't want to tip him over the edge.

John Joseph turned his eyes to Celia. "For Christ's sake, Ma. Talk some sense into her."

"Frannie, you can't leave," she said. "I know it's hard living here, but we're family, and what about Juan Esteban? He suffered while you were away. He needs you—we need you."

"I want Juan Esteban to come with me," I said.

"No," Pop said. "You and Juan Esteban alone—up in the panhandle? Too far away—no."

"What if you need help?" Celia said.

I looked at Juan Esteban seated next to me. He was the only one still eating and was chewing a piece of salted pork that he had used to flavor his turnip and potato stew.

"Juan Esteban will help. We'll figure it out. A person's got to have some-thing to be proud of. Here, I am *nothing*."

John Joseph pushed his chair away from the table. "I'm not hungry anymore." Then he walked outside, and I heard him whispering angrily to Hannah.

In John Joseph's absence, the pressure in the room fell, and I took on a more conciliatory tone with Celia and Pop.

"It will be good for Juan Esteban and me," I said.

Pop slumped like all strength had left his body, and he looked at Celia with a confused expression as if he needed her to tell him what to do.

Celia cleared her throat. "I don't like it," she said and paused, "but I understand. You are independent and strong, and I support you."

I blinked as if I were re-seeing the courageous side of Celia that I had witnessed several times before—like the day Mr. Slocum showed up with Juan Esteban in tow and implied that Juan Esteban was useless—the way she met Mr. Slocum eye-to-eye and said, "No child is a burden."

And the time when she confronted the schoolteacher who said Juan Esteban was too dumb to learn. She stood behind Juan Esteban with unswerving commitment. Like Celia, I wanted to be there for Juan Esteban—in the face of Jasper O'Brien or anyone else that threatened us.

~

The next day, I visited a horse dealer, and Juan Esteban came with me. There were several—two sorrels, a buckskin, a chestnut, a gray, and none were stellar, but the one Juan Esteban stood in front of—mostly white with a black patch on his rump—appeared the most haggard. Bones were protruding from his sides, and he had one blue eye and one brown.

Since I didn't have much money, I went for what I perceived to be the low bid and Juan Esteban's pick. "How much for that one?" I said.

The old man, who smelled like hay and sweat, said, "You don't want that one, he's temperamental. The chestnut would suit you better."

"What do you mean by temperamental?" I asked.

"Bites, bucks, kicks . . . anything to be ornery. Costs too much to keep him, so I plan to walk him to the butcher."

I could see he had a point when Juan Esteban reached out to scratch behind the horse's ear, and the horse thrust his head upward, cuffing Juan Esteban under the chin and knocking him off balance.

"See?" the man said. "Got an attitude even with a big fella like that. Diablo I call 'im."

Instead of backing off, Juan Esteban tried again. This time he moved his hand very slowly and made an *mmmm* sound. The horse blinked and allowed Juan Esteban to gently rake the hairs that protruded from his muzzle.

"How much will you get from the butcher?" I said.

"Thirty," he said, but when he saw I wasn't deterred by that amount he said, "Maybe forty."

I took a chance, and we bought Diablo for thirty-five dollars. Betting that Juan Esteban could reform him, I gave him a more dignified name—Moses.

The next day, Juan Esteban and I headed north on a wagon trail with dark clouds to the west and a dry wind from the east. Both of us walked while Moses pulled a cart filled with our belongings and three jars of Celia's pickled cucumbers, a slab of salted pork, and a sack of pinto beans. I felt a sense of freedom as we moved north, leaving behind Jasper's threat and my sullied reputation.

CHAPTER 21

A PLACE TO HIDE

1934

I feel a certain kinship to my home. At one time, Leilo had promise, but like me, it took a precipitous slide.

Back when Juan Esteban and I showed up, about ten people lived here. Then when the railroad came through in 1887, it rose to thirty—those were the heydays. We had a post office, two churches, a general store, a school, a grain elevator, and the town's founder, Jeremiah Leilo, built a hotel—the same one Dom lives in now.

Our town grew to about a thousand people, but progress didn't last long—the fire of '29 took out four buildings on Main Street, a tornado in '30 flattened the whole east side, and then the drought and dust storms started getting bad in '32. By then the population was back to three hundred or so, and no one in their right mind would have moved here. So that left me—the town's "crazy old bag"—feeling comfortable again.

I imagine Dom's grandparents must have settled here around 1910, when a bunch of Polish farmers bought land. I'll have to ask him about that next time he comes to work.

He hasn't been here for a week because he was sick—his mother sent a note saying he had a fever. While he was away, I had a new nightmare every night. Maybe I was worried about him and the fact that I had knowingly lied to him about shooting the professor after I had lambasted him for stealing the vase. Perhaps the pot calling the kettle black was weighing on my conscience. I've never felt this way before about someone outside of family—maybe because Dom is becoming something more than I expected—not just a friend, but a confidant.

I've been hoping all morning that he'd show today, so when I heard footsteps on the porch, I gave my hair a quick combing, straightened my skirt, and was ready to greet him like an excited grandparent.

But when I opened the door, someone else was slouched in my rocking chair biting his nails and spitting them on the floorboards. It had only been two months since his last appearance—when he had hassled me for money—and this time, he appeared even the worse for wear. His cheeks were hollow, and his arms looked like toothpicks emerging from his gray short-sleeved shirt. If he hadn't been the scoundrel I knew him to be, I might have felt sorry for him.

"Pretty day, ain't it?" he said. "I was just passing through again—thought I'd sit a spell. You mind?"

"I do mind. Get out of my chair, off my porch, and off my property."

He began to suck what was left of his teeth in his usual annoying way.

"I can't do that," he said, "not yet."

"Why do you keep bothering me?" I said.

Right then I saw Dom opening the front gate. He strolled up to the porch squinting the whole way.

"Who's this fella?" Jasper said. "Ain't you going to introduce me, Frannie?"

Dom had a stern expression. "I'm Dominik."

"Well, Dominik, what brings you here? You the paper boy or something?" Jasper spat.

Dom stood upright. "I help Mrs. Frannie with her chores."

"Now ain't that interesting, Frannie. I thought you were so proud of being able to take care of yourself. Proud Frannie—the hero."

I looked at Dom and said, "Head on around back and get started. I'll be there in a few minutes. Got some business to take care of."

When Jasper smiled, his lips caved in over his gums, "Now you're talking."

Dom turned and walked toward the back, but he looked over his shoulder and eyed Jasper like a hawk.

"How much do you want this time?" I said.

"How about we make a final deal. I promise I won't come back, and you give me fifty dollars."

"How do I know you won't come back?"

His eyes were bloodshot like he'd been drinking. "I'll give you my word."

"Your word? What a joke. You'll come slithering back like the snake you are."

"Where is he, Frannie? Inside . . . scared?"

"None of your business."

"I don't know why you lied for him. Granted he's missing a few screws, but shouldn't a man stick up for himself? He's a damn coward!"

"Get off my porch!" I yelled.

Dom heard me yell and came around the house with his shovel over his shoulder like he was ready to swing it. He glared at Jasper. "Mister, I believe Miss Abbott told you to leave."

"Well, look there . . . another hero," Jasper said, "What you gonna do little fella? Use that shovel to scrape me off this porch?"

I saw Juan Esteban at the window, and Jasper did too. "Well, looky there—Mr. Fraidy cat. *Meow, meow.*"

"Don't talk to him like that!" Dom said.

Dom's knuckles were white as he gripped the shovel handle. He looked at me like he was waiting for me to give him the signal. I shook my head, and Dom loosened his grip.

I glared at Jasper. "I'll go inside and tend to our deal. Then you're out of here."

"Now you're talking sense, Frannie." Jasper said.

I went into my room and rummaged through my drawers looking for the money I had stashed, but I only had thirty dollars. I walked back out and stuffed the wad of cash into Jasper's open hand.

"I only have thirty."

Jasper sneered. "How do I know you're telling the truth?"

Dom's eyes turned black as night, and he gritted his teeth. "Leave," he said.

"Let me tell you something, boy. This lady—if you want to call her that—is a liar. She has a history of it. You may have heard she killed a man. Well, let me get something straight. She didn't kill nobody. Her brother did it. I saw it with my own eyes. And she was dumb enough to take the fall for him. She's fucking crazy."

Dom looked at me. I turned my head and looked down the road, unable to meet his eyes.

Jasper got up, shoved the bills in his pocket and stretched his arms. "Guess I'll be on my way." Then he turned toward me with brown colored spit collecting in the corners of his mouth. "But no deal."

I watched as he walked off, closed the gate behind him, and winked. "*Arriva durchee*, Frannie."

I sat down on the steps next to Dom. He didn't look at me.

"Is that true what he says?"

"Yes," I said.

"Why didn't you tell me? You told me lying is bad—that it gets you in trouble."

I looked down the road as Jasper's figure got smaller and smaller. "It's complicated," I said.

Dom blinked. "I don't see what's complicated about it. Like you said, you either did or you didn't."

I put my head in my hands. "It was my fault. I drove him to it. He was so mistreated, wounded, and he was just defending me. But I'm sorry for lying to you. You're the only person who knows."

We sat for a minute and listened to the wind rattle the screen door. I looked down the road again as Jasper faded into dust.

I swallowed hard. "Do you forgive me?" I said.

He looked at his feet, then raised his head and peered into my eyes. "Guess so, don't know why I wouldn't. You forgave me."

I sucked in air like I was emerging from a deep lake after almost drowning. I let it out slowly.

"Thank you," I said. "I'm feeling kind of tired now. The day has worn on me, so I'm going inside."

194

Dom gently touched my shoulder before I got up. "Do you feel better for saying it?"

"I'm not sure. Feels different."

"How?"

"Less lonely maybe."

"I won't tell anybody, Miss Abbott. Not if you don't want me to."

"Thank you," I said. "If it makes a difference, next to Juan Esteban, you're my only friend."

CHAPTER 22

OFFICIAL BUSINESS

1934

After my confession to Dom, I felt different. Though my bones still weighed me down, I felt an airiness in my surroundings—like there was more oxygen. I could think clearly.

When Dom came by to work, I was wearing a flowered print dress, and my hair was combed and secured in a tight bun with hairpins.

Dom walked up and smiled. "You look nice, where're you going?"

"I need a favor," I said. "Can you stay with Juan Esteban while I go into town?"

"Sure," he said.

When I turned the key in the ignition, the Ford's engine sounded like it was grinding gravel. It sputtered, then stopped. I pumped the accelerator three times, and the smell of gasoline filled the shed. I waited a moment before trying again. The engine turned over, and I revved it to blow out any accumulated dust in the tailpipe.

As I drove into town, I turned on Main Street instead of taking the back roads. It didn't bother me when a cluster of barefooted boys playing in the street pointed as I drove past. I wasn't unnerved when my lawyer's receptionist appeared irritated that I had shown up without an appointment.

"Take a seat," she said. She shoved her pencil behind her ear and walked brusquely into Mr. Gaston's office.

"It will be a while," she said after she returned. "Maybe an hour. Mr. Gaston has urgent business and since you weren't expected . . ."

I interrupted her. "No problem. I'll wait."

When she offered me coffee, she came back with a cup that looked like it was filled with sludge. I didn't get angry. I put it down and picked up the newspaper. There had been a terrible tornado in Alabama, a hurricane that killed thousands in Honduras and El Salvador, and locusts had blown into Kansas, stripping crops bare. One farmer was quoted as saying, "The sky was black with them—it felt like Armageddon."

Armageddon. I whispered and rolled the word around in my mouth like it was a piece of hard candy. I should have winced from its sourness—all of its sadness—but I didn't.

Mr. Gaston opened his door, furrowed his brows, and said, "Come-in."

I responded, "Lovely day isn't it, Mr. Gaston."

He frowned and pointed to a wooden straight-back chair opposite his desk that wasn't designed for comfort. It wasn't plush like the wing chairs and small sofa nearby that I presumed he offered to his more desirable clients.

"How may I help you?" he said.

"I have some business to discuss . . . regarding my last wishes," I said. "I want to get it done today."

He took a deep breath. "Your visit is unexpected. I can't possibly fit it in today."

"I'll pay you extra," I said and gave him my best smile.

He leaned back in his leather chair, ran his hand over his slicked-back hair, then called to his secretary.

"Miss Clancy, please bring me Miss Abbott's file."

Mrs. Clancy waddled in and dropped the file on his desk. He opened the folder with the tips of his fingers like it was sullied.

"What's on your mind?" His face was smug.

I pushed a folded piece of paper his way with words penned in ink and signed, Frances Abbott.

He looked over his glasses and raised his eyebrows.

"Hmmm," he said. "Give me a minute . . ." Then he walked out the door. While he was gone, I heard the rappity tap of Mrs. Clancy's typewriter and the sliding clang of her returns, and then the final turn of the crank as she released the sheet of paper.

He came back in and laid the document in front of me. "Sign both copies," he said. "This one's for your files."

I read it over slowly, examining every word for proper spelling. "Is twenty acceptable?" I asked.

He nodded.

After handing him a check, I got up and walked out with a smile on my face.

~

When I got back to the house, neither Dom nor Juan Esteban was outside. I walked in with a pile of mail that I'd picked up at the post office. Coming from Juan Esteban's room, I heard Dom's voice.

"Dang, Juan Esteban. Look at all these drawings. You did these?"

Juan Esteban had all of his drawings on his bed and was brushing off the dust while Dom stood by his side.

"Look at that bear, that cougar. How'd you do that? They look real."

Juan Esteban picked up the eagle.

"Damn. That's a bald eagle," Dom said. He stared at it. "Look how he's taking off with his wings spread wide. He must have a seven-foot wingspan."

Juan Esteban carefully held the brush in his hand and dusted around the eagle's head.

Dom held out his hand. "Can I hold it?"

Juan Esteban kept dusting for a minute, then stopped, and what happened next gave me chills. Juan Esteban handed Dom the drawing.

Dom held it gently between his fingers, then walked over to the window and lifted the eagle up to the light. His eyes were wide. "Fierce," he said.

He walked back and handed it to Juan Esteban. "Show me more. You got a wolf in there?"

I knew immediately that my decision had been right.

CHAPTER 23

THE LETTER

1934

The next morning the wind came howling at thirty to sixty m.p.h. As I lay in bed it made me wonder if I'd be looking at sky instead of ceiling before it was all over. Juan Esteban was edgy, partly because of the wind but mostly because of my cough. Just breathing this morning felt like work.

I walked into the kitchen, made some coffee, then sat down at the table. In the stack of mail, there was a letter from John Joseph.

I hadn't seen John Joseph since Juan Esteban and I had moved to Leilo. We'd sent letters back and forth, and a couple of times he'd said he was going to visit, but it never happened. And now that we're both in our seventies, I doubted it ever would. Not because we don't love each other, just 'cause times are hard, life passes, and then the distance between you seems too far.

In his letters, he talked about his growing family—who did what, where they were, and it seemed like every time I got another letter, he had another grandkid. When I wrote back, I told him about what was going on in Leilo and tried to put a shine on the bitterness, so he wouldn't worry. In my last letter, I told him about Dom, hoping it would comfort him to know that we were managing.

Most of my letters ended with news about Juan Esteban—what he was drawing and how he was getting along. In the last letter I said,

> *He's on a cicada kick right now, along with all things flying, and his*
> *collection is probably way over a hundred by now. I bought him a*
> *trunk where he can store them and lock it up. He hides the key in*
> *different places. Sometimes when I'm putting clean clothes in his*

drawer, I'll find it among the socks, but the next time it won't be there. I know he moves it every few days because I'll see him rooting in a drawer or putting it inside a book.

One time, I nearly swallowed it when I took a big slug of coffee and felt something clank against my back teeth. He had hidden it in a mug, and I didn't pay attention when I poured the coffee.

When I scolded him ever so slightly for almost choking me, he gave me that toothy expression. I can't say for sure, but I think he was laughing. I broke out laughing myself once I realized that I hadn't chipped a tooth.

That Juan Esteban is something else—but you already know that. I can barely remember what day it is, and he's got a head full of things. Sometimes I wish I could peer inside, but that would spoil the marvel of it all. Letting him be who he is and watching his mind come out in his drawings is enough for me—and like I promised myself, I'll never let someone take that from him.

The letter I held in my hand today was John Joseph's response. When I opened it and read what was inside, I was taken aback. He didn't chit chat about his family, he got straight to the point.

I understand that you lied, Frannie, to protect Juan Esteban—you've always protected him. You knew that a boy like him would have been called crazy, and he would have been hanged for murder. You did what you thought was right, and I never questioned it because I knew you and Juan Esteban had something special between each other. You understand Juan Esteban in ways that no one else does—you don't see boundaries or a frame that defines him like other people do. You see limitless possibility with his mind.

I had to put my coffee cup down when I read what came next.

You might not want to hear this, but think about it, Frannie.

Maybe you're protecting him too much. A lot of time has passed, and maybe opening up and giving him the opportunity to show his

*talent to others would be a good thing. There might be somebody
at the University up there who might understand the enormity of
what he's accomplished. Maybe you should show the drawings to
somebody.*

*We're all getting old. Some of us more than others. You've
sacrificed so much, Frannie. Maybe it's time to crack open the door
and find joy—both for you and Juan Esteban.*

I put the letter down and stared out the window. The sun was shining
through the curtains, and a warm glow filled the room.

～

I didn't know it at the time, but that was the last letter I would ever receive
from John Joseph. His widow wrote the next time.

Dear Frannie,
*John Joseph caught pneumonia and passed on March 12th. Just an
hour or so before he died he said, "Tell Frannie and Juan Esteban that
I love them." We are surviving despite the sadness.*

*The funeral will be in Cedar Bend on May 7th. We hope to see
you, but if you can't make it, we understand.*

Hannah

～

The day after receiving Hannah's letter, I got up, fixed my hair, put on my
best dress, and packed mine and Juan Esteban's bags. Dom loaded the trunk
while I fixed a sandwich for Juan Esteban and me.

When I headed toward the car, Juan Esteban followed with a duffel
under his arm that held both his drawings and Pico.

Dom stood in the driveway wringing his hands as I opened the car door.
I sat down and groaned when I swung my legs in.

"You be careful," he said. "Don't drive too fast, your eyesight's about
shot."

"Thanks for reminding me," I said.

"I'm just saying, Miss Abbott, you're the one always telling me your eyes ain't what they used to be."

"We'll be back in a few days, don't worry," I said as I closed the door. Dom ran over to Juan Esteban's side.

"Look out for her, Juan Esteban. If she gets tired, make her stop. Just pull over and rest for a while. Then when she's rested, you can get going again."

I smiled. "You're a worrywart, Dom."

I backed out of the driveway, made it to the intersection of Highway 60, turned right, drove through Pampa, then White Deer, but when I got outside Amarillo, I started coughing.

I pulled over into a gravel drive and let the car idle, hoping my coughing spell would pass. When it did, I leaned back and closed my eyes for a minute, but then the coughing started again, and it got worse. When I spit up a tiny spray of bright red blood, Juan Esteban stared at it.

"I'm not feeling so good, Juan Esteban. I'll do like Dom said and rest here a minute more and then . . ." but before I could finish my sentence, Juan Esteban had opened his door and was walking around the back of the car to the driver's side. He opened my door, aimed his rear end my direction and pushed me toward the middle seat with his strong hips.

I looked at him in disbelief. "You can't drive," I said.

He didn't look at me. He sat down, closed the door, revved the engine, shifted into low gear, and with two hands gripping the wheel made the slowest U turn known to mankind. We crept through White Deer at ten miles an hour, at Pampa he pressed the gas and hit twelve, and then when we turned onto Highway 60, he drove about twenty on the gravel shoulder the way tractors do.

Cars whizzed past beeping their horns, but Juan Esteban stared straight ahead and never took his eye off the road or his foot off the gas until we pulled into our drive two hours later.

When we came to a stop, I was surprised to see that Dom was still there standing near the garden. He ran full speed toward the driveway when he saw Juan Esteban at the wheel. Then stuffed his head through the window on the driver's side.

"What happened?" His face was pale with alarm when he saw my body slumped against the side door.

"Had a coughing fit," I said. "Couldn't catch my breath. Juan Esteban got behind the wheel and drove. I didn't tell him, he just did."

"I didn't know he could drive," Dom said.

"I didn't either."

"Can't say what wore me out more—Juan Esteban's slow driving or my coughing attacks."

Dom helped me inside and held my elbow as I sat down on the edge of my bed.

"I'm not sure why the coughing came on so hard."

"Maybe you should see a doctor," he said.

He helped me lie down and put a blanket over my legs.

"No, I'll be all right," I said. "Maybe it was just stress of losing John Joseph. It's better we didn't go. I'm not sure I could've held up under the sadness anyway."

I looked at Dom. "You go on home. We've got those sandwiches I made, so we'll have them for dinner. I'll be better tomorrow, once I get a little rest."

That night I lay in bed thinking about the letter John Joseph sent and his plea to open up and search for joy.

CHAPTER 24
GRADUATE STUDENT

1934

The next day, I woke up still feeling weak, so I stayed in bed until Dom arrived.

He poked his head in my room. "Feeling better?"

"Sort of," I said.

"I got an errand for you, though," I said. "Go to the library and ask the librarian to help you find the address for the zoology department at Texas University."

"Why?" he said.

"I want to talk to someone about Juan Esteban's drawings."

His eyes got wide. "What about?"

"Don't know yet, but I want to find out if they might be valuable to someone?"

"Valuable?" he said. "You mean like worth a pile of money?"

"I don't know. I was thinking that somebody at the University might be able to shed some light."

"Okay!" he said, then he shot out the door and the screen door slammed.

I lay in bed and chuckled to myself. "You don't have to run. I'm not going to die today."

Within an hour, he was back with a slip of paper with a name and address scrawled on it.

"Here," he said. "The librarian said this guy's the department head." He stared at me. "Now what?"

I smiled. "You don't know any speed but fast do you, Dom? Go get a sheet of paper, something hard to write on, and a pen from my desk."

He handed me a paper and pen, looked around the room and scratched his head, then picked up a magazine from a basket on the floor.

"Will this do?" he said.

"That'll work fine."

He flopped down next to me and lay on his stomach, his elbows on the bed and his chin in his cupped hands. "What're you gonna say?"

I rolled my eyes. "For goodness sake. Give me a minute to think."

While he drummed his fingers on the blanket, I picked up the pen and wrote.

Dear Professor Crawley:

I understand that you are a professor of zoology at Texas University. I'm writing to see if you might be interested in examining drawings that my brother, Juan Esteban Slocum, has produced over his lifetime. He has over two hundred drawings of animals with a particular emphasis on species of the Texas Panhandle, where we have resided for the last fifty-nine years.

I recognize that my knowledge of your specialty is limited, but it appears that the works are exceptional and might be worth your inspection.

I am unable to bring them to you, but if you are willing, you can examine them at our residence. I've been ill and would like for you to see them as soon as possible.

Sincerely,
Frances Abbott

~

For two weeks we heard nothing, and every afternoon Dom greeted me with the same question. "Any news?"

After a few dust-free days, I started to feel better and was able to spend mornings doing small chores around the house without wearing out. By afternoon, though, I needed a nap.

The afternoon of April 23rd, we got a card. I read it out loud to Dom.

Miss Abbott:
Thank you for your inquiry. I will send a graduate student to
examine the drawings, as I am too involved in my research and
teaching to take time off. Please expect a visit on the morning of
Saturday, April 30th.

I tossed the card on the bed. "Graduate student? Why not him?" I said.
"What do you mean?" Dom said.
"He's sending an assistant to look them over. He's not coming."
"That's better than nothing," Dom said.
I took a deep breath. "Got a point, I suppose."
I closed my eyes. My exposure to professors had been limited to one, and I was beginning to think that maybe all professors were alike—arrogant sons-of-bitches.

~

On April 30th, I dragged myself out of bed, got dressed, spruced up my hair, which looked like an abandoned bird's nest, and sat in the living room and waited. I made sure Juan Esteban had on clean clothes and asked Dom to be there to calm Juan Esteban while whoever examined his drawings.

I had continued to marvel at how Dom had fostered a sense of trust with Juan Esteban and was as close to being a friend to him as anyone. Instead of always being near me, Juan Esteban had taken to Dom. The whole time Dom was at the house, Juan Esteban was nearby, either watching or helping. While I was washing dishes one day, I looked out the window and saw Dom huffing and puffing, hauling buckets full of water from the well that he handed to Juan Esteban for the watering part. Juan Esteban had a measuring cup in hand and gave every plant the same amount of water, showing no more generosity to the green beans than to the carrots.

I had to smile at the two of them—Juan Esteban with his six-foot stature, strong arms, and big hands gently tending to the plants while Dom—skinny, short, and wiry—did the heavy lifting.

While I waited for "the graduate student," I perched myself close to the window, so I could keep an eye out. I read a few magazines, battled through a few coughing spells, and listened to our old wall clock *tick tick tick*—9:00 a.m., 10:00 a.m., 11:00—no one showed.

When the clock chimed on the half hour at 11:30, Juan Esteban padded into the kitchen and started chopping carrots, turnips, and potatoes. He had a steaming pot of soup ready by 1:00 p.m.

All three of us sat at the table. Between slurps, Dom said, "Think anyone's coming?"

"Dunno," I said. "They sure are taking their time—I don't have much patience for waiting on folks."

Dom finished his chores, and at a little after 3:00 p.m. flopped down on the sofa and let out a big sigh.

"Tired?" I said.

"Not really. Bored mostly. Wanna play cards?"

"Cards? Been a long time since I played, plus I don't think I have any."

"I do," he said. He reached in his back pocket and pulled out a pack of red bicycle playing cards.

"I don't know, Dom. Not sure I feel like it."

"Why not? Maybe it'll kill some time. Take your mind off the waiting."

I looked into his dark eyes and sighed, "Okay. What'll we play?"

"Poker."

"You know how to play poker? Where'd you learn that?"

"School."

"That's what they're teaching you?"

"Nooooooo, we play at recess. Won a nickel yesterday."

"A nickel? That's a lot. Are you sure you should be betting? Does your mama know about this?"

"No. I don't tell her *everything*."

"Well, seems like she might not take a fancy to you putting your wages on the line."

"It'll be our secret," he said. "Okay?"

"I don't like keeping things from your mama, but just this once can't hurt. Go grab my penny jar in the kitchen cabinet. I'll give us each fifteen, and what you win you can keep—if you win, that is. I've played some cards in my time. My brother taught me how."

"Hmmm," Dom said. "We'll see."

Dom pulled a three-legged wooden stool up to the coffee table near me. He sat down and looked me over like he was sizing me up.

"What are we playing?" I said.

Dom was serious faced. "Let's start off with blackjack, then we'll play seven card stud, then five card draw, then high/low Chicago."

"You know all those games?" I said.

"Of course."

I raised my eyebrows. "Aren't *you* a little card shark!"

"I'm a player," he said. He furrowed his brow like I had insulted him.

"Okay then, you deal," I said.

While he was shuffling, Juan Esteban came in and sat next to Dom.

"Siding with him . . . instead of me?" I said.

Juan Esteban gave me his toothy expression.

"Well, well, well, loyalty has shifted, hasn't it?"

The first hand, Dom beat me with a queen and an ace. The second with double tens. In five card stud, just when I thought I had him with two aces, he won with three fives.

The next time I looked at the clock, it was 4:00 p.m., and he had all of my pennies except five. Not only was I annoyed with the fact that "the graduate student" hadn't shown, but I was even more annoyed that I was losing.

Dom dealt another hand of five-card draw. I splayed out my hand and held it close to my face. I took my time.

Dom tapped his finger. "Come on, Frannie. We ain't got all day," he said.

I smiled. "So, you're calling me by my first name now, eh?"

"I figure since we're playing poker, we should be on equal footing. You don't call me Mr. Rostenkowski."

"Okay," I said. "So be it. Call me Frannie from here on out." Plucking two cards from my hand, I lay them face down on the table. "Give me two."

I stuffed the two cards in what remained of my hand with a confident air: *two threes, ace, jack, five.* I thought to myself, "Come on, Frannie, you've lied all your life, surely you can bluff Dom."

I pushed all five of my pennies to the center of the table. "Hold," I said.

Dom pursed his lips and moved them from side to side. "Hmmm . . ."

He lay down three cards and gave himself three new ones, then rubbed his chin and stared into my eyes like he was looking straight through me. His expression was so intense that I flinched and accidentally raised an eyebrow ever so slightly.

Without saying a word, Dom counted out five pennies from his stack and pushed them my way.

"Call," he said and squinted like he was a Vegas dealer. "What ya got, Frannie?"

I flipped my cards over, and he let out a hoot. "Dang, Frannie! I kicked your rear!"

At first, I was taken aback. He read me like a book.

"Don't get all braggadocios on me," I said. "Not polite," but then I cracked a smile.

"Okay . . ." he said, "sorry."

I looked at the clock—4:30.

"Maybe this isn't going to happen, Dom. You can go home now. I appreciate your staying."

Dom cocked his head, then ran to the window. "Wait, I hear someone coming."

I got up and peered over his shoulder, but whoever it was too far for me to see. "Can you tell if it's him?"

Dom cupped his hands around his eyes. "It ain't a him, it's a her."

"A her?" I said. "Well, I'll be damned, that son-of-a-bitch sent his secretary."

"How do you know she's not the graduate student?" he said.

I cleared my throat. "Not likely."

Dom put his hands on his hips and gave me a stern look. "Frannie, maybe you should start trusting others a bit more. I know that fellow Jasper's a jerk, but that doesn't mean everybody is. Look at us—we're friends now."

I didn't say anything for a minute, then I tilted my head toward the door.

"Maybe you're right. Go on out there and welcome her—ask her if she wants something to drink. I imagine her throat's parched after driving out here."

Dom jumped up, threw open the screen door, and ran to the gate and held out his hand.

"Hello, my name's Dominik Rostenkowski."

I watched from the window as the young woman shook his hand.

~

Dom coaxed Juan Esteban outside to go for a walk while Cindy Foster—a lean, tall brunette—examined the drawings for about thirty minutes. She was wearing a robin's-egg-blue colored dress that highlighted her blue eyes.

"So, you're a graduate student, Miss Foster?" I asked.

"Yes, Ma'am," she said, "and please call me Cindy."

I smiled. "What do you study, Cindy?"

"My interest is in wildlife physiology. I study how animals operate under various environmental conditions and how these processes are regulated and integrated. I'm particularly interested in how species are adapting to these dusty dry conditions—which ones survive and how they manage it."

I had to admit that not only was I impressed, but I could relate.

"I've certainly put a lot of energy into survival," I said.

She smiled.

"Might my brother's drawings help with your work?"

"I'd say so, because his thorough documentation gives us evidence of which species are adaptable and which are not."

Cindy looked up. "Miss Abbott, would you mind if I take some photographs—to take back and study? I'd like to specifically look at the smaller creatures. The insects."

"That would be fine," I said. "But I'd like them back when you're done."

"Absolutely."

She pulled out a Kodak box camera from her bag, and as she photographed the collection, she handled each drawing with the tips of her fingers, then gently restacked them in their original order. While she worked, I sat down on the edge of Juan Esteban's bed.

"You know," I said, "my brother drew all of these from memory. He didn't capture anything to do so. He would observe and then draw them later. I've always found them to be beautiful."

Cindy took off her glasses. "They are remarkable, Miss Abbott, and your brother has a gift that is quite inspiring."

I smiled. "Yes, I think so."

She started collecting her things and said, "I'll need to talk to Professor Crawley—I'm not sure what his assessment will be, but we are grateful that you shared this with us, and we'll get back to you."

I started coughing again. "I'm sorry, Cindy. I can hardly get a word out edgewise these days without having a coughing fit."

"I'm so sorry, Miss Abbott. Perhaps you should see a doctor?"

I nodded and smiled. "Perhaps," I said.

"Before I leave, may I meet your brother?"

"Of course," I said, "but just know he's shy."

"I'm shy too," she said. "I understand."

"Yes, but he's more than just shy, his brain works differently from ours." I cleared my throat. "You do understand, right?"

Cindy looked at me with a soft expression. "Yes, Miss Abbott. It would have to for him to have produced such detailed and exquisite work from memory."

As she turned to leave Juan Esteban's room, I gently touched her arm and met her gaze.

"He's protective of his drawings," I said, "it's where he finds comfort. I don't want him to be distressed by all of this."

"We will take it slowly," Cindy said, "and if anything becomes too much or too difficult for him, all you have to do is say so. I have a sister who has a different mind—probably not the same as your brother, but I get it."

"You do?"

"Yes, Ma'am." She pushed her hair behind her ear. "Patience is everything, because intense intelligence can be fragile. You clearly have supported him. It shows. People with such challenges can be misunderstood."

I didn't know what to think. I was flabbergasted at her response. I suddenly felt tears in my eyes.

When we walked outside, I called for Dom and Juan Esteban to come to the porch. Dom reached out and gently grazed Juan Esteban's hand with his index finger.

"Come on," he said. "Let's meet the graduate student."

Juan Esteban ambled over and stood next to Dom and looked at his feet with his arms squarely by his side.

"Cindy," I said, "This is my brother, Juan Esteban Slocum."

Juan Esteban turned his head to the side and looked away from her. She held out her hand, but Juan Esteban didn't take it, so she carefully pulled away.

"Your drawings are quite remarkable, Mr. Slocum. I thank you for sharing them with me. I took some photographs and would like to show them to my colleagues at the university if that's okay with you."

Juan Esteban didn't move his head, but he shifted his eyes between Dom and me.

Dom looked up at Juan Esteban. "It'll be okay," Dom said. "You can trust her just like you do me and Frannie."

Juan Esteban put his hands in his pockets, then raised his head.

Dom raised his eyebrows. "Looks like a yes to me, don't you think, Frannie?"

I smiled. "It certainly does, Dom."

CHAPTER 25
MISS FOSTER

1934

I had recently tasked Dom with picking up our mail after school because our postman delivered only three times a week. For several weeks, Dom arrived with a handful of mail and a look of disappointment.

A few days back, he crossed his arms with a huff.

"It's been four weeks and two days since Miss Foster was here. What's taking so long?" he said.

"Dunno," I said. "Perhaps they're not interested."

"Oh, come on, Frannie. You know they're interested. You heard what Miss Foster said."

I shook my head and didn't say anything. I had not fully adopted the optimistic spirit that Dom was encouraging.

One week after his summation, on a surprisingly clear day, I sat on the porch with Juan Esteban and Pico and warmed my bones in the sunshine. Juan Esteban was working on a drawing of a dung beetle when I saw Dom pedaling toward us like a maniac on wheels. His arm was raised in the air, and he was waving a piece of paper and shouting.

"Frannie, Juan Esteban—a letter from the University!"

I don't know where it came from, but I stood up with the energy of a twenty-year-old. Juan Esteban looked up from his drawing and squinted.

Dom didn't bother to put up his kickstand but threw his bike down and ran to the porch. His face was red and sweat streamed down his cheeks.

He waved the letter in front of me. "Open it, open it!"

213

"You open it," I said. "I'm kind of nervous. Read it out loud to Juan Esteban and me."

Dom's hands were shaking as he carefully opened the envelope. "Don't wanna rip it. It's got the university's official seal—looks important."

He held the letter with two hands and read.

Dear Mr. Slocum and Miss Abbott:

I hope you are both well and enjoying springtime before the heat.

Professor Crawley has found the drawings to be exceptional and if Mr. Slocum is willing, he might be interested in using them in a future textbook publication. The timeline is uncertain, however, due to limited funding. We are hoping to obtain a grant, but thus far we have had limited success—we do, however, remain optimistic.

Should we receive funding, please let us know if you would allow us to purchase the rights to the drawings for publication.

I hope your cough is getting better.

Sincerely,
Cindy Foster
Graduate Assistant

Dom's eyes were sparkling. "Told you, Frannie. Good news, I think. Don't you?"

I sat back down and fanned myself. "I'm a little lightheaded from all of the excitement, but yes, I think it is good news."

Dom walked over to Juan Esteban and stood by his side. His voice was calm and gentle.

"Your drawings are going to be published, Juan Esteban, if you want them to be."

Juan Esteban didn't look up.

"This is good, Juan Esteban, not bad," Dom said.

Juan Esteban kept drawing, and Dom shrugged his shoulders and looked at me with a what-do-we-do-now look?

"Give it some time," I said. "We're excited, but it might take Juan Esteban a little longer. You know him. And remember what Miss Foster said. Patience."

"I know, I know," Dom said, "but when are you going to write her back? You gotta do it soon."

"Let's give it a day or so."

"A day or so? Dang, Frannie, I don't know if I can wait that long."

I laughed. "You'll be fine, just start your chores to get it off your mind."

Dom dragged his feet and groaned. "Oooookay. Come on, Juan Esteban, let's get started on the garden. I expect there are some green beans that need picking."

For about an hour, I heard Dom whispering to Juan Esteban between trips to the well and back. I couldn't hear his exact words, but he was talking in a soothing tone, like a dove cooing. Juan Esteban was bent over the green beans and was filling up a paper bag. A few minutes later, he came and sat on the porch and separated them out into the straight ones and curled ones. He snapped the straight ones in half but let the curled ones be—as if their curled form signified something worth preserving.

"Looks like we'll have a nice dinner tonight," I said.

I stared in the distance toward our hedgerow, where several redbud saplings were showing off pink buds.

"You know, Juan Esteban, you and I are old dogs—I'm seventy-three and you're seventy-two, and though we aren't used to new tricks, this may be worth considering."

Juan Esteban got up, went inside, and started banging pots.

$\sim$

The next day, when Dom came back to do his chores, I could tell he was doing more than yard work. He was working on Juan Esteban. I listened from the kitchen window.

"It'll be good," he said. "You should be proud. Not everybody gets to be in a book."

Juan Esteban poured water on the tomatoes.

"We can sit on the porch together, and I'll read the book to you. All about your drawings. And Frannie, she'll listen too."

Juan Esteban had his back to me, but I saw him straighten up. Then Dom's eyes grew wide, and he backed slowly out of the garden, then kicked his feet up and came running inside.

"Frannie, Frannie! He made that face. He said, YES!"

~

With Dom looking over my shoulder, I wrote back to Miss Foster.

> *Dear Miss Foster:*
> *Thank you for your letter. Mr. Slocum has decided that he is interested. Please let us know what we need to do next and when.*
> > *Fondly,*
> > *Miss Frannie Abbott*

I put the letter in an envelope, licked it, gave it to Dom and handed him a book of stamps. "You pick the stamp," I said. "Find your favorite."

He perused the book, considering the profiles of famous men, scenic views of western mountains and lakes, Old Glory, then tore one out.

"Here," he said. "This is perfect."

I held it in my hand before licking it. It was Babe Ruth hitting a home run.

~

I'm not much one for praying—for most of my life, I've had trouble talking to most folks, much less God. But that night, even though my bones were stiff, I got down on my knees next to my bed and thanked God for John Joseph, Dom, and Juan Esteban.

CHAPTER 26
MOON FACE

1934

The next day when I stood in front of the bathroom mirror, I scared myself. My face was pale as the moon, my legs were weak, and my hands shook when I brushed my teeth.

I didn't bother to get out of my nightgown. I went back to bed and lay still while the morning breeze fluffed my curtains. I drifted back to sleep but awakened when I heard Juan Esteban rustling in the kitchen. Then he came into my bedroom with a bowl of oatmeal.

I thanked him, then sat up and leaned against my pillow and raised the spoon to my lips. My chest was tight as a knot, and my breathing so shallow that I had to take a break between spoonfuls. Juan Esteban sat in a straight-back chair next to my bed and watched me eat until I couldn't eat anymore because of all the coughing. I closed my eyes, and when I woke up two hours later, Juan Esteban was still there.

I knew what he was thinking.

~

That afternoon, Dom came into the house whistling, but when he saw me in bed he stopped in his tracks.

"Frannie, please don't take this wrong, but you don't look so good."

I could barely get the words out. "Not feeling good either."

He looked panic stricken. "I'll go get Mama. You're making me worried."

"Take the car," I said. "It'll be faster. Keys are on the dresser."

"But I can't drive," he said.

"Juan Esteban did it. You'll figure it out."

I heard my old Ford start up, then Dom revving the engine. He shifted into gear, gunned it, then slammed on the brakes. He tried it again, this time more slowly, and I heard the gravel crunching under the wheels as he crept out of the driveway.

An hour later, he was back with his mama. She appeared in the doorway.

"Miss Abbott? May I come in?"

I looked at her and blinked and whispered, "Yes."

"I'm Sheila, Dom's Mama." She had the same dark hair and eyes as Dom.

I smiled. "I'm glad to . . ." then I started coughing and couldn't finish my sentence. Sheila put her hand on my forehead.

"You're very hot, Miss Abbott. I think you need a doctor."

I nodded.

Sheila turned to Dom and whispered. "Go back to town and get Dr. Smalling—room five. If he's not there, he'll be next door in his office. Go quick!"

Dom shot out of the house like a cannon. I heard my car again, and this time he didn't take it slowly. I heard my tires slip against the gravel when he floored it out of the drive.

I tried to tell Sheila what I was thinking, but the words caught in my throat. "He's a good . . ."

Sheila put her finger up to her lips. "*Shhhhh*" she said. "You need to rest, but you're right. He is a good boy."

~

I must have drifted off to sleep because I was awakened by a cold sensation on my chest. I opened my eyes.

"Hello, Miss Abbott. I'm Dr. Smalling."

I swallowed—my eyes burned, and I couldn't see clearly.

"Freezing. Blanket," I said.

I heard Dom run into Juan Esteban's room, open a few drawers, then come back with a quilt that he handed to his mother. She gently tucked it around me.

The doctor put his hand on mine.

"You have a case of dust pneumonia, Miss Abbott. I will be back a little later with some medicine and to check on you."

I heard the doctor talking with Sheila on the porch, but their words sounded blended together. All that I understood was Sheila saying, "Of course we will stay."

~

Every time I opened my eyes, Juan Esteban was there in the chair.

"Go rest," I said, but he didn't leave. I looked at his wide face, his dark eyes, the gray hair that was taking over his sideburns, and the flecks of white mixed with dark on top of his head.

"I love you, Juan Esteban," I said.

~

The next day, I felt more lucid. Juan Esteban had fallen asleep and was leaning against the wall with a blanket covering his chest.

Sheila brought me a cup of chicken broth and spooned it into my mouth as she sat on the edge of the bed.

She gestured toward Juan Esteban with a nod and said, "Dom tried to move him to his room, but he wouldn't go, so we didn't force him."

"He'll go when he's ready," I said. "That's his way."

I looked into her eyes, "Your son is our only friend—he understands Juan Esteban like no one else," I said.

"He's told me so much about both of you," she said. "You are very special to him. I've watched him grow in the time that he has worked for you. He's gained confidence. I am grateful for your hiring him. We would not have survived without his pay."

I reached for her arm and held it as tight as I could.

"I know I'm dying," I said. "I have made plans—in my will, I've left what I have to Juan Esteban for his care, and when he dies, the rest goes to Dom— the house, our land, and what little we have left in the bank."

She put her hand on her chest and took a deep breath.

"Don't feel like you have to keep the property. Sell it for what it's worth, if you'd like. I want whatever there is of it to be used toward Dom's future. Perhaps his schooling. Whatever he wants. I hope that you will accept this gift."

Sheila's eyes grew watery, and her lip quivered. "Miss Abbott . . . you have no idea."

~

I was having a dream—I think. Someone was talking to me, "Frannie, Frannie, wake up."

I blinked. My room was a blur except for the bright light from the window that shone on Juan Esteban's bulky figure sitting in his chair. He had on a white t-shirt that lit up like a beacon, and he sat upright with his hands on his knees as if he were paying close attention to something in the room. Under his dark hair, his eyes were a penetrating black, and he was staring with an intensity that was frightening.

I raised my head and blinked to see his face more clearly. "Juan Esteban . . . what's wrong?" My voice had a quiver.

Someone else started gently shaking my shoulder on my opposite side. "Frannie, turn this way, it's me Dom." His eyes were wide.

I licked my lips. "What, Dom? You're scaring me. Is someone here? Is it Jasper?"

Dom's voice softened when he saw my panic. "No . . . everything's okay. It's just you, me, and Juan Esteban."

I took a deep breath. "Damn, Dom. You sure know how to scare the crap out of an old lady."

He started to get excited again. "Look I found something . . . you *have* to look."

He held a piece of paper in his hand and pushed it close to my face.

"My glasses . . . " I said, "I can't see." I reached for them on the side table, but they dropped to the floor. Dom bent over to pick them up and slipped them behind my ears and onto my nose.

His hands were shaking, and he was pointing.

"What?" I said.

"It's in the drawing, Frannie. Juan Esteban's drawing. See?"

I blinked again, then squinted.

"I found it in a wooden press between some cardboard mixed in with some others that I've never seen before," he said. "One was of a bear and a donkey, and there's also this one."

He held it up.

"Do you see?"

"Yes," I said, "Looks like a horse."

He pointed. "And look, in the background . . . it's a man on the ground . . . and there's a gun . . . somebody's holding it . . . your Jaeger rifle. I can tell by the scrollwork on the stock . . . see?"

"Barely." I adjusted my glasses again but had trouble focusing. "Get me that magnifying glass on my desk."

Dom wheeled around, ran through the doorway, then in an instant was back by my side with his arm stretched out and the magnifying glass in his hand.

"Look closely . . ." he said, "a trail of smoke is coming out of the barrel. The guy's skinny . . . his hair's curly."

"What?" I said.

Dom's voice was shrill. "It's not Juan Esteban! His hair's straight. He didn't do it. Somebody else did."

I moved the magnifying glass back and forth until I could see more clearly, then took a deep breath. The magnifying glass fell from my hand when I recognized who it was.

"I'll be damned."

I looked at Juan Esteban. My whole body went limp.

~

I don't understand why it happened when it did—why so many years had passed before the truth was revealed to me about Jasper shooting the professor, or that I had never found that drawing within Juan Esteban's collection. And if anyone had asked me why Juan Esteban didn't try to

221

show me earlier, I would have answered, "That wasn't his way. He didn't use his drawings for any motive—what he drew is what he saw, and what he saw was life."

I could have been angry about the years I spent in prison because of Jasper and how he harassed us for so long, but when you're dying, being angry seems like wasted time. What happened is over. And I'd like to believe that maybe it was all meant to be—our fate—so that Dom would be part of our life.

EPILOGUE
DOM

1945

Frannie died on a Thursday. I had fallen asleep in her rocking chair, and I awoke to Juan Esteban touching my arm from where he lay next to Frannie. Juan Esteban wasn't crying—he looked peaceful. As if he knew it was going to happen and had moved on.

I looked out the window, and the sun was just coming up. It was dusty out, but a pink glow the color of a wild rose lit up the sky.

Did I cry? I bawled my eyes out. But I had Juan Esteban and Mama, so I knew we were going to be okay.

When Frannie's lawyer read the will, I was proud. Not because of the money, but that she trusted me with Juan Esteban—along with Mama—to be his friend and caretaker for what remained of his life.

That fellow Jasper never came back, but if he had, I was ready. I was only thirteen then, but I was sure I could have punched him in the jaw and given him a good-sized welt.

Hauling water for years on end makes you strong, and I was putting on the weight of a middle school kid. I had Frannie's Jaeger rifle too, and though I would have loved to have given him a scare Frannie-style, she wouldn't have approved.

Enough, she would have said.

Not long after Frannie died, Mama read something in the paper about a fellow by the name of O'Brien who was killed in a bar fight in Terlingua. Seemed consistent with his nature, so I put any worries of him to bed.

Juan Esteban died three years later, at age seventy-five, but not before the textbook was published with his drawings.

The title was: *The Physiology of Animals in the Texas Panhandle*.

At the bottom of the title page it noted in bold text, "Illustrations by Juan Esteban Slocum."

Over eighty of Juan Esteban's drawings were photographed and printed for publication. Though they were impressive within the context, I knew their depiction in printed form didn't hold a candle to the originals.

As I had hoped, I had the chance to sit with him on the porch and read aloud the section written by Cindy Foster, "Adaptive Species of the Dust Bowl Years." Juan Esteban listened, but not the whole time. Halfway through, he got up, went inside, brought out some paper and pencil and started drawing a cottonwood beetle borer with its black and white coloration. I'm not certain where he saw it, but perhaps it was among the cottonwood tree roots that stretch out like long arms on the banks of a draw near Frannie's gravesite.

We were frequent visitors there in the years after she died and before Juan Esteban was laid to rest next to her. When Juan Esteban was alive, our visitation timing and procession was the same.

Every Thursday at 6:15 am he stood at the edge of my bed, and if I didn't wake up, he'd poke me in the arm. At precisely at 6:43 am—the moment Frannie died—we would drive under the metal arch that marked the cemetery entrance—Leilo Memorial Cemetery.

Though many a Thursday morning I might have preferred to sleep in, Juan Esteban made sure I didn't. We drove three and two tenths of a mile to the outskirts of Leilo and parked the car in a grassy open area, then walked fifty-two paces towards a Mondel Pine that was at the head of Frannie's grave.

I learned later in my studies that this tree wasn't native to our home— someone had come here and planted it for a reason. Its evergreen upright structure added a sense of confidence to the surrounding low-lying landscape. I felt as if it beckoned and spoke to me—*come see, here lies a person who lived with purpose.*

On our Thursday journeys, I carried a bucket of water, and Juan Esteban had a pocket full of seeds. It didn't matter to him if the seeds survived; it was the ritual that seemed to give comfort. In the fall and early winter, Frannie's grave would be covered in a mix of cabbage, beet, and mustard green leaves until a frost knocked them back. Late spring brought a twisted mass of string beans, cucumbers, and radishes that reached at least ten feet beyond her grave marker. Juan Esteban watered and tended to them but didn't take any home. I believe he wanted to leave them for Frannie.

When Juan Esteban died, I continued his ritual as best I could on his behalf, but my life started to change, and I was drawn elsewhere. Since then, I have started college—I have entered the Wildlife Management program at Texas University.

Mama sold Frannie's home in Leilo so I could go to school—she kept the promise that she made to herself to make good on Frannie's wishes. Mama's apartment is near the university, so I check on her regularly.

Juan Esteban's drawings are in the archives there for anyone to see. Mostly, it's those interested in animals, but sometimes it's those who study the minds of others. In the archival index, they are labeled the "Juan Esteban Slocum and Frances Abbott Collection." It's not only Juan Esteban's drawings; Frannie's journal is there too. The university believed both to be important to the story of Juan Esteban's work and Frannie's commitment to supporting his talents.

She told me where the journal was—under the floorboards in a metal box—the day I showed her the drawing that proved Juan Esteban's innocence.

Sometimes I go to the archives myself for research, but mostly I lay the drawings out like Juan Esteban used to do and marvel at their intricacy and beauty.

The librarian knows me by name and my connection to Frannie and Juan Esteban—when I walk through the wooden doorway with its gothic framing, the familiar air of academia fills my senses—a hint of dust mixed with the scent of old wood—bookshelves, long tables, and straight-back chairs that creak against my weight.

Mrs. Greenberg greets me with a confidence that reminds me of Frannie. As light from an arched window brightens her face, she smiles and stands straight-backed behind the long wooden checkout desk. Her words are always the same.

"Good day, Mr. Rostenkowski," she says. "Back again to study brilliance?"

ABOUT THE AUTHOR

CATHERINE O'CONNOR is a writer and landscape architect. She holds a Bachelor of Arts in English Literature from Duke University and a Master's in Landscape Architecture from Harvard University's Graduate School of Design. A native Texan and Austinite, she is the founding principal of Co'design, LLC and has served as an adjunct faculty member at the University of Texas School of Architecture. Catherine lives in her hometown with her husband, Jim, and they are proud parents of Claire and Patrick.

Printed in the USA
CPSIA information can be obtained
at www.ICGtesting.com
CBHW062236121124
17345CB00006B/159

9 780875 658834